MURDER IN TIME

An Ellie Quicke Mystery

Veronica Heley

This first world edition published 2014
in Great Britain and the USA by
SEVERN HOUSE PUBLISHERS LTD of
19 Cedar Road, Sutton, Surrey, England, SM2 5DA.

Trade paperback edition first published
in Great Britain and the USA 2014 by
SEVERN HOUSE PUBLISHERS LTD.

British Library Cataloguing in Publication Data

Heley, Veronica author.
  Murder in time. – (The Ellie Quicke mysteries)
  1. Quicke, Ellie (Fictitious character)–Fiction.
  2. Widows–Great Britain–Fiction. 3. Murder–
  Investigation–Fiction. 4. Absentee fathers–Fiction.
  5. Detective and mystery stories.
  I. Title II. Series
  823.9'14-dc23

ISBN-13: 978-0-7278-8398-8 (cased)
ISBN-13: 978-1-84751-518-6 (trade paper)

Typeset by Palimpsest Book Production Ltd.,
Falkirk, Stirlingshire, Scotland.

ONE

Tuesday, early evening

Ellie opened the front door with her grandson in her arms . . . and recoiled.

She'd never laid eyes on the man before but she knew who he was. Or rather, who he must be.

Tall and slender, dark-skinned and handsome with fine features. A high forehead. Wealthy. British-Somalian?

He was expensively dressed in a brown cashmere jacket over a white polo-necked jumper which was either silk or silk mixture. Well-cut dark-grey jeans, NOT off the peg. Boots, shiny.

Hard, black eyes. An air of command.

He was the very image of . . . no! No! NO!

He couldn't be. She was seeing things. She blinked. He was still there. The baby in her arms twisted around to inspect the newcomer and said, 'Gawk!' around the spoon he was thrusting in and out of his mouth.

'I'm looking for Vera. Are you her mother?' A well-educated voice. English might not have been his first language, but he'd been to good schools here. He twitched a smile. He wasn't accustomed to being kept waiting but was holding impatience in check.

She made no move to let him in. 'Vera . . .? Well, yes; she does live here, but . . . I'm Mrs Quicke, Mrs Ellie Quicke. Not her mother. And you are . . .?'

'You're the housekeeper, I presume?'

Ellie reddened. She'd worn her oldest clothes to look after baby Evan that day, and yes, her short, silvery hair was probably all over the place and she knew there was a patch of baby sick on one shoulder. 'No, but this is my house. At least: my husband and I live here with our housekeeper, Rose.'

Also with single-parent Vera and her son. Perhaps it would

be best not to mention them till she'd found out what the visitor wanted.

'Rose? Ah, *she's* Vera's mother?'

'No, Rose is an old family friend, and our housekeeper.' Ellie was angry with herself. She was handling this badly. If this man was who she thought she was, then what ought she to say about Vera? Should she admit that the girl lived there, studying for a business degree while paying for her board by helping Rose to look after the house? Or, should she deny that she even knew Vera? Yes, that might be best. Except that, oh dear, she'd already admitted that Vera lived there.

The stranger ducked his head, not smiling, and moved forward until she gave way, letting him into the hall. 'I've come to the right place, then. I'll wait for her, shall I?' It wasn't a question.

He looked about him, assessing the evidence of inherited wealth; the panelling and the tiled floor; the door propped open to give access to the kitchen quarters, other doors leading to the dining and sitting rooms, the fine old staircase, and the view through to the conservatory at the back of the house.

'Pleasant,' he said. Patronizing. Raising his eyebrows. 'Is the baby another of Vera's little mistakes?'

Ellie flushed. 'No, of course not. He's my grandson. I look after him one day a week when his nanny has her day off.'

Ellie wanted to scream at the man to leave, get out, not to upset their quiet lives. And didn't, because . . . well, it wasn't her business to intervene between husband and wife, was it? Well, not husband and wife exactly.

What had Vera told her son about the man who had fathered him? Perhaps the truth was too harsh for a small boy to hear and, as far as Ellie knew, young Mikey had never raised the subject.

Little Evan struggled in Ellie's arms, dropping the spoon he'd been playing with. He was a strong lad for his age, and she was not as young as she had been. She tried to put him into his buggy. He resisted. She could never get him into or out of it without a wrestling match.

She sought for something to say. 'Does Vera know you're coming?'

The man shook his head. 'A pleasant surprise.'

Ellie didn't think it was going to be a pleasant surprise. She didn't dare think what Vera was going to say when she saw the man who'd raped her when she'd had too much to drink at an end of school year party.

Evan was working up to one of his famous tantrums, so Ellie rescued his spoon and, careless of germs, thrust it back into his mouth. She had learned the hard way that there were times to be flexible about bringing up a child as strong-minded as Evan. Only then did he allow himself to be strapped into his buggy. He'd been awake for hours. Perhaps he'd sleep now.

Without waiting for an invitation, the visitor walked across the hall and into the sitting room. Ellie seethed at his bad manners, but followed with the baby buggy, hoping against hope that Evan would collapse into sleep. One cheek was bright red and his nose needed wiping. She did so, tenderly. He was teething.

The visitor went to stand by the window, looking out on the garden in all its brilliant end-of-summer splendour. 'Will Vera be long?'

Ellie looked at her watch – which had stopped at three. Had she got water in it while changing Evan's nappy? If so, it would have to go to be repaired. She said, 'I don't know.' She decided against offering refreshments. She wondered if she could possibly get hold of Vera on her mobile, to warn her . . .

And Mikey! Vera's brilliant imp of a son would be home any minute now.

What had he been told about this man? Surely not the truth?

Panic! Ellie wondered if she could make some excuse to go out to the kitchen, to tell their elderly housekeeper not to let Mikey come into the sitting room. But Rose would hardly be awake from her afternoon nap yet and might not take in what Ellie was saying.

Meanwhile, the man selected a chair and sat. He crossed

one elegant leg over the other and steepled his fingers. 'I gather Vera's had a somewhat chequered history since I last saw her.'

The nerve of the man!

'She's doing well for herself.' A short answer. Ellie rocked the buggy, a little too hard. If only her husband were around. Where was he today? At a meeting somewhere . . .

Perhaps Vera had told Mikey some story about star-crossed lovers parted by hostile families? A Romeo and Juliet affair?

She said, 'Vera is part of our family.'

'Splendid.' Fake politeness. He was not interested in what Ellie thought.

A door in the kitchen quarters opened and shut with a bang. Mikey was home from school. The man turned his head to listen.

Mikey was a growing lad who needed a constant intake of food. When he came in he'd raid the cake tin, take a handful of biscuits, an apple, raisins, anything. Rose scolded and indulged him. Yes, Ellie could hear raised voices, laughter from Rose and from the boy, a radio turned on, a sharp cry of triumph from Mikey and a clatter as the lid of the cake tin fell to the floor.

Ellie ceased rocking the buggy. Red in the face, baby Evan struggled for a moment to free himself from his harness and then collapsed into sleep.

Ellie's mind whirled with various scenarios. How about impaling the stranger on her garden fork and hiding his body in the garden shed till her husband could get home to dispose of him? She said, 'Mikey's always hungry when he gets in from school.'

The visitor, previously relaxed, froze into a statue. '"Mikey"? He is to be called Mohammed in future.'

A rush of feet down the corridor from the kitchen, more laughter from the boy and from Rose. Perhaps he'd go straight up the stairs to the flat he and Vera occupied at the top of the house? Ellie prayed that he would.

He paused in the doorway to the sitting room, in mid-flight. He'd shot up several inches since he started his new school, but the strong bones he'd inherited from Vera saved him from looking fragile.

A piece of cake in one hand, he stared at the visitor. Did he realize he was looking into a mirror?

What had Vera told him?

The man held out his hand to the boy. 'Ah. My son. Mohammed.'

Ellie could see knowledge flash into Mikey's bright, dark eyes. Yes, he understood who the man must be, but he wasn't sure how to react. He switched his eyes to Ellie, seeking information.

Ellie said, 'I don't know, Mikey. When your mother gets back—'

'Come!' said the man, leaning forward, still holding out his hand. Clearly, he expected the boy to obey him.

Mikey, however, was not your average boy. Mikey had always thought for himself and was not accustomed to obeying orders unless he saw good reason to do so. This had got him into trouble on many occasions and would no doubt continue to do so.

'Surely you're not afraid of me!' The man smiled, scornful.

Ellie's heart leapt. Most boys would react negatively to a slur on their courage. Mikey started, but checked himself. His eyelids contracted. Again he flashed a look at Ellie. One she found hard to read.

WHAT HAD VERA TOLD HIM?

A look of annoyance crossed the man's face. Then he smiled. A false smile. Ellie wondered if he had a sharp temper and whether if she hadn't been there he might have slapped the boy for disobedience.

She was horrified at herself. How could she have thought such a thing?

More noises off. Vera had returned, was talking to Rose in the kitchen. Also laughing.

A big girl, taller than Mikey, but as fair as he was dark, Vera appeared in the doorway. She rarely bothered with make-up and smoothed her hair up into a sleek ponytail. She was dressed as usual in a blue sweater and jeans, a tote bag swinging from one arm.

She was smiling, saying, 'You'll never guess who I saw in—'

She saw the man.

And froze.

The man stood up. 'Ah, Vera. No need to introduce me to my son. Mohammed, come here and let me look at you.'

Mikey turned his head to look up at his mother, frowning, unsure what to make of the situation.

Vera took a deep breath. 'What do you want, Abdi?'

'The boy, of course. I wasn't able to help you before, but I can take him off your hands now.'

Vera gaped. 'What?'

'I don't have any children of my own, so I plan to adopt him, formally. I shall, of course, compensate you for your trouble in looking after him to date.'

With a scream that raised the hairs on the back of Ellie's neck, Vera flashed across the room and brought her knee up, sharply . . . accurately . . .

Abdi grimaced, folding into himself. He subsided on to the carpet.

Mikey grinned, wild and triumphant.

Vera, fair hair flying, grabbed her son and dragged him out of the room.

Ellie found she was grinning, too.

The man made huffing noises. Spider-like, his limbs contorted. Tears spurted.

Tut-tut.

Ellie said, 'I'll leave you to recover.' Smiling, she pushed the sleeping baby in his buggy out into the hall.

Only just in time, as someone was leaning on the doorbell. Ellie knew that ring. Only one person demanded entrance that way. Diana, Ellie's difficult, ambitious daughter, the mother of little Evan, whom she'd woken up with her prolonged attack on the doorbell.

As arranged, Diana had arrived from work to collect him.

Ellie checked Evan – was he a bit smelly again? She wiped his nose with a tissue she then tucked into the waistband of her skirt . . . and oh dear, she ought to have changed her own clothes before Diana arrived, because her daughter would be sure to comment on Ellie's untidiness. But there was no time to do anything else but open the door.

Diana didn't bother to greet Ellie, but swooped on her son. 'Who's my little chickadee, then! Have you missed your Marmee?'

Evan responded with a grin showing off all three of his teeth. He chattered, and threw his arms and legs around. He adored his mummy, and Diana – to the astonishment of all her friends and relations, who hadn't believed she could adore anyone but herself – was devoted to her son.

Diana scooped him out of the buggy and held him high in the air. Her smile vanished. 'Oh, Mother! He's definitely whiffy. He needs changing. Have you given him something to eat that you shouldn't?'

'No, I—'

Thomas's key turned in the lock of the front door and he came in, shaking off his jacket. He was a big, bearded bear of a man, and the two women automatically turned towards him; Ellie with a smile, and Diana with a nod. Even little Evan waved one hand – still holding the spoon – in his direction.

Thomas said, 'Phew! Chilly out today! Whose is the limousine outside? Chauffeur-driven, no less. We have a visitor?' He dropped jacket and briefcase on to a chair and gave Ellie a hug. 'Nice and warm in here. Had a good day?' And then, in more guarded tones to his stepdaughter, 'Hello, Diana. How are you doing?'

They were polite to one another, nowadays. Well, Thomas was always polite, being the possessor of an equable temperament and, although it didn't automatically follow, a minister of the church. Thomas had seen pretty well everything that men and women could do to one another, and still tried to think the best of people.

Diana bared her teeth in a social smile but wasn't actively unpleasant to him since he did, after all, hold the key to Ellie's heart and, incidentally, to her moneybags. Ellie had inherited money from various sources, and her daughter was always trying to access the source of the goodies . . . so far without success.

A groan from the sitting room drew their attention.

Diana clutched her son closer. 'What's that?'

'Someone in trouble?' asked Thomas. 'The owner of the limousine?'

'Uninvited and unwelcome,' said Ellie. 'He got what he deserved.'

Abdi, bent double, crossing over at the knees, stumbled to the doorway and leaned against it, gasping, 'Hooroo!'

'Whatever's the matter?' Thomas was alarmed.

'I'm out of here,' said Diana, efficiently collapsing the buggy with one hand while clutching little Evan to her with the other. 'Ring you later, Mother. Small problem this weekend. May have to call on you to babysit. Whew, baby! You stink!'

Evan crowed with delight and clutched the lapel of his mother's black suit with a hand which was probably sticky. Diana had never allowed anyone else to mishandle her this way, but Evan was different. Cooing to her son, she swept out of the front door, letting it bang to behind her.

Their visitor addressed Thomas. 'You! Get . . .!'

Thomas's eyes widened as he, too, identified the stranger. He looked to Ellie for information. 'Who . . .?'

Ellie said, 'Now, Mister-whatever-your-name is—'

'You saw what she . . .?'

'After what you did to her,' said Ellie, hoping she'd interpreted correctly, 'I think you got off mildly. Oh, find a chair and sit down, do. I'll get you a cuppa if you like. And then you can go.'

'"Did to *her*?"' Thomas was confused.

Vera, who was standing halfway up the stairs, confirmed, 'Did to me.' She had her arm around Mikey's shoulders. The boy was clutching their marauding ginger cat, Midge. Ellie could see that Mikey needed something to hold on to at the moment and only hoped Midge wouldn't object.

'You . . .!' The newcomer emitted a string of words in a foreign tongue which none of them could speak, but all interpreted correctly.

'That'll be enough of that.' Thomas projected sufficient authority to stop a bus, never mind one foul-mouthed intruder.

The newcomer managed to get upright, almost. The look he shot Vera was pure poison. 'Whore! I'll be back for the boy tomorrow!' He measured the distance to the front door, and sidled towards it, crab fashion.

Thomas hesitated. 'Are you sure he's all right?'

Ellie said, 'If he isn't, he can sit outside in his car till he is.'

Thomas interpreted the expression on his wife's face correctly and opened the front door wide. A uniformed chauffeur hastened to his master's side and helped him, carefully, into a back seat. After a moment, the car drove away.

Only then did Thomas shut the door on the outside world. 'Now, suppose someone tells me what's going on.'

Ellie said, 'He wants to buy the boy.'

'What?' Thomas almost laughed but, seeing their faces, decided against doing so.

Vera said, 'I can't believe that he . . .! How dare he!'

Thomas looked from Vera to Ellie and back. 'Will somebody fill me in?'

Vera took one step down, then stopped to look at Mikey, who hadn't moved. 'Mikey, did you understand that that man is . . . was . . .? Oh!' With a burst of angry laughter, she said, 'I suppose I ought not to have . . . He's evil! How dare he come here and . . .!'

Mikey looked back at her with a face of stone. In times of stress, he forsook speech and was mute, sometimes for days at a time. Now he seemed to be judging his mother – or perhaps was merely withholding judgement?

Vera closed her eyes for a moment. But she was no weakling, and Ellie could see her decide to face the problem head on. 'All right, Mikey. I haven't been quite straight with you about—' Her voice broke. 'About how you came to be.' She looked at Ellie and Thomas. 'Nor with you. But I never thought I'd see him again. As for wanting Mikey . . . He can't be serious!'

He'd looked pretty serious to Ellie. She glanced at her watch. It was still stopped at three. 'I think the time has come to tell us everything.'

Thomas led the way to the sitting room. 'Council of war.'

Ellie went to her high-backed chair by the fireplace, while

Thomas settled on to his La-Z-Boy. Vera sat on the settee and patted the cushion beside her, but Mikey chose not to obey her. Instead, he sat on the floor nearby, with the cat stretched out on his knees. Mikey was definitely withholding judgement. Oh dear.

Vera produced a nervous smile, her hands working at her sweater. Tears were not far away. 'I couldn't tell you the truth, nor Mikey. It was too difficult. It still is. I don't know if I can, even now. Mikey, I told you that I'd had a wild love affair with a foreign student, who'd promised to marry me but who was killed in a car accident. I thought that was better, much better than . . . Sorry, Mikey. Try not to think too harshly of me. I thought, maybe, one day . . .' A gesture of frustration. 'I didn't want you to know what kind of man your father was.'

'I knew all along,' said Mikey, speaking for the first time. His voice was breaking and could go high or low on him. Now, it was low. 'What did you expect? Of course I knew. I got it thrown at me at my old school all the time. You can't keep things like that secret.'

'What things?'

'You got drunk at a party and had it off with whoever wanted it. Everyone knew.'

'No, Mikey: no!' A cry from the heart. 'It wasn't like that at all. Who told you that?'

A shrug. 'Some boys in my class. They were all talking about it. Somebody's mother knew someone who'd been at the party when you passed out. They thought it was funny that I didn't know. They told everyone else in the class, too. I didn't ask you about it, because you'd made up that silly story about your boyfriend being killed.'

Vera clutched her head. 'Tell me their names! I'll kill them!'

Thomas said, 'Mikey, was that why you got into so much trouble at school?'

Mikey shrugged. 'There was a lot of bullying at that school. I'm glad to be out of there.'

Vera swiped tears from her eyes. 'It was only partly the truth. If only you'd said!'

'How could I? You'd told me a fairy story, and I believed it at first. Then, when I understood you'd lied, I—'

Vera wrung her hands. 'Don't think too harshly of me, Mikey.'

'There's lots of boys who don't know who their fathers are. You might have trusted me with the truth but you'd decided not to, so that's it.'

'That wasn't the whole truth, or even half of it. You should have asked.'

'If you didn't want to tell me, that's OK. It's how it is. There's lots worse off than me. I can take it,' said Mikey. And meant it.

Ellie intervened. 'Tell us how it really was, Vera.'

Vera closed her eyes. 'It's so hard . . . even now.' She looked at Mikey. She put out her hand to reach him. She patted his shoulder. He made no move to reassure her. She winced, accepting his rebuff. 'All right. I'll try. Mikey, listen. There was a birthday party and school leaving "do" combined. A whole crowd of gatecrashers. Someone gave me a drink. I thought it was Diet Coke, but there was something else in it. I passed out. I didn't wake up till hours later. I realized straight away that I'd been raped, but I didn't know who . . . There was such confusion . . . I got home under my own steam. End of story.'

Thomas said, 'You went to the police?'

Vera's mouth formed the shape of a bitter smile. 'No. I didn't.'

'Why not?'

TWO

Vera lifted her ponytail, shook her hair free and scooped it back into its clasp. 'You have to understand how it was in my family. Mikey, you never knew your grandfather and grandmother. I've not talked about them much, have I?'

Mikey didn't look at her. 'You were ashamed of them because they ran a fish and chip shop.'

Patches of red burned on Vera's cheeks. 'I never said that. My father was a self-made man who worked hard all his life. He was proud of the reputation of our shop. He'd wanted a son, but there'd been several miscarriages before I was born, and my mother was in her forties when I arrived. She was never strong, always at the doctor's. Back trouble. Stomach trouble. Finally, cancer.

'My father was a solid Labour supporter because that was what his father had been. He didn't hold with women going to college or, worse, to university. He expected me to work in the shop whenever I wasn't at school or looking after Mum. As luck would have it, we were in the catchment area for a good local school, and there I learned that bright girls could go on to higher education if they wished.

'My father disapproved, but I set my heart on going to university. I studied late at night and early in the morning. I got a provisional offer of a place at Leeds University. If I got the grades I expected, I had a place to go. There were terrible rows at home, but I stuck to it that this was what I wanted to do. Looking back, I can see that my father was frightened, worrying how he'd cope if I left him to it, because he needed me in the shop and my mother was getting frail. And yes, I did feel a bit guilty about that, but not very because . . . I had a boyfriend who encouraged me to dream.'

'Abdi?'

A grimace. 'Not Abdi. A very different sort of boy. We spent as much time together as we could during that last year at school. We'd walk in the park, eat our sandwiches together at lunchtime. Only to talk, you understand. Nothing else. His parents weren't happy about it. They didn't want him marrying the girl from the chippy. He was a doctor's son, due to study medicine himself. We were both going away to university. We knew it would be years before we could marry, but we said there'd be the holidays and we could write and phone one another.

'We didn't have sex. I was a bit shy, being so big and awkward. And, I was scared of my father. Dan and I agreed I'd go on the pill as soon as I left school. We were going to go out for the day into the country and . . .' She shook her head. 'Love's young dream. As if.'

Mikey squirmed.

Vera said, 'Sorry, Mikey, but you have to know how it was.'

Thomas said, 'Your boyfriend's name was Dan?'

Vera passed her hand across her eyes. 'Dan McKenzie. His eighteenth birthday fell at the end of term, and we had a party at his house. His parents had gone out for the night. A crowd of rowdies gatecrashed, wanting drink and drugs. Dan confronted them, asked them to leave. They laughed at us. We were no match for them. They laid into us. I mean, physically. Threw us around.

'And before you ask; no, Abdi wasn't one of the gate-crashers. He'd been invited by one of his friends who went to our school. Some of us got away through the kitchen into the back garden, which was divided by hedges into different "rooms". The McKenzies had also bought a piece of someone else's garden off to one side, and there they'd put in a swimming pool and changing hut. We joined some of our lot in the hut, barred the door as best we could, and tried to work out what to do. Nowadays we'd all have mobile phones and be able to call the police, but very few of us had them in those days, and none of our group had one. We could hear the gang charging about and yelling, but they didn't find the pool. We were all very shaken. When I'd calmed down, I remembered there was a door in the hedge nearby leading on to an alley, from which you could reach the main road. Two of the boys volunteered to go and see if it was locked, or if we could force our way out through the hedge.

'Someone passed me a drink. I thought it was Diet Coke. I was thirsty. I drank it . . . and passed out. I don't remember anything after that until I woke up in the open air. I was lying on my back on the lawn near the hut. I was alone. Everyone else had gone. I remember looking up at the moon. Half a moon. I felt most peculiar. Then I realized the state I was in. No panties, and blood all over my thighs. A lot of blood. When I tried to move, I realized I'd been raped.'

Mikey was stone-faced.

Thomas glanced at him and glanced away. He said, 'You got help?'

She shook her head. 'Two of my school friends came running down the garden from the house. I tried to get up, to call out to them. The girl jumped a mile and screamed. She said the police had arrived and there was all hell to pay. She said her father would kill her if she got arrested because they'd been smoking pot in one of the bedrooms. They'd got away by scrambling out of the window on to the flat roof of the kitchen and jumping down into the garden.

'They could see what had happened to me. The girl asked if I were all right, but the boy was backing away, didn't want to get involved. He asked if I knew of another way out, and I told them about the gate on to the alley. He ran off, without waiting for us. To give the girl credit, she tried to help me. She was dying to get away, but she helped me into the changing hut so that I could wash myself. She asked who'd raped me, but I didn't know. She said she'd wait for me if I was quick, but I was too slow. She ran away, too. After a while, I took a towel to wrap around me and staggered out. I felt so weak . . . but all I could think of was about getting home. I walked. Resting now and then. I'd lost my purse so I hadn't any money for a taxi. Not even for the night bus.

'My father had waited up for me. He was furious. He beat me. He said I was filth, had disgraced him, that he'd never be able to hold up his head in the community if it got out that I'd had sex in public at a party. My mother wept. She did suggest I see a doctor, but he wouldn't have it, because then everyone would have known what a slut I was.'

'A doctor wouldn't have told on you,' said Thomas, 'and he would have arranged for you to be seen by the police.'

Vera covered her eyes with one hand. 'I was so ashamed. That was the last thing I wanted, believe me. Or my father. But, what with the beating he gave me and all, I don't think I was in my right mind for a while. Several days. During that time the news broke that Dan's father, the doctor, had been killed by an intruder at the party.

'I crawled to the phone with the intention of ringing Dan,

just to say . . . I didn't know what I was going to say, but I
wanted . . . I hoped . . . I was desperate to hear his voice, but
I knew we could never go back to what we'd had before. I was
no longer fit for purpose. Dan was out. I left a message with
his mother and she said she'd give it to him, but he didn't ring
me back. He must have thought I'd cheated on him, that I'd
consented to have sex with his friends. I had to accept that he
didn't want to know me any more.'

'You still didn't go to the police?'

'My father said I must keep quiet, that no one would ever
want to marry me if the news got out. He said the police
would say I was drunk and asking for trouble. He said the
best thing to do was to put it behind me and get down to
the shop to help out. So I did. I worked at the chippy
all through the holidays, evenings as well. I didn't see any
of the old crowd. I read the papers for news of the murder.
First they were asking for anybody who'd been at the party
to come forward. I suppose some of them did. I didn't. They
took in a known drug-dealer for questioning. My father said
that would be it. Case solved. But the police let him go without
charging him. The following week they questioned another
man . . . and let him go, too. So far as I know, nobody has
ever been charged with the murder.

'The only thing that kept me sane was looking forward to
October when I could get away to university, where nobody
knew my story. And then . . . I discovered I was pregnant. I
phoned a girl I knew from school, someone I thought might
not judge me too harshly, to ask for news. She was embarrassed, said that I'd gone and done it good and proper, brazenly
entertaining so many men in the open like that, and she thought
I'd do best to keep my mouth shut and move away. That was
the first I'd heard that there was more than one man involved.
The idea that when I'd lain there, helpless, several men had
used me . . .!'

Mikey shuddered. He lowered his head to his knees and
stayed like that.

Thomas said, 'She gave you names?'

'I asked if one of them had been Dan, and she thought that
was a hoot. She said it wasn't. She said she didn't know who

it was for sure and if I were wise, I'd not ask. Forget it, she said. Every time I went out of doors I imagined people were looking at me, knowing what had happened. I tried not to look into men's faces, in case one of them might have taken part in the rape. I told myself it had to be someone who'd been invited to the party, but that didn't make sense. I couldn't imagine any of them doing . . . that.

'It became easier after a while as I realized that all the old crowd had scattered to university or taken a gap year, and that I wasn't likely to meet up with any of them in the street. In the end I had to tell my parents that I was pregnant. My father . . .' She closed her eyes for a second. 'I can't blame him, really. Mum had just been diagnosed with breast cancer. Second time round. He was disgusted. He washed his hands of me. He sold up and moved down to the south coast. He said I was on my own, and that he didn't want me bothering them again. I did what everyone else does; I went to Social Services, they gave me a bed-sitter and finally allocated me a one-bedroom flat, really run down but at least I could shut the front door on the world. I tried to find work. My A-level results were good, but I couldn't get a proper job with a baby on the way and no parental support. I took whatever jobs I could get. Cleaning, mostly.'

She laid a hand on Mikey's shoulder. 'When you were born I realized whose son you must be. What a shock! I'd never in a thousand years have thought that Abdi was interested in me. He'd been to one or two of our parties in the past but I don't think I'd ever even had a proper conversation with him. We had nothing in common. To think that he'd been one of the men who'd raped me! For maybe sixty seconds, Mikey, I hated you . . . and then you opened your eyes and looked up at me. They say babies can't focus that early, but you did. And I loved you with all my heart.

'I tried to contact your father, of course. I looked in the phone book and there was his address. Not far away. I delivered a note to the house telling them that I'd had a baby and that he was the father. I didn't expect much. I thought he might make me some sort of allowance . . . but that was stupid of me, wasn't it? I'd given him my address. He came to see me there. He said I was trying to blackmail him, to force him into marriage, that it wouldn't work, that he didn't believe me, anyway. He said that if I persisted in trying to damage his reputation, he'd have me killed.'

'Killed!' Ellie repeated.

Vera nodded. 'He'd been spoiled. Too much money. Brought up to think he could do whatever he liked. He told me the family was moving away and warned me not to try approaching him again.'

'But now he wants to make amends?'

'No,' said Vera. 'I don't think so, do you? Mikey, tell me you understand how it was.'

The boy didn't look at her. He slung the cat over his shoulder and got to his feet in one smooth movement. And removed himself.

Vera grimaced, on the point of tears. But she was a brave lass and used to bearing her troubles alone. So she ducked her head at Ellie and Thomas, and followed her son out of the room and up the stairs. Quietly.

Silence.

Thomas went to stand at the window, looking out on to the garden. 'I'm trying to think where I was twelve years ago. July 2002. A sabbatical? Yes, that's it. All that summer, I was in a terraced house in Cambridge. Pleasant enough. I was working on that textbook, and my first wife was . . . That was the year in which she began to fade away. Did Dr McKenzie's death make the national papers?'

Ellie looked back into the past, too. Her first husband had still been alive, and they'd lived in a pleasant three-bedroom semi near the church where they'd both worshipped . . . the same church to which Thomas had been appointed after his wife had died, when he'd been told to take it easy for a while. As if Thomas ever took anything easy. Even now, in his semi-retirement, he was editing a national church magazine and filling in at local churches when the incumbent was on holiday or otherwise unable to take a service.

She said, 'I really can't remember much about the murder. It must have been in the local papers, but I only have a hazy memory of it. My first husband was still alive then.' And kicking.

Frank had considered wives ought to know their place . . . which was in the home. Just as Vera's father had done.

Ellie had believed him until he'd died and she'd learned to think for herself. Their only surviving child, Diana, took after him in spades. She said, 'That was the year Diana got married, first time round. Baby Frank was born that September – and look at him now, in the football team and doing well at school.'

He grinned. 'I shouldn't ask, but was Diana still as . . . demanding . . . then?'

Ellie gave a sad little laugh. 'Worse. Her expectations were always high, and she gave her first husband a bad time of it. I suppose that that marriage never really had a chance. To think of it, there's you and me and Diana all happily married second time round.'

'Well, Diana's second is a man who's up to her weight, and she's got herself a new baby whom she adores.' He grimaced. 'I shouldn't have said that about Diana's husband.'

Ellie grinned. 'It's unlike you to say anything bad about anyone. But yes, it's true. He *is* a better match for her than her first husband, who was inclined to give in to her at every point. A bit like me and my first husband. In the old days, I believed it was right to give him his way about everything. It's only later I realized that that comes at a price.' She went to stand beside Thomas, nudging his shoulder with hers. 'How very fortunate we are to have met one another.'

He put his arm around her. 'And here we are, getting along fine. Our lines have indeed fallen in pleasant places. Living in this big old house, waited on hand and foot—'

She looked at her watch, which still said three o'clock. 'Except, oh dear, we won't have any supper unless I do something about it. Cold meat and salad do you?'

'I'll do some chips. I don't think Vera's going to be up to cooking tonight, and Rose—'

'You shouldn't have chips.' Thomas was supposed to be on a diet, but he wasn't serious about it. 'Rose was going to bake a cake this afternoon, but she may not have been up to it, either.' Ellie was worried. 'That man wants Mikey, and he's backed by wealth and power. If Abdi takes his claim to court, what chance does Vera have? She worked as a cleaner for years, and it's only this last year she's been able to go to college and study for a business degree.'

'Mikey's a strong enough character to make his own way in the world without asking his father for favours.'

'But will he see it that way? He's young. If he has the chance of living in a world where money is no object, if he's offered foreign travel and the latest in gadgets, if he knew he could go to university without having to work too hard, wouldn't he plump for that?'

Thomas was silent.

Ellie scrabbled around in her head for an idea. And one popped up, just when it was needed. 'But . . . if . . . just suppose that it was Abdi who killed the doctor?'

'What?' He dropped his arm from her shoulders. 'Ellie, what grounds have you for thinking that?'

Her smile was innocence itself. 'I just thought it would be a neat solution if he turned out to be the murderer.'

'Now then . . .' He shook his head at her. 'You mustn't start rumours.'

'Er, no. But you must agree it would be a satisfactory solution.'

'Don't even think of it . . . Ellie, I know that look of yours. You mustn't interfere. Vera and Abdi need to work things out for themselves.'

'Don't you think Vera could do with a little help up against a man like that?'

'Indeed.'

She knew what he was going to say about it, and he did.

'I shall put in some praying time.'

She nodded, the very picture of a submissive little wifey. But, she told herself, she was no longer the browbeaten woman of her first marriage. She'd learned to stand up for herself. She had resources in the millions she'd inherited and which she administered through a charitable trust. She had friends. And she had many contacts in the community. Prayers were just fine. Thomas was a powerful prayer, and she believed in prayer. But she also believed that God had given us a lot of tools to use in times of distress: such as a tongue, and a brain, and hands and feet.

'I'll get supper started,' she said, wondering which of her acquaintance she could approach first. She did recall something about the doctor's murder, but not much. She hadn't been particularly interested at the time.

Rose had started to make a cake, but hadn't got as far as putting it in the oven, so Ellie did that for her, and rummaged in the fridge for salad stuffs. Thomas joined them to set about peeling potatoes to fry some chips. Ellie didn't mention his diet, thinking they needed carbohydrates for the shock they'd had.

Rose asked if Vera and Mikey were joining them. Ellie had to say she didn't know.

Rose had a new toy, a mobile phone with pre-programmed numbers in it. Rose loved it dearly. There weren't many numbers on her phone, but Vera's was one of them. Before Ellie could say that Vera might prefer to be alone that evening, Rose had produced her mobile and got through to Vera. 'Are you two coming down for supper? Thomas is doing chips.'

Ellie could hear Vera making excuses.

Rose put the phone down. 'Now what's up? And don't tell me nothing's the matter, Ellie Quicke, because I'm not as gormless as I look.'

'You're not gormless, Rose. You're as sharp as they come. And yes, you need to know what's happened. Vera had a visitor this afternoon, who . . .'

Between them, Ellie and Thomas brought Rose up to date.

Rose was distressed. 'He can't take Mikey away from us, just like that. Can he?'

'I shouldn't think so, but if he takes it to the courts . . .' Thomas was not happy about it.

Rose folded her arms across her chest and rocked to and fro. 'Whatever next!'

The cat Midge came prowling to see what there was for him to eat, and Ellie put some food down for him. Midge was a noisy eater.

Ellie wondered who she could ask for information about the deceased doctor. She was in a different medical practice and always had been. She'd heard . . . searching her memory, which did let her down now and then . . . that one of her

friends had gone to him and thought him excellent. Now who
was that?

Ah, she had it. Her old friend Mrs Dawes, who had not
only been the redoubtable head of the flower arranging team
at Ellie's old church but was also a first class gossip. Now,
wait a minute! Hadn't she heard through someone . . . something about Mrs Dawes having been housebound the previous
winter? Ellie had meant to visit her, but this and that had
happened, and the weeks had slipped by.

Oh dear! Ellie knew she ought not to have let old friends
drift out of her life, and in this case she was pretty sure that
Mrs Dawes would have noticed that Ellie had not been to see
her and would be holding it against her. Well, that gave her
two reasons for a visit.

Before getting ready for bed that night, Ellie stood in front
of the full-length mirror in her bedroom. She imagined herself
facing an intruder who wanted to have his wicked way with
her. Well, all right, he probably wouldn't want to rape her, not
at her age, and with a far from perfect figure, but . . .

All right. Suppose she was faced with an intruder who
wanted to mug her. Now, Vera had brought her knee up . . .
so . . . and he'd collapsed. Vera's aim had been perfect.

Ellie practised the same manoeuvre. Or tried to. It didn't
work with the tight skirt she was wearing. She ought to be
wearing trousers. Only, she didn't possess any trousers. Or
jeans. She had never felt comfortable in them, although she
realized that if she went on a diet, she might shed enough
pounds to consider wearing them. But, she wasn't going to
go on a diet, was she? Any more than her dear
Thomas would. He really ought to take dieting more seriously, but . . .

All right. Suppose she wore a full skirt?

Mm. Might be all right. She shed her skirt and stood there
in her slip. And tried again.

Yes, that was more successful, but she'd needed to hold on
to the mirror to steady herself while she brought up her knee.
That couldn't be right. You couldn't expect a man to stand
still while you held on to his shoulders in order that you
might knee him in the groin.

Perhaps she ought to leave such movements to the young and nubile?

She brightened up. What about getting a pepper spray? Or . . . were they illegal? She must ask Thomas.

Wednesday morning

Breakfast was difficult. Rose was restless, worrying about Vera and Mikey, deploring her uselessness in the face of the threat to their peace and quiet. Rose was getting frail. She hadn't been out of the house for months and could fall asleep as soon as she sat down in her big chair in the kitchen, or in her bed-sitting room next door. This morning she was on the verge of tears. 'I hardly slept a wink, thinking what I'd like to do to that nasty Abdi. If only I were ten years younger, I'd give him what for.'

Ellie tried to soothe her. 'Dear Rose, keep on loving and scolding us and worrying about us. You're better than a grandmother to us all.'

'Grandmother, indeed!' But Rose was pleased by the compliment.

Ellie dreaded the day when Rose would need nursing, but so far, fingers crossed, she hadn't fallen and broken anything, and her little ailments remained just that, little. On her good days she did some cooking, and it often turned out all right.

The only odd habit of hers which did cause a frown was that she occasionally 'saw' and 'spoke to' her old employer, Ellie's Aunt Drusilla, who had died years ago. This only happened nowadays in moments of stress, when Rose would report that Miss Quicke was worried about Ellie doing this or that. Sometimes the warning had proved timely. It was an eccentricity which the household could take in its stride. Was Rose going to 'see' Miss Quicke today?

Nowadays, Vera and Mikey usually had their breakfast upstairs before going respectively to college and to school. Ellie was keeping an eye out for Mikey, but he slipped silently down the stairs and out of the house before she could catch him. And Vera . . . oh dear! Vera swept through the kitchen, her manner so cheerful and her smile so bright that it hurt. 'I'll get some fresh veg on the way back, all right? Ta-ra, all.'

Evidently, Vera did not want to talk about Abdi, or Mikey, or . . . well anything. So what could Ellie do about it?

Well, there were more ways of killing a cat than by confrontation, and Ellie decided to try one. So, once she had seen Thomas settled down to work in his study, she went into her own office to consult the phone book. And then had to find a magnifying glass to read the teeny-weeny print. Why did they bother to produce a phone book if no one could read it without a magnifying glass?

No Doctor McKenzie. Well, of course not. He was dead, wasn't he? And his son must long ago have graduated and got a job anywhere in the world from Aberdeen to Addis Ababa. She checked to see if there were an entry for a Dan or a D. McKenzie living locally, but there wasn't. Of course, he might be ex-directory.

With that out of the way, Ellie set off to see her old friend, Mrs Dawes, who had once been a patient on the old doctor's list. It was a fine morning for a walk, or it would be when the sun broke through the early morning mists. She wondered what she'd take to Mrs Dawes for a present. Fudge? Perhaps. No, a box of chocolates would be better. Soft centres, of course.

Ellie didn't often visit this part of town nowadays. As she walked along she identified the places she had once known so well. There was the church, encircled by its lawns and enclosed in trees . . . that was where she'd first met Thomas. Across the road was her own dear little house, the ordinary but pleasant little semi in which she'd lived all the years of her first marriage, the house in which Diana had grown up.

Next door had had a big loft conversion done. That house looked trim and well-cared for, whereas the one which had once been Ellie's had been sold on and now looked a bit neglected. Ah well. Never look back.

Ellie went on round the road and up the hill to Mrs Dawes' house. Another semi-detached, three-bedroom house, slightly smaller than the one which had been Ellie's. Mrs Dawes was a keen gardener, and . . .

Oh. The front garden had been paved over, and the curtains at the window had been replaced with those wooden shutters which were supposed to tilt this way and that to let in or exclude the light. Mostly, they worked. Yes, this lot looked new. Mrs Dawes would never have paved over her garden. So what had been going on here?

Sinking feeling.

Ellie rang the doorbell, which had a dog-barking chime. If 'chime' was the right word. Probably not.

A frizzy-blonde head appeared in the doorway. Not Mrs Dawes. A bony woman, fiftyish. T-shirt, jeans, trainers and a tan which must have been acquired on a recent holiday in a warmer climate . . . or by use of a beauty parlour. 'Yes?'

'I'm sorry to intrude,' said Ellie. 'I used to live down the road by the church. I'm an old friend of Mrs Dawes, but I hadn't seen her for a while, and I wondered . . . She doesn't live here any more, does she?'

THREE

The woman opened the door wide. 'Come on in. You don't remember me, do you? Geraldine. I used to help out at the church in the old days, when Thomas was there. You're Mrs Quicke, that used to be a friend of Mrs Dawes? Then you came into money and got married to Thomas and moved away?'

'Yes, indeed. I seem to have lost touch. It happens when you move out of the parish.'

'Like a coffee? I've got the lunch sorted and was just about to have one before I start on the ironing. I work at the beautician's in the Avenue, but I don't do mornings.'

In Mrs Dawes' time, there had been two reception rooms downstairs. The front had been the kept-for-visitors sitting room, while Mrs Dawes had used the cosier dining room at the back to sit in while she watched the birds through her binoculars. Now the two rooms had been thrown into one and everything was light and bright, though cluttered with photographs of an extensive family: parents and babies, ancient and modern; wedding photos galore; plus two gowned and capped diplomas.

What a change.

'Take a seat, do,' said Geraldine. 'That's my husband over there, that passed two years ago, and my children and grandchildren, quite a tribe we are now and still find time to visit . . . Do you prefer decaf?'

Ellie sat on a squashy armchair, while her hostess ran in and out of the kitchen next door . . . Yes, the kitchen had had a makeover, as well. And the planting in the garden had been tidied up almost to extinction.

'Funny you should drop by. I found something of Mrs Dawes' the other day, a photo album which must have been dropped at the back of the built-in cupboard upstairs. I'd like to get it back to her some time, and you can take it to her if you like. She's in sheltered accommodation now, the one on the main road going up to the Broadway, where they give you a sherry before meals if you care for it, not that I do . . . care for it, I mean. Sherry's not exactly my tipple but there's no accounting, is there?'

'No, indeed. The old people's home, you mean? The Cedars?'

'That's it.' Geraldine bustled in with two mugs, both spark-ling clean. 'Milk and sugar, too? I always say, a little of what you fancy . . . Yes, poor Mrs Dawes. It was her hip, you know. She had this operation but it didn't go right, and, well, her weight told against her as we all said it would, but she would not diet, would she?'

Ellie shook her head. 'Very true.'

'She did manage to keep going for a while, with us taking it in turns to get her food, and then she had those carers, not that they amounted to much. Promise the earth and do as little as they could if you ask me, and she did struggle to church on Sundays, but her temper!' She rolled her eyes.

Ellie nodded. 'Ah.'

'So she had to give in and go into care, and those relatives of hers, vultures more like, if you'll forgive the harsh words—'

Ellie nodded again. She'd come across Mrs Dawes' relatives, too.

'Well, they said they wanted her to go to live with them, or them to move in with her, but her grandson, the only one worth tuppence—'

'The best of the bunch.'

'He was realistic. He said from the start it was a no go because when she fell, it took two trained people to lift her up. So I was looking to move after my husband passed away. Such a big house we had with all the children growing up, but after he'd gone it wasn't the same. So she sold up and went into care, and I sold up and moved in here. I visit her every now and then, when I can, though it's not as often as I should, really, and take her a bunch of something, not that they haven't got everything you can think of there. But it's sad, isn't it? No way out of there except in a box.'

'Talking of health care,' said Ellie, sipping bad coffee and trying not to grimace, 'one reason I wanted to see Mrs Dawes was that I've a friend just moved into this area and she asked me which doctor I'd recommend. I know Mrs Dawes used to be with Dr McKenzie, but I don't know who took over his practice and whether he's any good or not, so I said I'd ask. That practice would suit her best, being so near.'

'Ah, well, it's lost the personal touch and gone downhill since he died. Four or five doctors there now, but you never see the same one twice.'

'That wouldn't suit her. What about the son? Wasn't he going to go into medicine, too?'

'Now there was a change of direction.' Geraldine relished giving bad news. 'Went haywire he did, after his father . . . You know about that?'

'I remember the father died, yes.'

'Murdered, he was. On his son's birthday. Drugs, they said. Some bad lad thinking the doctor had drugs on the premises, which of course he never. But I'm thinking there was more to it than that.'

'Really?'

Geraldine winked. False eyelashes? 'All that hoo-ha about the hedge. Storm in a teacup, but it led to blows at least once, didn't it? I reckon he was done in to stop the court case, right?'

'What I've missed, moving out of the parish! Tell me more.'

'Well,' said Geraldine, bony hands slapping the arms of her chair, 'I suppose I ought not to say this . . .' A sideways glance to see if Ellie appreciated gossip.

Ellie leaned forward. 'The only way to discover the truth is to explore all the possibilities. Sometimes even to say the thing that you ought not to say . . .?'

Geraldine thought that was amusing. 'That's right. It was always the bit of gossip my husband used to say I shouldn't repeat that's the most interesting—'

'Tell me *all*!'

Geraldine drew her chair closer to Ellie and dropped her voice, though there was no one else in the room. 'Well, I got this from my Friday-afternoon customer that was a friend of theirs, played bridge with her, that sort of thing, and of course it was all in the papers, the local papers, I mean, though it never got as far as the High Court, which it was going to do, both parties being determined to have their pound of flesh. You know where the doctor lived? One of those big houses up the hill, the other end of the Avenue, over by the Cricket Club? Big houses with their own driveways and long gardens at the back. Well, apparently the doctor bought a bit of someone else's garden at the side of his that they didn't want, and he had it dug out and put in a swimming pool. But when he did so, the contractor tore out some of the hedge between him and his next-door neighbour. The doctor said the hedge was on his property and he wanted to put in a fence instead, to give him privacy around the bathing pool, you see?'

'And the boundary was in dispute?'

'That's just it. The deeds showed the line of the hedge, but it looked as if it had been put in a couple of feet to the west or the east of the boundary line, I can't remember which, and it wasn't clear who owned it. The doctor said it was his, and the solicitor next door—'

'Any name for the solicitor?'

'Or was it a barrister? I'm never sure of the difference. A bigwig, you know. Big car, big stomach, big ego. A second-hand wife; that's what they call these women that have been through the divorce courts a couple of times, isn't it? I think they broke up soon after. Anyway, there was a right ding-dong and it came to fisticuffs at the golf club one evening, which I wouldn't have heard about but my Friday-afternoon appointment that I told you about – she's moved away so I don't see her any more – anyway, she was there on the next table, and her dress was ruined when the Sauternes went flying around the place. I said she should have sued him for the cost of cleaning, but she said she'd never liked the dress that much, and didn't want to bother, especially as the Sir was such a tightwad and she didn't think it was as much as her life was worth to complain.'

'The Sir was a K?'

'A Queen's something; they made him a Sir.'

'So it went to court?'

'Magistrates'. And then on to County. We were taking bets on it at the salon, I can tell you. We all liked the doctor and hoped he'd win, though my Bill, my husband that was still with us then, he said him and his friends that worked in the council thought the Sir would probably win. Being who he was and knowing all the right people. My Bill said the costs would be enormous and whoever lost might have to sell his house to pay.'

'I can't quite see a Sir killing the doctor, though. Did anyone see them fighting? Was it an accident, perhaps? A bit of shoving and pushing getting out of hand?'

Geraldine sighed. 'Didn't you read the papers?'

'Sorry. A lot was going on in the family then. My daughter was being difficult, pregnant, wanting . . .' Ellie gestured helplessness. Diana had indeed been exceptionally demanding at that time, pushing even her doting father too far. Tears, rage, screams . . . frantic phone calls . . . Not a good time to remember. 'I do recall that there was a big party on that night, but the details escape me. Did they make too much noise? Did the Sir complain?'

A shrug. 'He was out. Both him and his wife. *And* the doctor and his wife were out and the youngsters were let loose, which I'd never have allowed if it had been me, because

Heaven only knows what they can get up to when the adults aren't around.' She nodded, looking wise. 'Drugs and such.'

Ellie sought in her memory for details. 'Didn't they think the doctor was killed by someone who'd gatecrashed the party and was looking for drugs?'

'That's what they said in the papers. They tried hard enough to find someone, but did they manage it? No, they didn't. But, they didn't look at the Sir next door, did they? I reckon he and his wife, that tart, and the doctor and his wife, who wasn't too well at the time, they say, although she's chipper enough nowadays, I believe . . . Anyway, it seems they all got back home about the same time, and the wives went in, leaving the men to put the cars away. The Sir says he went straight back indoors and didn't speak to the doctor, but I reckon that's when he did it. He clocked the doctor with a spanner or something, and left him in the garage, pushing the door shut so no one would find him for a while. Which they didn't. Find him, I mean. Not till the morning.'

'Hadn't Mrs McKenzie missed her husband?'

A wink and a nod. 'They didn't sleep in the same room, apparently.'

'What about the Sir? Didn't the police look at him?'

'His wife gave him an alibi, didn't she? "He was with me every minute after we got back, officer." And they believed her just because she was upper crust. Excuse me a minute . . .' Geraldine consulted her watch and, with a shriek, bolted into the kitchen. 'Sorry, sorry! I forgot the stew. I'm expecting one of my grandsons for lunch today, so you will excuse me, won't you? He won't like it if I don't have it ready for him, with him only having an hour off in the middle of the day.'

Ellie knew it was time for her to go, but hadn't finished yet. 'Wasn't there something about a foreigner making trouble that night?'

'They're everywhere nowadays, aren't they? Not that I'm against them, understand, for one of my other grandsons is going out with the prettiest little thing, and she can cook, too, though her people come from somewhere out in the East, not India, it will come to me in a minute . . . Oh, are you going? Well, it's long time no see, don't be a stranger any more, will you? And where did I put that thing for Mrs Dawes? The Cedars, remember? Give her my love and tell her I'll pop in after the weekend, got the family coming, another birthday, and they don't like to leave their old gran out, do they?'

Ellie was swept out of the front door and on to the path. She decided that what Geraldine had said was just gossip. What's more, it didn't make sense, did it? Or, it made sense, but only if Ellie adjusted her timing for the events. She frowned. At what point had the police been called in? Who had summoned them? Not Sir, because he was out with his wife, 'that tart'. Not the doctor, ditto.

Ellie looked at her watch. She'd put it on that morning without thinking, and it still registered the wrong time. She must take it in to be repaired. Or . . . embarrassing thought . . . did the battery need changing? She couldn't remember when she had last had that done, which meant it was probably a long time ago and the battery did need changing . . . which meant a trip to Ealing Broadway, because there was nowhere in the Avenue which sold the tiny batteries for watches. Which meant another errand to run.

In the meantime, could she fit in a visit to Mrs Dawes in the retirement home?

Ellie had a struggle with her conscience. Why bother? Why not go straight home and help Rose sort out the food situation? Or do some of the paperwork which drifted on to the desk in her study every day? She hadn't seen Mrs Dawes for ever, and she could drop off the photo album any old time. Mrs Dawes hadn't missed it, or she'd have made a fuss, wouldn't she?

Besides which, Ellie realized she'd been asking for information of the wrong age group. The people she needed to talk to would be those who'd been at the party; the school-leavers of that day, and the gatecrashers who might or might not have been dealing in drugs. Not the older generation who'd been parents then, for they knew nothing about what had gone on there. It would be a waste of time to visit Mrs Dawes.

Ellie shook her head at herself and set off down the hill. She'd neglected Mrs Dawes, and she was ashamed of herself for doing so. Mrs Dawes might not be the most congenial of companions, but she was an old friend and had looked after Ellie in the days when the old lady had ruled the flower arranging team with a pair of sharp scissors and an even sharper tongue. True, Mrs Dawes had been in the habit of using Ellie as something of a slave . . . *Do this, fetch that!* But even then, Mrs Dawes had not been quite as spry as she might have been.

It would be best to take the bus. Ellie smiled, wondering if Mrs Dawes still dyed her hair and wore dangling earrings.

Two bus stops later, Ellie got off at The Cedars. She rang the bell and announced herself as a visitor to Mrs Dawes.

'What?' Mrs Dawes was in a chair with a high back and arms, seated at a table. 'Who?' A Zimmer frame was at her side. Her eyes were not as sharp as before, her hair was now silver, and she no longer wore her dangling earrings. 'Ellie Quicke, is it? Well, stranger: what brings you here? Your conscience smiting you? I didn't think you of all people, and married to a vicar, would have neglected your old friends. You're all the same, marry into money and forget your old friends.'

Ellie hid her distress at seeing how her old friend had deteriorated and stooped to kiss her cheek. 'I know. I have been meaning to. But moving away, even only half a mile . . . I dropped in to see you at your old house, to bring you a little something, a box of chocolates, I hope you like them. It was only then I heard you'd come here. Geraldine found this photo album, too, which she says must have dropped behind a cupboard.'

'Chocolates. Soft centres, I hope. Can't do with nuts at my age. They get under my plate. The photo album? Geraldine should have brought it round herself. Did she say when she was coming?'

'Not this weekend. A family do of some kind.'

Mrs Dawes' eyes strayed. 'It'll be lunch in a minute. A good cook, most days. It saves my legs, them cooking for me. Proper printed menus they give us, and a choice, too, and they understand about teeth not being up to much nowadays. They even have a dentist visit here. And a chiropodist. But the telly's on all the time, unless you ask to be in the garden room where it's quiet and . . .'

'Splendid,' said Ellie, resigning herself to hearing a litany of complaints.

'So what finally brought you here, eh?'

'A query from a friend. She's just moved into the area, wanted to know if she should join Dr McKenzie's old practice.'

Silence. Mrs Dawes worked her jaws. 'Bad business, that. A doctor from that practice comes to see us here. One of them, anyway. One's as bad as the other.'

'I hoped the son would have gone into the practice.'

'No backbone. Gave up at the first hurdle. Went in for something else, can't remember what. The church, was it? My memory's not what it was.'

Ellie let a laugh escape her. 'You mean he became a minister? Like my husband?'

'Who?' A stare. 'Oh, yes. I forgot. You married again, didn't you? Is it working out all right?'

Alzheimer's, here we come. 'Very much so,' said Ellie. 'So, what about the McKenzie lad? He wasn't stupid, was he? I thought he was a bright lad, went to university?'

'Tried something else. Not the church. Sometimes I get confused.'

'Never mind, dear,' said Ellie.

'But I do mind.' Tears welled in old eyes. 'It comes and goes. Will you come to see me again? On a good day, mind. There's days when it's . . .' Her voice trailed away.

Ellie patted the old woman's hand. 'I promise.' An aide was coming round with trays of food. Another was distributing large bibs. A tray of food was placed front of Mrs Dawes, whose hands trembled as she reached for a glass of orange juice. Her eyes were on the plate of chicken and vegetables. All soft food. It looked delicious. 'About the doctor,' she said. *'Cherchez la femme.'*

'What?' Ellie wasn't sure she'd heard correctly. Look for

the lady? What did that mean? The old lady seized her knife and fork and lost interest in Ellie.

Home again. The Tesco delivery van was in the driveway and the front door was open. The weekly order of shopping had arrived. Vera was clever about ordering online, something neither Rose nor Ellie was good at. Ellie hoped that Rose hadn't been trying to carry the bags in herself, which she had been known to attempt in the past.

Ellie called out, 'Yoo-hoo, I'm back!'

The delivery man emerged from the kitchen quarters, smiling. 'Cheers, missus!' He banged the front door to on his way out.

There was a strange coat on the chair in the hall. Oh. So now what?

Thomas loomed in the doorway to the sitting room. He was stroking his beard and frowning. This must be an important visitor, for he didn't usually leave his study at this time of day. 'Ah, Ellie. I hoped you'd be back early. Our visitor from yesterday is here again.'

Ellie dropped her shopping and her jacket, and joined him in the sitting room.

'Forgive my informality,' said Abdi, half rising from his seat in deference to the fact that a woman had entered the room, but sinking back on to it straight away. 'I believe we were at cross purposes yesterday. I wanted to set the record straight.'

Ellie seated herself in her high-backed chair by the fireplace. She wondered whether or not she should offer refreshments, and decided against doing so. She placed her hands in her lap and waited to hear what their visitor had to say for himself. She didn't suppose there would be an apology . . .?

Thomas didn't let himself down into his favourite La-Z-Boy chair, but took an upright one instead. Perhaps Abdi would prefer to talk to a man, rather than a woman? Ellie assumed Abdi would be a Muslim. They didn't think women were equal to men, did they?

Abdi produced a smile and a certain amount of charm.

'Yesterday . . . So much drama. So unnecessary. I seem to have taken you all by surprise. Perhaps I ought to have approached Vera through my solicitors but I had not thought it necessary, given the circumstances.' He seemed to expect a reply. Excellent teeth.

Ellie and Thomas exchanged glances.

Thomas was as puzzled as Ellie. 'What circumstances, may I ask?'

The newcomer spread his hands. 'My mission is simply to right a wrong. To give my son a future. But your reaction . . . Forgive me, but only afterwards did it occur to me that Vera may not have been perfectly frank with you about her somewhat chequered past. Has she represented herself to you as a victim of fate? Understandable, if she wishes to pass herself off as more sinned against than sinning, though not precisely accurate. It occurred to me that you may have taken her in and, as I understand it, almost adopted her, under false pretences. I tried to put myself into your shoes. I came to the conclusion that she could not possibly have told you the truth, or you would have seen things from my point of view and not taken her part. Hence my calling on you today. I need to put the record straight.'

Thomas said, 'We have been acquainted with Vera for a number of years and know of nothing to her discredit.'

'I understand why you feel so protective of her, but if you had known her better—'

'Get to the point.' Thomas was losing patience.

Abdi smiled. He seemed to think he held all the cards. Ellie felt uneasy. What did Abdi know, or think he knew, that could shake their trust in Vera?

'Put simply, I will go to court if necessary to reclaim my son. I can offer him opportunities in life which he is denied as the child of a woman of doubtful virtue, who works as a domestic servant, and who is suspected of murder—'

'Murder!'

'I am sure the courts will agree.'

FOUR

Ellie couldn't believe her ears. 'You think Vera is a murderer? You are out of your mind! And how can you say her reputation is in doubt?'

'She can hardly have concealed her lack of virtue from you, when by her own admission she allowed so many men the pleasure of her company. Or perhaps she has never seen fit fully to inform you of what happened? I suppose she has been equally reticent about her involvement in the murder of the doctor, the man who stood in the way of her love affair with Danny boy? I can see she has. What a clever little thing she is. Allow me to enlighten you.'

Ellie struggled with a feeling that she was being sucked into a quicksand of lies. For one thing, Vera had referred to her boyfriend as 'Dan' not 'Danny'. The diminutive 'Danny' made Dan sound unimportant. 'She has told us what happened that night, yes. There was a birthday party which you attended along with other school leavers. Some gatecrashers disrupted the party and—'

Abdi laughed. 'I should say so. Poor Danny was in a terrible state.'

'They were after drugs, weren't they?'

A shrug. 'Not my scene.'

'You, along with others, fled the house, and in a secluded part of the garden you saw a girl lying on the ground, being visited by other young men.'

'Correct. And enjoying it.'

'You must have realized she'd been drugged.'

An indulgent smile. 'Is that what she told you? A fine story. I was there, remember. I saw it all. Four of us . . . maybe more . . . taking a turn at pleasuring themselves and her.'

Four of them! How dreadful! 'So you joined the queue?'

'Why ever not? We were all of an age. Drink flowed. The gatecrashers had thrown us out of the house, so we took our pleasure where we could. It was exciting. She was lying there in the open, waiting for us.'

'She was unconscious.'

'If you believe that . . .' He laughed.

'Did she open her eyes and scream to you all to get on with it? Or did she lie there like a rag doll, unresisting? Comatose?'

His eyes narrowed. 'It wasn't rape. She was a whore, a slut.'

'She didn't have that reputation before that evening, did she? If anything, I believe she was regarded as a prude. Her father was careful of her, wasn't he?'

'How should I know?'

'Did you recognize her?'

'Of course. Danny's little bit on the side.'

'You knew her, but not well.'

'I'd seen her at parties but she was not the sort of girl I would ever have taken seriously. Naturally, I would have preferred the mother of my son to have a better character. But it is not to be, and I'm stuck with who she is.'

Ellie heard Thomas grind his teeth. 'I'm surprised you want the boy, if you have so little respect for his mother.'

A grimace. Momentary discomfort. 'Ah, well. You must understand that in our culture a man without offspring is, well, at a certain disadvantage in family affairs. True, I am currently living in Britain, but in due course I will return home to Somalia to take up my position as my father's eldest child. Without a son I would be at a certain disadvantage vis-à-vis my brothers, who already have several sons each. I married, of course, within a year of leaving school. An arranged match. A delightful girl from a good family. Unfortunately, she failed to conceive, and eventually tests proved that it was I who had overindulged in the delights of the flesh and not her.'

Thomas was appalled. 'Are we to understand that you contracted a sexual disease at some point in the year after you left school and before you got married? You mean you are now infertile?'

Abdi swept his hands outwards. 'So it seems. And what a shock that was! After some thought, it occurred to me that I might possibly have been fortunate in one of my early . . . er . . . adventures. There were several possibilities.' He smiled to himself. 'I engaged a detective to discover if by any chance one of my early couplings might have led to a happy conclusion. One had had an abortion. Two were married with young children. Only one of my partners from those days had had a child within the possible time constraints, and that was Vera, who had produced the boy you call Mikey. The detective obtained DNA samples from both Vera and her son without their knowledge. They had carelessly left their ice cream cups on the table when they'd indulged in a little treat at McDonalds, and he managed to remove them for testing. Unfortunately or otherwise, there can be no possible doubt about it. Mikey is my son.'

Thomas said, 'And you assumed you could just walk in and buy the child?'

Abdi smoothed out a smile. 'Of course not. That would be crude. No, there will be a certain adjustment of finances. Some compensation to Vera for bringing up the boy so far. I will formally adopt him and provide him with a standard of living which she cannot possibly give.'

'He's doing pretty well on his own merits,' said Ellie. 'He got a bursary to one of the top schools in London.'

'Living in rented accommodation . . .? No doubt you've been kind to him, but it's not the same, and you can't pretend that it is. His mother will never be anything but a domestic servant, even if she does now call herself a housekeeper.'

Ellie realized she was spitting into the wind, but persisted. 'She's going to college, doing a business course.'

Thomas said, 'Let's get this clear. Does your wife agree to your adopting Mikey?'

An airy gesture. 'She understands the situation. Either she accepts the boy into our household with good grace, or there will be an amicable divorce. Even if she does accept him, there will be very little contact, as I will be sending him to one of the best boarding schools in the country. In the holidays he will return home to my grandfather's place and become accustomed to his new position in life. It will be as if he were the offspring of a previous wife, now deceased.'

Ellie was getting angry. 'Mikey is not a toy to be picked up and laid aside at will.'

A soft laugh. 'I hear he's been in one or two scrapes before now. All the better. I like his independence of character. But he will soon learn what is expected of my son. He will adjust.'

Thomas took a turn around the room. 'You are assuming too much. I suppose it is true that you can offer Mikey a more affluent lifestyle than the one he has at present, but I do not think you will be able to separate him from his mother as easily as you think.'

'If I cannot convince you all that what I suggest is for the best, then we will have to let the courts decide.'

Ellie shook her head. 'You think the courts would give you Mikey? I don't think so. The truth is that before the party Vera was a virgin with a steady boyfriend . . .' She held up her hand, seeing that he was about to intervene. 'I understand what you would say. Possibly, it was an unequal match, the doctor's son and the girl from the chippy, but they were both going on to university and their relationship might well have developed into marriage. Only, at the party she was given a date rape drug and was out for the count. She was raped. You, among others, raped her.'

'Ridiculous! What a story! Is that what she told you? Every whore cries, "Rape!" when they've had too much to drink and want to justify what they've done. She's a cunning little liar, I'll give her that. Pulled the wool over your eyes, Mrs Quicke. Sweet as pie, and twice as treacherous! And, you've conveniently forgotten her involvement with murder.'

Ellie was getting angry. 'What involvement?'

'Why, the death of the good doctor. Didn't you know? Ah, I can see she hasn't told you about that, has she? There was a confrontation between them later that evening, after the police had been and gone, long after the other partygoers had left. She was seen arguing with Danny's father . . . no doubt over her conduct that evening. They were seen, I tell you. Struggling. Shouting. In the garage. She hit him with a tyre lever, or some such, and killed him.'

'What!' said Thomas.

'No, I don't believe it.' Ellie was horrified, and yet . . .

what was it Geraldine had said? No, no. That was something to do with a neighbour.

Abdi shrugged. 'There was a witness.'

'Who?'

'Someone my detective found.'

'Why didn't he or she come forward at the time?'

Abdi shrugged again. 'I believe it was someone who didn't want to bother with going to the police. On night duty or some such. Or just come off it. Something like that.'

Thomas was incredulous. 'Your man found someone who wouldn't go to the police about it before, but who has been persuaded to speak about it now?'

Ellie's eyes narrowed. 'Someone you've bought off. That's it, isn't it? You paid this private detective of yours to find someone, anyone, who can dig up some dirt on Vera. Which makes me ask: why is this witness now prepared to go to court when he wouldn't do so before? How much did you have to pay him to testify against Vera?'

'I doubt if there will be any need to go as far as that.'

'In other words, he is so unreliable that you daren't produce him?'

'I mean that Vera won't want to risk her past being brought up against her. I only have to lay information to the police about her involvement with the doctor's murder, and they'll have her in for questioning.'

'On such flimsy evidence?'

'I suppose it may well be in the papers the following day that she is being questioned for murder.'

'You mean that you would leak it to the papers, in order to turn public opinion against her?'

A bland smile. 'How dreadful for Vera, to be pilloried in the press, to have everyone know what sort of good-time girl she was, and to hear that she is now under suspicion of murder. What will that do to her course at college? She will be forced into hiding. The university will not want her on their premises if she's being followed around by the press, will they? Only think what this would do to Mikey.'

'You . . .!' Hot words sprang to Ellie's tongue. She refused them voice with an effort.

Thomas said, 'You mean that you are going to hold an unreliable but potentially incriminating witness over Vera? Either she gives up the boy, or she risks being accused of murder in the press?'

A wide smile. Abdi spread his hands. 'I think that between us we can persuade Vera to see reason, don't you?'

Ellie could see exactly what he meant. Vera probably thought that the very worst had happened to her that night so long ago. Never mind that the events of the party had changed her life and she'd been unable to take up the place she'd earned at university. Never mind that her father had disowned her and made her homeless when he discovered that she was pregnant. Never mind that the father of the child had then refused to help her, had accused her of trying to trick him into marriage . . .

Worse, she was going to be accused of murder unless she gave up her only child.

'You didn't mention anything about murder when Vera applied to you for help when Mikey was born.'

'I was about to be married myself, to a suitable girl.'

'So she was left to support herself and the child. She might have had him adopted, but she didn't. She found work, mostly cleaning jobs. She brought Mikey up as best she could. She married, eventually—'

'I heard she took advantage of a dying man—'

'Your private detective, if that's who has been feeding you incorrect information, needs his ears syringing. Yes, he was dying and knew it. She loved him, cared for him, nursed him to the end. He didn't leave her much, but he asked me to keep an eye on her and to help her get the education she deserved, and that's what I'm doing. She is no slut. No whore. She is a good woman who's been dealt some terrible blows by fate but has made the best of what she's got.'

'That's her story, is it? Well, we'll see what happens when we go to court. I hear the boy's been in trouble with the law already. That shows precisely how good she's been as a mother.'

Thomas said, 'You don't like hearing the truth, do you? He was exonerated of all charges and helped to bring a couple of villains to justice. As for you, you rape an innocent young girl, refuse to help her when she discovers she's had your child, ignore her and your son for twelve years, and expect the courts to be sympathetic towards you? The boy is at a good school now and doing well.'

'Go back to your private detective,' said Ellie, 'and ask the right questions this time. Tell him to look elsewhere for a boy to adopt.'

His lips drew back over his teeth. 'There is no one else of my blood.'

Ellie said, 'You should have thought of that before you scattered your seed in so many different directions.'

'That was then, and this is now. The boy will be fine, once he realizes what he is going to inherit. I must admit that at first I did wonder how costly it was going to be to pay off his mother, even if she did have a distinctly unsavoury past, but the evidence my man has turned up is more than just useful. Potentially, it's a knock out, don't you think?' He stood up, stretching, very much at his ease. 'Do tell the girl that I'm willing to be generous, won't you? My solicitor says Vera hasn't a leg to stand on. Not that you'd wish this matter to go to court, any more than I would. I am sure that between us we'll be able to make Vera see reason. I'll be back tomorrow to make some preliminary arrangements.'

He got out a mobile phone, and said, 'I need the car now.' Phoning his chauffeur?

Ellie didn't offer to let him wait for his car indoors, but opened the front door for him. It was beginning to rain. Good. Let him wait outside.

The clock in the hall chimed the hour. Was it only one o'clock? It felt like bedtime.

Rose hovered in the doorway to the kitchen quarters. A little brown wren, inquisitive but anxious. 'What's that man doing here again? I said to him that you were out but he pushed in past me while the Tesco man was delivering, and then I went and fetched Thomas because I didn't want to leave him alone, and I thought about ringing Vera to say he was here, but then I thought I shouldn't spoil her day unless I had to.'

'You did right, Rose.'

'There's some soup for lunch and some of that quiche left over, if you fancy.'

'Yes, in a minute.' Ellie returned to the sitting room, where Thomas was standing at the window, looking out.

He said, 'We have to fight him, don't we?'

'Do you doubt it?'

'No.' He didn't sound sure of it, though. 'I've heard three different versions of what happened that night . . . No, four if you count Mrs Dawes' comment. And none of them make any sense, including Abdi's.'

'Would your policewoman friend help?' He answered his own question. 'No, you can't ask her or she'd want to have Vera in for questioning about the murder.'

'The murder must have happened before Lesley joined the force. She's a good friend, but I don't want to involve her unless I can think of a way of keeping Vera out of it. I'd like to ask her to look up the police records, but I'd have to be careful because her boss – who is as awkward as they come – would like nothing better than to annoy me by tossing a murder charge in our direction.' She tried to lighten the atmosphere. 'You usually tell me not to when I want to look into a problem in the community, yet here you are, cheering me on.'

He pulled a face. 'My first reaction was to say I was at your disposal, and then—'

'You realized the magazine has to be put to bed next week, and you've hardly time to eat or drink before that. Which reminds me; Rose has rustled up some lunch for us.'

He followed her out to the kitchen. 'Where will you start?' And to their housekeeper, 'Prayers needed, Rose.'

Rose wrung her hands. 'That's exactly what Miss Quicke has been saying to me, ever since yesterday when that man arrived on the doorstep without so much as a by your leave. She's been popping up all over the place, in the conservatory which is usual with her, and then in the back garden when I was out hanging up the dishcloths, and here in the kitchen with me last night. Gave me a bit of a fright, then. I thought it was the wireless, but it was her, saying that we've got to look after those that have taken refuge with us, here in this house. Which is a bit odd as I never thought she'd really taken to young Mikey, him being a bit of a loose cannon, as you might say, but she's adamant that he's in danger and we're to watch out for him specially, and there's a dish of beetroot salad instead of the quiche if you'd prefer it.'

'Thank you, Rose,' said Ellie, giving the older lady a hug. 'Trust me, I'm going to see what I can do to protect both Vera and Mikey.'

Thomas slurped soup.

Ellie collected the memo pad they used for shopping lists and started to make notes, speaking her thoughts aloud as she did so. 'Questions to ask: what time did the party start, and who was invited? How did the gatecrashers know about the party? How many of them were there? Did they bring drugs with them, or did they come looking for them?'

Rose put some soup at her elbow. Ellie had a couple of mouthfuls, then said, 'The police must have asked these questions, before. After twelve years, the partygoers may have scattered to the four winds. How on earth can we get answers to them now?'

Thomas looked at his watch. 'I mustn't be long. So much to do.'

Ellie wondered, 'At what point in time did everyone arrive? Vera would have been there early, I suppose, as Dan's girlfriend. Who was it who helped her home? Who gave her the drugged drink, and who raped her? Apart from Abdi. I don't think she knows.'

Another glance at his watch. 'Some of the other guests may be able to enlighten you.'

'Abdi's not going to tell us anything which might cast doubt on his carefully edited version of events.' She attacked her soup, thinking. 'I wonder, at what point did the police arrive? Who called them, and what did they do when they did attend the scene? Was anyone arrested? Taken away for questioning? Was it drug dealing that triggered a call to the police?'

Rose cleared their soup plates away. 'You can find out, Ellie, if anyone can.'

Ellie served up pieces of quiche. 'Vera says she woke up

when the police arrived and that the guests had nearly all disappeared by that time. Vera must know who it was who helped her. Probably a pillar of the community by now. It's just occurred to me to wonder what Dan was doing all that while. Was it he who called the police? We've been told the parents were away for the evening. Why? And for how long?'

Thomas joined in for once. 'What time did they get back, and what happened then?'

'A neighbour was supposed to be at loggerheads with the doctor about a hedge which got torn down or planted in the wrong place. They were angry enough to go to law about it. I wonder what they were doing that night? And then, if anything that Abdi's man has dug up is correct, there was some sort of fight when the doctor returned home. This must have been after the police investigating the gatecrashers had gone. Long after the guests had disappeared . . . or was it? It would have been useful to talk to the good doctor. So inconvenient that he died.'

'As did Vera's father and mother.' Thomas attacked his plateful. 'Mm. Good quiche. What's in it?'

'Asparagus. Twelve years on . . . Memories play us false. Especially inconvenient ones. Dan might have been a right raver at eighteen, up till all hours, just passed his driving test, hormones rampaging, a nuisance to all and sundry . . . He might well be an assistant bank manager by now, with a wife, a mortgage and two point four children. The girls who were at the party, ditto.'

Thomas said, 'You need to speak to Dan first, don't you?'

'If I can find him, yes.'

'Amen,' said Rose. 'And I'll try to remember to put in a spot of praying this afternoon, though it looks as if it might be sunny and I was thinking of deadheading some roses if the rain keeps off.'

Rose hardly moved out of the kitchen nowadays, and Ellie didn't take her plan to work in the garden seriously.

Ellie was talking to herself more than the others. 'Dan McKenzie, where are you? You didn't follow your father into the practice, and you're not in the phone book. Are you working in a hospital somewhere? What has become of you?'

'Cycling from John o' Groats,' said Rose, putting the dirty plates into the sink instead of the dishwasher. 'Land's End to John o' Groats. I hope he's as fit as he thinks he is. It's terrestrione, that's what it is. Always wanting to show off their muscles.'

Thomas was amused. 'Did you mean "terrestrial", as in protecting territorial rights, Rose? Or "testosterone", as in the male desire to prove themselves alphas in society . . .? Though I suppose it could be both, in the case of cycling.'

Ellie said, 'What was that, Rose? You know where Dan McKenzie is?'

'He was in the local paper last week. Don't you remember? You'd sent some money to his school for something, and you thought it was interesting that one of the teachers was now doing something to help others. There's far too many small charities, in my opinion. All wanting to help some minority group which may be very deserving for all I know, but if they can't raise enough money to make a difference then what I say is, the money should go to the bigger charities that know how to spread a little kindness around.'

Ellie hit her forehead. 'Was that him? I did send some money to a school, yes, to help their choir to go to some event or other. But his name didn't mean anything to me then, and what he did wasn't about music, was it?'

Rose was far away. 'I remembered it because I had a neighbour once was called MacSomething who was into sport, but I think that was motorbikes. I thought it might have been him, but it wasn't. McSweeney? McCartney?'

Ellie scrabbled in the pile of newspapers which had been set aside for recycling. When did the dustbinmen come? Thursday. And this was Wednesday, so last week's local paper should be here somewhere. Or not, if it had been used to line the waste food bucket . . . Hopefully not. 'Ah.' She drew it out of the pile and smoothed out the creases on the table.

She turned pages. No. No . . . goodness gracious! Every week there seemed to be someone objecting to something . . . Probably quite right to do so, but . . . 'Ah, here it is.'

A photo of a youngish man wearing goggles and a cycling helmet, dressed in the usual Lycra and sitting on a good-looking racing bike. He was holding out a large cheque to a pudding-faced man in a decent suit. 'He was raising money for Help for Heroes. Wounded soldiers, that sort of thing.'

Thomas looked over her shoulder. 'From here to eternity, or Land's End to John o' Groats. Which end is he starting at?'

'He's done it,' said Ellie, reading further on. 'Collected his money and handed it over. I suppose he was wearing cycling gear because it made a better photo opportunity for the papers. I can't tell what he looks like from the picture. It says he's the Deputy Head of the new secondary school. Feather in his cap. And yes, that *is* the school that I sent the money to.'

Thomas said, 'He lives in Perivale, Middlesex. Next door to, but not *in*, Ealing.'

'"Father of one,"' said Ellie. 'Why do they always say that, as if it's the most significant thing about them? Or,' she corrected herself, 'maybe it is. But it doesn't mention his wife, and she's not in the picture. Maybe she doesn't approve of his taking half term off to cycle the length of the land.'

'Well, at least you know where to find him now.'

FIVE

Wednesday p.m.

Ellie opened the gate. It squeaked. Or rather, it squealed. She imagined that it was protesting at being opened. It was a good enough squeal for a movie featuring vampires, but this part of London was a far cry from Hammer Horrors. It was a road of nineteen sixties semi-detached houses, on the small side but well-kept. Pebble-dashing was everywhere, and most people had concreted over their gardens in order to park their cars off the road.

Dan's garden still had some plants in it, mostly roses. No car in the garden, but there were some parked in the road.

Ellie had come by bus, which had dropped her off almost outside his house, but if Dan were a cyclist then he probably didn't bother with public transport.

Ellie was puzzled. She hadn't imagined Dr McKenzie's son living in this part of London. This was a world of cheap furniture from Ikea, where holidays were taken in a caravan, at one of the cheaper Spanish resorts, or back in Pakistan. These houses were tiny with thin walls, and they all looked alike. They were a world away from the solid, five or six bedroom house in which Dan McKenzie had been brought up. There would be no swimming pool and garage here. Perhaps a paddling pool in the back garden for the child?

The school had given her his address. Normally, they wouldn't have given it out, but her recent gift had opened doors, and when she'd said she wanted to meet Mr McKenzie before deciding whether or not to add something to the amount he'd raised on his recent bike ride, they'd arranged for her to call on him at home after school.

She rang the bell, and he opened the door. Tall and whiplash thin. Casual clothing, of good quality. Handsome enough in a bony sort of way. Greying prematurely. Laughter lines.

Laughter lines were good.

An attractive personality? Rephrase that. The man had personality.

He wasn't what she'd expected, but then, she hadn't really known what to expect. A weakling who had given Vera up at the first sign of trouble? He'd been eighteen years old, then. This was a man, and a mature man at that.

His eyes were sharp and didn't miss much . . . such as the fact that she'd shrugged on a jacket which had a button missing. She thought he'd have made a good doctor.

The years had taken him even farther away from Vera-at-the-chippy than they might have done. He looked erudite, charming, steely . . . and seemed out of place in this humdrum road. He was definitely a 'Dan' rather than a 'Danny'.

He ushered her into a brightly painted but bare hall. The only furniture was two good-looking bicycles. *Not* the sort you did the shopping with.

'Mrs Quicke? The school said you wanted to talk to me about my ride for charity. A long-held ambition of mine, thankfully fulfilled without accident.'

'Did you have to do a lot of training for it?'

'Almost every day, yes. I'm glad it's over, in a way. It took up a lot of time. May I say how grateful we were for your earlier gift, which helped us to send our youth choir to the Eisteddfod? Would you care for some coffee? Only instant, I'm afraid.'

'"Yes" to a cup of tea, if you're making one. That was the first time we've provided money for a school project, but we might do more of that sort of thing in future. The choir did well, I believe. Congratulations.'

The two reception rooms had been thrown into one. More bright paint, more clean-looking cheap furniture, no art or mirrors on the walls, no pot plants. Paperback books, higgledy-piggledy; hardbacks in a solid oak bookcase. More books in piles on the floor. A stack of CDs.

Was this a rented house? There were several items of furniture here which didn't match the image: an antique walnut desk with a laptop computer up and running on it; a couple of good watercolours propped up on the mantelpiece; a La-Z-Boy chair. There were stacks of files in office-type trays. A pile of papers . . . from school, ready for marking? A telly smaller than she might have expected, a CD player with speakers. No children's toys.

He raised his voice, speaking from a galley kitchen at the back. 'Apologies for the disorder. I'm renting this place for six months while my own house is being underpinned. Subsidence. One of the consequences of building on clay. How do you like your tea?'

'No sugar, a little milk.' A rented house. That explained it.

There was a photograph of a dark-haired toddler, a girl, on the mantelpiece between the two watercolours. The fireplace itself had been blocked off, but there was an efficient-looking central heating radiator under the bay window. Curtains also from Ikea.

'Coming up.' A kettle shrilled, and he appeared with a tray containing tea in matching china mugs – surprise! – and some biscuits on a plate. 'I'm not terribly domesticated, but I do like a biscuit with my tea.'

Ellie quoted from the nursery rhyme, 'I do like a bit of butter with my bread.'

Warily polite, he waved her to a seat. The chairs were comfortable enough, and the tea hot. Time to talk. She said, 'I read about your bike ride in the local paper. Congratulations. I thought you might like me to add something to the amount you collected.'

'That's good of you.' Warmth in his tone for the first time, but bright eyes said she could have sent a cheque. Why was she here in person?

She felt embarrassed, looked away. 'All right, I had an ulterior motive and used that as an excuse to get to talk to you. But I did bring a cheque as well.' She fished it out of her handbag and laid it on the coffee table.

He dropped his eyes to look at the amount and produced a real smile. 'Thank you. That is most welcome.'

'Twelve years ago—'

He nearly spilled his tea. He set the mug down with care. He put his hands – capable, long-fingered hands – on the arms of his chair. Ellie imagined he'd have no trouble dominating a class or even a hall full of children. He had that intangible thing called authority.

He tried to smile. 'The night the earth shook?'

'The night everything changed, and not necessarily for the better.'

'No, indeed.' His smile faded. 'Let the past bury the past. I decided a long time ago that I had to draw a line under what had happened and move on.'

'Unsolved mysteries have a habit of returning to upset the present, and now there's a need for answers.'

'I'm sorry, Mrs Quicke. I can't talk about it. So, may we change the subject?'

'Someone has dug up a witness to your father's death.'

That shook him. 'What? Who? No, I don't believe it.'

'The witness concerned may not be speaking the truth, but can do a lot of damage even if the case never comes to court.'

'To court? You mean . . .? No, surely . . .! Why would
you joke about . . .? The police . . .' He controlled himself
with an effort. 'Perhaps you'd better start from the beginning, Mrs Quicke.' A formal tone.

'I wish I knew where the beginning was. A man has been
found who says he witnessed your father's death. He – or
she – is prepared to put a name to the person concerned.'

His breathing quickened. He got to his feet and took a
turn around the room. She thought that he was used to larger
rooms and didn't like being confined to this small space.
With his back to her, he said, 'Who?'

'A private detective has been paid to come up with
evidence against a friend of mine. Such evidence is tainted,
but could cause her a great deal of trouble.'

His whole body jerked. 'Her?' He turned, slowly, to face
her.

'Yes.' Ellie watched him struggle with the name.

'It can't be . . .?'

'Vera, yes.'

He coloured up. A flush that receded only slowly. 'Well,'
he said, in a flat voice, 'there's a turn up for the books, or,
as you might say, a blast from the past.' He went to stand
by the French windows that looked on to the garden, hands
behind his back, looking up at the sky. So that he didn't
have to meet Ellie's eye?

'Don't you want to hear why she's been accused of murder?'

'I have no feelings on the subject. I haven't seen her for
years. I don't suppose I'd recognize her if I saw her in the
street. I wouldn't have thought she'd have . . . But what do
I know? I suppose she might have been caught up in an
abusive situation and lashed out, or . . . Forgive me. I really
don't want to talk about it.'

Ellie persisted. 'I'm afraid it's too late for you to hide
your head in the sand. People are telling what they think is
the truth, but *their* truth may not be someone else's truth,
and . . . I'm getting into a muddle here. All I know is that
a certain person is blackmailing Vera. He says that either
she gives him something he wants, or he'll see that she's
accused of murdering your father.'

'Ridiculous!' He pressed his hands over his eyes for a moment. 'Great heavens above! Has the world gone mad?'

'Would you be prepared to give me a statement to the effect that Vera had long gone home by the time your father was killed? That should do it.'

'I . . . No. I can't do that, not of my own knowledge.' He made a despairing gesture with his hands.

She guessed, 'You weren't there either?'

'No. I wasn't.' He turned a frown on her. 'What is your interest in this, Mrs Quicke?'

'Vera was one of my cleaners for years. I found her honest, hard-working, quick-witted and reliable. She had a short and tragic marriage, nursing a dying man who left her in rented accommodation and badly provided for. Before he died, he asked me to find some way of helping Vera get to college. My husband and I have a big house on the far side of the Avenue, not far from where you were brought up. Our housekeeper is an old friend but getting on in years, so I asked Vera if she'd like to move in with us and help out. She and her son—'

'Ah. I thought you were going to miss him out.' So he knew Vera had a child?

'It would be hard to miss him out. Vera and Mikey have a flat at the top of the house, and they're, well, family. Vera's a great girl who's pulled herself up by her bootstraps. He's an imp, a mathematical genius. Vera's now putting herself through college, part-time. A business course.'

His tone was polite but distant. 'I'm glad to hear she's making something of herself at last. A business course? Splendid.'

Ellie set her teeth at his condescending tone. 'Twelve years after she was supposed to start, yes.'

He got the point all right. He put the empty mugs on the tray. 'Another cup?' And removed himself. To think?

Ellie followed him into a sparklingly clean kitchen. A frozen meal for one was defrosting on the side, next to a coffee-making machine. A glazed back door gave a glimpse of a whirligig clothes drier, festooned with white shirts, in the middle of a neat lawn. 'You knew she'd had a son?'

'I'd heard.' His hands were busy. He was making himself a coffee. His brain was probably working overtime.

Ellie said, 'Can you bear to talk about what happened?'

'I regret. No.'

'For old times' sake?'

For a moment he allowed her to see his pain. 'After what she did to me?'

'Or was done to her.'

He frowned, not understanding. Didn't he know what had happened in the garden that night?

He made a visible effort to control himself. 'Mrs Quicke, I really can't help you. The police at the time couldn't find the person who killed my father. You say there's new evidence which incriminates Vera? I thought she'd left long before my father returned home, but I can't give her an alibi for that evening. You must look elsewhere.'

He finished making his coffee and poured it out before exclaiming, 'Now look what I've done!' He took a step back. 'I never drink coffee after four in the afternoon.'

'You feel the need for it?'

He pushed the cup away. 'No, I don't. Mrs Quicke, what's going on? Why, after all these years . . .? So much pain.' He tried to laugh. 'My mother will go spare if it's all raked up again.'

Was he trying to distract her by mentioning his mother? Well, Ellie thought, she should make use of the opening he'd given her. 'Tell me about her.'

She thought he'd refuse at first, but he'd been jolted off balance. Leaning against the kitchen cupboard and looking out on to the garden, he said, 'My mother. Well, she's a fragile-looking, self-centred little person with a will of iron. She can't understand why anyone should upset her by opposing her wishes.'

A deliberately cool tone. He loved his mother, yes. But there was a good deal of frustration mixed with the love. And pain? Yes, pain.

He said, 'My father indulged her, avoided doing anything to upset her. "Take care of your mother, now; she's having a bad day." That sort of thing. She felt she'd married beneath her. She'd brought money into the family, you see, and was sister to a baronet who didn't even bother to use his title. She'd hoped that young Dr McKenzie would end up in Harley Street, but he turned out to be just an ordinary, old-fashioned GP. No clock-watcher, mind.'

The wind was getting up outside. It might well rain soon, but he made no move to bring the washing in.

'What was he like as a father?'

'He taught me to drive. Taught me to appreciate music; jazz, mostly. He was good company. He worked long hours. Perhaps he drank too much. Mother thought so, but I never saw him lose control.'

'There was some trouble with a neighbour?'

'The swimming pool? Mother's idea. It cost a fortune. Yes, there was a fuss, something about the height of the new fence, that it ought to have been a hedge, or it had been sited six inches to the left or the right . . . I can't remember which, now.'

'Someone was going to sue?'

'It was talked about, but never came to anything after . . . after. You must understand that I had just turned eighteen and was about to go to university. I thought of nothing but the summer holidays and Vera.'

He was talking freely now. Good. 'Your mother was pleased you were going to be a doctor?'

'I was to fulfil all her dreams. I was to marry the daughter of the baronet, have a practice in Harley Street, and she . . .? She would live round the corner from Harrods.'

'Vera was not included in her plans?'

His mouth thinned. 'No.'

'It was a Romeo and Juliet romance?'

A glancing, painful smile. 'Yes, perhaps that's what it was. A youthful fantasy. We must have seemed an odd-looking couple, the naive boy from the big house and the big, bold girl from the chippy.'

'How was Vera treated by your friends?'

'Fine. She had a mouth on her, was always ready with a quick retort, or a laugh. She cared about people. She was warm and loving. She was my girl. Or so I thought.'

'Nobody set out to make her feel unwanted? Nobody special had it in for her?'

A hesitation. 'Certainly not.'

'Meaning . . .?'

A rueful smile. 'Well, some of my friends didn't think it would last, and they were right, weren't they?'

Maybe. Maybe not. 'Whose idea was it to have such a big party?'

'Mother's, of course. She invited my cousins to stay. Sam was older, in his mid-twenties. He was supposed to see to it that the party didn't get out of hand. Daphne was mother's little favourite, seventeen years old. Mother got someone to lay on a buffet, and I organized a disco.'

'Daphne was your mother's choice for you?'

'Mother got her own way, as she always did. Unfortunately, Daphne didn't like being married to a mere schoolteacher.'

'You are divorced?'

'There was a baby. I'm fond of the child, but . . . Tell the truth, I'm not at all sure she's mine. Daphne was playing around by the time the child was born and left me a year later. She remarried, a Frenchman with a title. Much more *suitable*.' He pulled a sour face. Then laughed at himself. 'As if it matters.'

'Your mother is still alive?'

'Living in luxury in a flat near Harrods. Her lifelong dream come true.'

'How many people did you invite to the party?'

'Those in my set at school studying sciences, those I used to play around with in a jazz group we formed that year, plus their girlfriends. Three of us had been accepted to study medicine. There was supposed to be about twenty people, but some brought friends. Maybe thirty of us in all? A disco. Some sandwiches and beer. It was all pretty innocent.'

'No drugs?'

'I had heard that drugs were being sold at the school gates, but our lot was clean. Definitely.'

Was he a little too emphatic about that? Possibly. 'Why

did your parents go out? Wasn't it considered best to have an adult on hand at such parties?'

'There was a clash of dates. Father was being made president of the golf club that night. Mother had a new dress for the occasion. My birthday had actually been the previous week, but this was the only date the DJ could manage. My mother and father left before the party got going. She said I must be sure to look after Daphne and not let her be "swamped by all my great big rugby-playing friends". We didn't play rugby at our school, but that was the way she talked.'

'And then . . .'

'And then.' He sighed. His eyes were unfocused. He was way back into the past. 'It was about eleven, half past. The disco was up and running, the beer was flowing, the sound was right. We were all hyped up, with excitement and with drink. We were dancing in the hall, and yes, it did get a bit crowded. We'd turned the overhead lights right down. Every now and then a couple would break away to go off upstairs or outside into the garden at the back. For a drink, for a snog. It was a hot night, so why not? I was thinking of taking Vera out there myself, but Daphne kept interrupting, wanting me to look after her.

'The doorbell rang, and someone opened it. Bad mistake. About fifteen louts in various stages of inebriation surged in, blocking the door, shouting for the doctor, demanding drink and drugs. We knew them. They were from a rough, neighbouring school. There'd already been scuffles at bus stops and in the town centre between us and them. It was so sudden. So frightening. In the dark, it was difficult to see, and the music was so loud that . . . Half of us didn't know what was happening . . . We were being pushed around, jostled. Then someone turned the lights up and we saw, all right.

'Ryan was at the front. A massive lad, only seventeen but he must have weighed eighteen stone. I shouted at him to leave. He grinned. He said they'd been invited to join the party – can you believe it? He linked arms with a couple of his gang, and they rammed into us, forcing us back to the wall. The girls screamed. Jack picked up the phone to ring the police. Ryan picked him up and tossed him aside. Just like that! Then he tore the phone out of the socket.'

'Jack who?' Ellie made a mental note of the name.

His train of thought interrupted, Dan took a moment to come back to her. 'Jack the Lad. Nickname. He was up for any lark in those days, so we called him Jack the Lad. Mad about guitars. Has a music shop, with a guitar repair service. Runs workshops for them in schools.'

He shuddered. 'We didn't stand a chance. Didn't know how to cope. Vera knew. I can see her now. She put her hands on her hips and yelled at Ryan to get lost. He backhanded her, and she went down, too. The gang thought that hilarious. They clapped and cheered. I tried to reach her, but Daphne hung on to my arm . . .'

Ellie heard him grind his teeth. 'They'd blocked the front door, so I yelled at Raff to get our lot out through the back—'

'Raff?'

'Sam – my cousin, remember? – helped. Someone turned up the sound on the disco, instead of turning it down. It was bedlam. You couldn't hear yourself think. Some people froze, some fled upstairs. Daphne clung on to my arm, screaming. She could scream for England. I heard Vera shout, "No!" Ryan had picked her up and . . .' He shuddered. 'I tried to reach her, tried to get him off her. He was built like a tree trunk. He threw me off as if I was a child. I landed up on the floor at the bottom of the stairs. But Ryan had had to let go of Vera to deal with me . . .'

He was breathing hard, reliving the moment. 'The last I saw of her, Gail was towing Vera out of the door to the kitchen. She looked back at me. She shouted something . . . That was the last time I saw her.' He closed his eyes.

'Gail? Gail who?'

His eyelids fluttered. Some thought had passed through his mind . . . about Gail? If so, he wasn't about to share it with her. 'Gail went on to become a doctor. Where was I? Oh yes. Vera. I thought she loved me.'

'Yes, she did.'

He opened the back door to let the air in, and stood there,

looking on to the garden. The grass at the back had been newly cut, and the scent drifted into the kitchen.

Ellie prompted him. 'What happened after Vera went?'

'There was just me, Sam, Daphne, and the DJ left. Some of our lot had fled upstairs and barricaded themselves into the bedrooms. I could hear the gang banging on doors, yelling for them to come out. Others had got out of the house through the kitchen. Some of those found the door through the outhouses into the garage and escaped that way. Others were chased down the garden, but the newcomers didn't know their way around, so they soon came back. Others foraged for drinks. They found wine in the kitchen, and then they came across the hard stuff in Dad's drinks cabinet. They passed the bottles around, egging one another on, saying they'd fought the toffs and come off best. Hurrah for them.

'Ryan was the muscle, but the leader of the gang was a weaselly little fellow called Lenny. As soon as he saw I was struggling to get up, Lenny turned the music down and started on me. He knew I was the doctor's son. He told me to produce the drugs for them. I refused. Lenny told Ryan to smash up the disco equipment to make me see sense. Ryan enjoyed smashing things. The DJ tried to object, so Ryan knocked him out, too. But at least the drumbeat stopped. It would have saved me a beating if I could have given him what they wanted. That's what they tell you nowadays, isn't it? If you're mugged, let them have whatever it is they want. I knew where the safe was, but I didn't know the combination because Dad changed it often and didn't tell anyone what it was. We had to get a specialist in to open it, after . . .'

He sighed, looking back in time. 'I used to have nightmares about that night. I haven't had one for ages, but I suppose I'll have one tonight, now you've brought it all back. Ryan held me up with one hand and punched me with the other. Sam tried to intervene, so Ryan knocked him out. Daphne went on screaming, till Ryan backhanded her. She fell backwards and hit her head.

'I've never felt so helpless, so angry, so scared in all my

life. In the end I said I'd show them where my father's study was, so that they could see for themselves that there were no drugs on the premises. Hoping against hope that they wouldn't find the safe. Which they didn't.

'Lenny's failure to find the drugs made him furious. He rounded up his followers and told them to stop drinking and to strip the house of valuables. Jewellery, television, anything they could sell for drugs. He ripped Daphne's earrings off and pocketed them. He took the watch that I'd just been given for my birthday. He told Ryan to put me out of my misery. Ryan hit me again, and that time I blacked out. End of story.'

'Not quite,' said Ellie. 'What happened when you woke up?'

SIX

D an sighed. 'I've tried not to think about that night for so long . . . What good does it do to rake it all up now?'

'You know as well as I do that once someone has started asking questions, there's no knowing where it will stop. Maybe even with the arrest of your father's murderer.'

'The police tried hard enough.'

'If a witness really is prepared to say your father was quarrelling with someone late that night – or rather, early next morning – the case will have to be reopened. Give me what you can. Lenny set his gang to ransacking the house. Daphne and Sam were out for the count. You woke up?'

'I was lying on the floor. Every part of me hurt. There was a blue light flashing somewhere. I couldn't make out why. Someone shouted, "Police!" The gang thundered down the stairs and in from the other rooms. They were shouting, didn't know how to escape. They milled around, carrying stuff they'd collected . . . my mother's jewellery, my father's best watch, a bottle of whisky, my old teddy bear, for heavens' sake! Stuffing them into pockets, panicking. Then they vanished. The hall was eerily silent. I only had one working eye. Couldn't move. Someone was knocking on the front door. Ringing the bell.

'The hall looked like the aftermath of a battle. Blood, broken glass, beer spilt, turntables wrecked, foodstuffs tipped on to the floor, plates smashed . . . Nightmare Abbey. Bodies here and there. Daphne began to stir. She was bleeding from a nasty cut at the back of her head. I tried to reach Sam, pulled myself over to him. Tried to wake him. Couldn't. I realized it was up to me to get to the front door to let the police in. Tried to stand. Couldn't. Crawled there.

'They caught Ryan blundering around in the utility room. Lenny and some of the others had broken through a hedge into next door's garden and from there got out into the next street. The police picked them up later. At the time I was more worried about Sam and Daphne. The police sent for the paramedics, who carted them both off to hospital . . . I was on my feet by that time. Unsteady, but on my feet. Daphne cried out for me as she was taken away. I promised I'd follow as soon as I could.

'The police wanted statements, wanted me to go through the house, say what was missing or had been broken. I couldn't think straight. I was desperate to see if Vera was all right. I insisted that the police search the house and garden for her, and they did. But there was no sign of any of the guests or of the gang. Just the odd beer can, a girl's jacket. I was relieved, because it meant Vera had got away safely.'

Ellie sighed. She knew what had happened after Vera had fled to the garden. But Dan didn't?

He said, 'The mess was horrendous. The DJ came out from under the table. His equipment had been smashed to pieces. He wanted compensation on the spot. The phone in the hall was out of action. I used the one in the study to try to reach my father at the golf club, but they'd switched over to an answering machine. I wanted to go to the hospital to make sure Daphne and Sam were OK, but I couldn't leave the house and the police kept asking questions. All I could think of was how devastated my mother was going to be when she got back and found out what had happened. They recovered most of her jewellery and my father's watch, but I never got mine back, nor my teddy bear . . . as if it mattered.

'The police finally left about two in the morning. I still couldn't raise my father, so I rang an old family friend, Mr Scott. You know him, perhaps? He lives locally. Raff, his son, had been at the party. Raff had got home all right and was telling his father what had happened when I rang. I said I needed to go to the hospital to look after Sam and Daphne but I couldn't leave the house open. I asked if one of them could come over and look after things, be there to break the news to my parents when they returned.'

'Your friend's name was "Raff"?'

'Short for Raphael. Raff hadn't yet got his driving licence. I hadn't either, at that point in time. Took me two goes, later . . . Anyway, his father got the car out and they came round. Raff stayed in the house while Mr Scott ferried me to the hospital. He left me there just in time to see Sam and then Daphne taken off for brain scans. They thought at first I'd been knifed, because there was so much blood on me. But it was Daphne's blood. Mostly. I had a lot of bruises but nothing broken. Daphne was hysterical. Eventually, they sedated her, but she took ages to drop off. Sam came to after a while and started cursing. His scan proved clear. So did hers. In the morning Daphne was stitched up and allowed to leave, though they kept Sam in for another twenty-four hours. I got a cab to take Daphne and me home . . . and that's when the nightmare turned into a horror movie.'

'Your father's death?'

'Yes.'

A spatter of rain fell, sprinkling heavy drops on the garden.

He started. 'She'll kill me!' He rushed out into the garden and began to take down the washing. Ellie dumped her handbag and helped him. Together they rescued the shirts and carried them inside. Dan closed the kitchen door and leaned against it, panting, to explain.

'It's her next door. Three children under the age of six,

husband working nights, and she still finds time to clean this place and to scold me if I forget to bring the washing in.'

Like Vera . . . Ellie did *not* say. She imagined Vera sweeping into the house, laughing, loving, picking up things and putting them away, dumping a basket of laundry in the kitchen, shaking up cushions, giving Dan a hug and a kiss as she brought him up to date on what she'd been doing that day. Vera would make any house a home.

What a shame, what a crying shame they'd been parted! Ellie began to fold and stack the washing. Dan reached for his cup of cold coffee and drank it off. Then realized what he'd done. He managed a smile that looked painful. 'I'll be up half the night, now.'

Ellie prompted him. 'Tell me what happened when you got back from hospital. You said the nightmare turned into a horror movie?'

He sighed. 'Let's go and sit down, make ourselves comfortable.' He led the way back to the living room, waved her to a chair and took a seat himself. Not in the La-Z-Boy. He was not going to relax, was he?

'Where were we? When I got back with Daphne, there were police everywhere. A different lot of police. Homicide, not Burglary. Lots of questions. Few answers. My parents had got home late, about half two. My mother had been tired, had gone straight into the house, leaving my father to put the car away. Mr Scott had met her in the hall and explained what had happened. She fell apart. She asked him to go up to her bedroom with her to see what the damage was. Fortunately, the gang hadn't made too much mess in her room. She and my father had separate rooms, by the way.

'After Mr Scott had seen my mother settled, he returned downstairs and, while waiting for my father to come in, he fell asleep. He woke at six, decided he must have missed my father's return, but thought it odd that he hadn't been roused and that all the lights were still on. So he investigated. He found my father in the garage. Dead.'

'The police thought one of the gang had come back, been challenged by your father, got into a fight, and that he'd got the worst of it?'

'They had Ryan in custody already, so they knew it wasn't him. They went after Lenny . . . and, later on, after his supplier. Couldn't make anything stick. Eventually, they moved on to other cases, and we were left struggling to make sense of what had happened.'

He was quiet, looking out at the garden again. The sun had gone in, and the wind had picked up. Ellie wondered about putting the washing back out, but didn't offer to do so.

'Mother was distraught. Bereft. She didn't know how to change a light bulb or read the gas meter. She had no idea how to get things replaced or repaired. My father's accounts were in a tangle. His will left everything to me provided I looked after my mother, so I had to take over his role in her life.'

'At the age of eighteen?'

'A rude awakening to reality. I had a permanent headache. Stress. Mother couldn't bear the idea of my leaving her alone for as much as a day. I was too weary . . . too confused . . . I dropped the idea of going to university that year. The police were in and out. There were court appearances. Insurance claims. Sam and I identified various members of the gang. We had to testify. Daphne made quite an impression in the witness box. It soothed my mother to have her stay over every weekend.

'You'd think it might have turned me off humanity, but trying to understand the reasons why the gang had acted as they did, I began to realize what Vera had always been trying to tell me, about how the other half of the world lived. I learned about the gang's background. Our school had been able to pick and choose who they took. These lads were not from privileged backgrounds and their expectations were low. They were mostly from dysfunctional families with a history of drink or drugs. They'd drifted into petty crime for lack of anything better to do. They had few role models. I'd never been exposed to no-hopers with that sort of background before. It changed the way I thought about life.

'The following September I enrolled at Imperial College to read sciences. By the time I got my degree, I wanted to help the poor creatures who'd wrecked my life. So I went on to teacher training and found that I was better suited to that than I'd expected.'

'Your mother approved?'

'No, but by that time she had a new set of friends to go about with, and I had grown a protective shell. Daphne and I ended up in bed together one night, and there was a wedding rather too hastily arranged for my mother's wishes, but there . . . we married in haste and repented at leisure.'

'While Vera—'

'I'd been completely taken in by her, hadn't I? I'd thought she was a virgin, waiting for a special occasion to sleep with me, but she didn't even wait to see if I was all right when the gang came, but had it off with whoever fancied her in the garden. That very evening! While I was trying to deal with the intruders and then with getting Daphne and Sam to the hospital . . .'

Ellie opened her mouth to speak, but he wasn't listening.

'Apart from anything else, if she'd been going to entertain other boys, she should have taken precautions. I could have told her Abdi wouldn't take her seriously. Mrs Quicke, I really don't want to talk about this any more. Having to face up to what she was really like half killed me in the early days. I should have listened to my mother when she said Vera was trouble, but I thought I knew better. I believed in her.'

'Who told you what happened?'

'Raff. He was there, saw it all.' He shuddered. 'I couldn't believe it at first. I rang her, but she wouldn't come to the phone. Ashamed, I suppose. Her father told me she didn't want to see me again. I was devastated. Couldn't believe it. But when Abdi confirmed that he, too . . . That was the final straw. I told myself it was fortunate I'd found out in time, that it would never have worked, her and me. Eventually, I decided to draw a line under the past, not allow myself to think about it any more.

'It's been twelve long years since then, Mrs Quicke. We are not the same people. I honestly don't think the real killer can be found after all this time. I can't confirm that

Vera had left long before my father was killed, so leave me out of it. And now, if you please, I have a pile of paperwork to do.'

'One question. Which of your friends brought the date-rape drug to the party?'

'What? What on earth are you talking about?'

'Believe me, someone did.'

'Really? Well, if anyone . . . I suppose one of Lenny's lot.'

'It was someone who was hiding from Lenny's lot in the garden. Someone you'd invited to the party.'

'Ridiculous. None of our crowd was into drugs.'

'You said you knew drugs were being sold at the school gates. So which of your guests brought some to the party?'

He froze.

If she'd waved her hand in front of his face, he wouldn't have responded.

He knew.

A twitch of an eyebrow. No, he didn't know. But he'd guessed . . .?

His eyes narrowed. 'I have no idea.' Deliberately.

'You could find out?'

'Are you trying to make out that Vera was drugged that night? She's not really claiming that, is she? Everyone knows she allowed several boys to pleasure her—'

'I repeat, who fed you that story?'

'Why, it's common knowledge. Raff said. Later, Gail confirmed it, and Abdi, of course. I met him at someone else's birthday party soon after. A black tie affair, rather different from mine. He boasted of how much Vera had enjoyed his attentions. Mind you, he ought to have helped her out when she had his baby, but—'

'Abdi was a particular friend of yours?'

A stare. 'Not particularly, no. But he wouldn't lie. Why would he?'

'It was rape. Vera was very shaken when she got out of the house and took shelter in the changing hut by the pool with some of your other guests. Someone passed her a drink. The next thing she knew, she was gazing up at the stars, in pain and distress. She'd been raped. Yes, Abdi was one of those who took part in it. He says they were queuing up to enjoy her. He says she invited them to pleasure her. She says she knew nothing of it. Who would you believe?'

He didn't want to consider that. He'd convinced himself that Vera had behaved like a whore, and he'd learned to live with the idea. He didn't want to have that belief disturbed, because if he'd been wrong all this time . . .

A horrified stare. 'No, no. Surely not. She reverted to type, that's all. I don't mean to sound like a snob but, as my mother said, she came from a group who traded their virginity in early. I'd failed to protect her at the party, and so she let herself go, abandoned herself to the excitement, the drink, did what other girls of her type did.'

'As you've already pointed out, she hadn't taken any precautions before the party because she was waiting for a special date with you. She hadn't expected to be raped! She had fought hard for the opportunity to go to university. So why would she risk everything that night?'

He didn't want to believe her. He shrugged. 'How can I tell? Yes, she'd told me she was a virgin, but it's obvious that was a lie. I was lucky to find out what she was really like before things got serious between us.'

'You'd known her for years, and you really thought she would lie down for anyone?'

He didn't like that. Another shrug. 'You say she was raped? She went to the police, I presume?'

'Her father beat her and kept her in. He was too ashamed to let it be known that his daughter had been raped. And so was she. For that reason, he wouldn't bring the police into it.'

'That's nonsense. Her father told me she never wanted to see me again.'

'He lied, of course. He wanted the match as little as your mother did. Vera didn't realize she was pregnant for some time. When he found out, her father disowned her. Sold up, moved away, left her homeless and pregnant. When the baby was born and she realized whose it must be, she asked Abdi for help. He refused. She might have had an abortion. I think many girls might have done, in her position. But no, she kept the baby, worked long hours at anything she could find, mostly cleaning jobs, and brought the boy up herself. Now Abdi wants the boy because he can't sire another child. He's threatening to produce someone who saw her killing your father, unless she gives Mikey to him.'

A long, hard stare. He didn't want to believe it. 'That's a good sob story, but—'

'You need to check it out. Yes, do that. If it can be proved that Vera was out of it and could not have killed your father, it will at least get Abdi off her back.'

She watched him weigh up the options. His eyelids flickered. His mouth firmed. He produced an almost genuine smile. 'What a fertile imagination she has, to be sure. It almost makes me angry to hear it. You don't really think one of my friends would have brought drugs to the party? And Abdi is a blackmailing villain? Mrs Quicke, really! No, no. You've been conned. Vera took a chance to have some fun, and it went wrong. Tough. But you can't expect me to . . . And as to what happened to my father, so long ago . . . Well, we can leave that to the police, can't we?'

He was angry. Angry with himself, or angry that someone was trying to upset his long-held view of the past? He held on to a veneer of politeness, but only just. He picked up the cheque she'd brought him and put it down again. He said, 'Thanks for the cheque, it was most kind of you to think of us. Have you an umbrella? It looks as if it might rain again.'

He moved her towards the front door. She could feel his anger and, yes, his distress.

She stopped in the doorway. 'Don't tear up that cheque, just because you're angry with me. It's not for you, but for your charity.'

'As if I would.' Another social smile. 'I know a fairy godmother when I meet one.'

Nicely put, meaning that he was in control of his temper in spite of her impertinent questions. Oh well. She said, 'Thank you for the cup of tea.' And, 'Yes, it does look like rain again, doesn't it?'

He said, 'Not that it's any business of yours, but I'm seeing someone else at the moment.'

'Someone *suitable*, I assume?' She couldn't help it. She knew she'd sounded sarcastic.

'Quite.' Showing his teeth.

She stepped out on to the path and heard the door shut behind her. She decided to catch the bus to the Avenue and walk home from there. She rather thought she'd meddled to no good purpose. But there . . . you had to try to help people, didn't you?

Dan was right. There was no point ripping open old wounds. Maybe Vera had gone with the flow that night and . . . No, she had not! Vera was genuine.

What a mess.

How had the gang known that there would be drugs at the house? There must be a link there, if only she could see it.

Well, if the gang had learned that the party was being held at a doctor's house . . .? Yes, but who would have told them? Perhaps Vera might have some ideas on the subject. Who else might know? This Dr Gail? And Jack the Lad . . . Silly name.

There were other people already waiting at the stop, so a bus might come along soon. Ellie tried to perch on a bench which was too high for her. Not for the first nor the hundredth time, she wished she were an inch or two taller. Had she her mobile phone with her? It was possible she'd left it . . . Ah, no. There it was. Switch on.

Ellie considered most modern technology a field too far, but today it would have been useful to have had one of those gadgets which gave you the phone book and a map of town and GPS – whatever that might be, though she'd heard it was very useful if you were lost – though of course she wasn't lost, sitting at the bus stop here in Perivale. However, it was no good wishing . . . and here she laughed at herself, because even if she'd bought one of those newfangled instruments, she wouldn't know how to use it.

An elderly woman next to Ellie leaned over. 'Someone texted you, did they, dear? Sometimes I think those phones are more trouble than they're worth. I keep telling my grand-daughter not to text me, but will she listen? The number of times she's told me how to do it, but what I say is, my fingers can't manage all that dancing around at my age.'

'I'm with you. I was trying to find someone called Jack who sells guitars, and to make an appointment with a Dr Gail Something, but I haven't the phone numbers with me.'

'Jack the Lad? Him that's by North Ealing Station? Sells guitars, all sorts and music and stuff that the youngsters like, though I've heard he has some proper musicians go there, too. My grandson almost lives there, wants to form a group and play dates in the pub when he's old enough. Shouldn't think he's good enough, myself, but what do I know about it?'

'There really is someone called Jack the Lad?'

'That's the name of the shop. He's a hippy type, know what I mean? Hair tied back and shoes down at the heel, though it's mostly sandals even if it is winter. But, Dr Gail? I don't know no Dr Gail. I'm with the surgery at the end here.' She indicated an elderly man using a stick who was inching along the pavement towards them. 'Here's old Nick that lives two doors down from me. Nick, do you know where a Dr Gail Something hangs out? This lady needs to see her, urgent.'

'Bail? I don't know no Bail.' He sank heavily on to the bench beside them.

The woman raised her voice. 'Doctor Gail, I said.' And to Ellie, 'Deaf as the proverbial.'

'Doctor Gail Trubody?' said the old man. 'Why didn't you say so? My sister goes to her. Posh practice, just off the Avenue. Seven or eight doctors, and you take your chance who you see.'

'That's the one in the new building, sticks out like a sore thumb, innit?' The woman repeated the words to Ellie. 'All the latest mod cons, but a steep ramp to get to it. Can't be doing with ramps, myself.'

'My sister likes it,' said old Nick. 'There's a young doctor there she says would put a spring in the heart of a plastic doll, he he, heeee!' He broke off in a paroxysm of coughing.

'Thank you,' said Ellie, putting her phone away. This might be the right Dr Gail or it might not, but the bus was coming and she needed to get on it. This bus would take her to the Broadway, and from there she could catch another to North Ealing Station. What kind of man would carry the joke through into adult life?

'*JACK the LAD*'.

There it was, across the shop front. There was a guitar in the right-hand window. *Not* a classical guitar, but something in Day-Glo paint and sequins, which you couldn't play without an amp, whatever that might be. The entire outfit was probably worth as much as a two-bedroom flat and would produce enough sound to deafen the total population of Ealing: man, woman and child. The guitar was posed in front of a huge poster, showing a man wearing very little except for some tattoos and a pair of tight jeans, surrounded by an adoring group of young teenage girls. The idea seemed to be that if you played this kind of guitar, you got the chicks thronging around you. Or were they called 'groupies' nowadays?

In the left-hand window there was a miscellany of recorders, instruments for tiny tots, manuals and piles of CDs. The effect was one of a successful niche in the marketplace.

Jack the Lad apparently knew what he was doing.

Ellie entered. An earnest-looking youth was explaining to a pretty girl – fake blonde and piercings, but still pretty with it – that he needed something technical done to his instrument before Saturday. A youngish woman, possibly a music teacher, was trying out a classical guitar under the watchful eye of a middle-aged man. Ellie waited her turn to be served, observing that the shop was kept spick and span and there were even – thank the Lord – some chairs for customers to sit on. She sat.

'Can I help you?' He sounded doubtful. Hippy type, soulful brown eyes, lumber jacket over collarless shirt, and yes, sandals. This must be Jack. Except that he didn't really look like a 'Jack the Lad'. Something sharp was flickering at the back of those beautiful eyes.

Remember, Ellie; this man is running a successful

business. He may pretend to be an artless bohemian, but that is just a front.

'I'm—'

He nodded. He already knew who she was. Which meant he'd been warned to expect her. By Dan?

'Come into my office,' he said. 'Tea or coffee?'

A superficially untidy office, with a computer, a scanner and a printer, all in working order. This was no paperless office, as there were filing cabinets ranged along one wall.

Sensible, thought Ellie, as both she and Thomas had experienced problems when they hadn't kept up to date with paper records and their computers had broken down.

There were two chairs, upright, and a tray containing equipment for tea and coffee sitting on top of a small fridge.

One window looked on to the shop itself, so that whoever was in the office might observe what was happening there. Another window at the back provided a view of a large workshop, where an elderly man was doing something delicate to an antique mandolin. The workshop walls were hung with a variety of instruments, and several more were in pieces on the worktops. A thriving business, well run.

She settled herself. 'Tea, please.' And then, 'Dan rang to warn you?'

SEVEN

Jack was guarded in his tone. 'Your visit came as a shock. After all this time. He's not sure what to think, and neither am I. In some ways I wish you'd never gone to see him. Surely he's suffered enough.'

'And you?'

He put the kettle on, concentrating, not looking at her. 'I don't like looking back. The last time I talked about it to him was when I gave a short statement to the police. I'd gone long before Dr McKenzie was killed.'

'Did you tell Dan what happened to Vera, or mention it in your statement to the police?'

'No, I didn't. What good would it have done? I'm not sure I'm prepared to open up that old wound even now.'

But he'd invited her into his office and was making her a cup of tea. He was sending out contradictory signals: he was saying that he didn't want to talk, and yet he was doing just that.

He said, 'When Dan rang me, he sounded all stirred up, not his usual imperturbable self. I hope you know what you're doing, Mrs Quicke, throwing a grenade into people's lives like this.'

'Is that what I'm doing?'

'You wouldn't like to go back home and forget this, would you?'

'No, and you don't really want that, either, or you wouldn't have invited me into your den.'

'Ah. Yes. Dan said you were to be taken seriously. I know who you are, of course. Lady Bountiful.'

'Hardly.'

He nodded. 'Lady Bountiful. Good deeds get rewarded, if you're pure of heart.' His tone hovered on the edge of sarcasm. He was not meeting her eye. Or enjoying this. But he was going to be polite and, she hoped, he was going to talk. 'Milk, sugar?'

'Milk, a little.'

He handed her a mug of tea and made one for himself, too. And sat. Scratched his cheek. 'Dan said Vera was being threatened by Abdi. Surely, that can't be right.' His eyes were anxious. Why?

She said, 'You remember Abdi?'

A non-committal nod.

'Did you like him? Have you seen him recently?'

'"Like him?"' A shrug. 'I could take him or leave him. Not a particular mate of mine. "Seen him recently?" No. Our Abdi moves in different circles nowadays.'

'Abdi wants Vera's boy, because he can't have any more children of his own. He's paid a private investigator to check that the boy is his and proposes to buy him off her—'

'What! But that's . . . Surely not!'

'Sorry. I exaggerated, didn't I? He's prepared to give Vera a certain sum of money by way of compensation for handing the boy over to him.'

He stroked his chin. His eyes lit up with mischief. 'From what I remember of her, she wouldn't take kindly to—'

'No, indeed.' Ellie grinned, recalling Vera's accurately aimed knee. 'I expect he remembered enough about her, too, to realize he might need more than money. In consequence he employed a private investigator to dig up some dirt on her. The man claims to have discovered a witness to Vera killing the doctor. Abdi says that he'll give the private investigator's report to the police if she doesn't hand the boy over to him.'

A frown. 'But that's not possible. Or so unlikely that . . .' Jack shook his head. 'From what I saw, from what I remember, Vera was in no position to . . .' He looked away. 'But perhaps you don't know about that? I mean, if that got out, it could embarrass a lot of people.'

'By "embarrass" you mean "seriously upset", perhaps "damage reputations"?'

'Yes.' He considered his fingernails. 'I mean, after twelve years. People have moved on. They are in positions of trust, perhaps even standing for election.'

'Aah. Someone who was involved is standing for election to the council? Or for Parliament?'

He winced, didn't reply.

She said, 'Yes, I see. There's no statute of limitations on rape, and you don't want to drop any of your friends into it. But, you did agree to talk to me.'

'Ever since Dan rang, I've been trying to think what to say. I've always felt so guilty about . . . Perhaps I do need to confess. Oh, not to rape. No, I didn't. Wouldn't have. No way. Only, if I can do something to help Vera, who out of all of us that night . . . But without dropping any one in it . . .' His eyes dropped away from hers. 'Listen to me. I sound like a child . . . "It wasn't me, missus." But I cannot tell on the others. They've all got too much to lose nowadays.'

'Do you think it right that Vera lost so much, and that none of the others should suffer?'

'Life isn't fair, is it? If only . . .'

'If only what? What did you do, exactly?'

He set his mug down, avoiding her eyes. 'It's what I didn't do that counts. You see, when I got there . . . Well, it was too late.'

'Start at the beginning. You were all in your last term at school together. Were you one of those who thought Vera and Dan were mismatched?'

'Mismatched?' He stared into the past. 'We all, or most of us, paired off in our last year, but it wasn't supposed to be a lifelong commitment. Mine definitely wasn't. Dan and Vera were floating around on cloud nine, but if I'd thought anything about it – which I didn't – I'd have said their romance probably wouldn't last their going to different universities. It was the same for everyone, wasn't it? I mean, I had fixed myself up with a girl, but by Christmas she'd moved on to someone else, and so had I.'

'You liked Vera?'

'What's not to like? She was as straight as they come. Hard working. We called her, taking the mickey, "the Lippy from the Chippy". She didn't know how to dress, and her accent was definitely "Sarf" London, but she was a bit of all right was our Vera. She didn't deserve what happened to her.' He shook his head. 'That night changed the course of many of our lives.'

'Beginning with you?'

A sigh. 'Not as much as Vera, but yes. I was supposed to go to uni to do media studies but, after I'd recovered, I took a reality check. I was no longer so happy-go-lucky. I realized I didn't want any more years of study. I decided to be practical, instead, and to learn how guitars are made. Eventually, I opened this shop, on a guitar string and a wave of generosity from my father. And never looked back.'

Ellie said, 'Returning to that night, can you bear to tell me what you saw? I'm hoping that if I can only get enough statements to prove Vera had left long before the doctor was killed, we can tell Abdi to get lost.'

'I told you, I can't give you names.'

'I understand, but you've already admitted to feeling some guilt about what happened. I'm giving you a second chance to help her.'

He wiped his face with his hands. 'You're right, of course. But even so. No names.'

Ellie thought about that. 'Dan mentioned someone. A Raff Scott. Was he one of those who raped Vera?'

He gasped. 'Who told you about Raff?' He recovered himself. 'Dan doesn't know. For pity's sake, don't tell him. They were good friends.' He bit his lip. 'Ouch. I see. You were just guessing. I'm not saying any more.'

Which meant that Raff had definitely been in on it? 'What was he like?'

'All right, I suppose. Not particularly academic, practical joker, curly hair. Fifty push-ups before breakfast, that sort. He always dreamed of going into the Army. The tragedy was that he didn't last long when he got there. Killed in Afghanistan.'

Oh. One down, and how many to go? 'I believe three boys took part in the rape. Abdi was one. Raff was another. I believe the third was the one who brought Rohypnol to the party.'

'Nonsense.' But his eyes switched away from hers.

'Dan says drugs were being sold at the school gates. He said he didn't know who was involved, but I think he did. You knew, didn't you?'

A long sigh. 'It might have been . . . Not that I have any proof. This is purely gossip, and I'd deny it if you say I told you. It might have been someone called Spotty Dick.'

'"Spotty Dick"?'

'Acne. We called him Spotty Dick. Dick Prentice. He's an accountant, quite high up, works for the council, no children, divorced.'

He'd given up Dick's name without a struggle. Perhaps he didn't like Dick much?

'What was he like?'

A shrug. 'No friend of mine. A hanger-on to whatever group would have him. Brilliant with figures. He smelt a bit. Anxiety.' He wrinkled his nose. 'He used to paw the girls. Ugh.'

She considered his answer. He hadn't liked Abdi much, had he? Or Spotty Dick. And Raff was dead. Jack hadn't minded talking about them, but . . . 'There was a fourth?'

'No, no.' His eyes dropped away from hers.

Ellie thought he knew very well that there had been a fourth and who it must be, but for some reason he didn't want to say. 'How much of the action did you see that night?'

He didn't mind talking about that. 'It was a good party. Parents out for the evening, not a bad disco, plenty of beer, plenty of girls. And then, crash, bang and wallop. The Invasion of the Body Snatchers. Dan stood up to them. I tried to phone the police and was sent airborne. I tell you, my feet left the ground. I hit my head on something, don't know what, landed in a tangle of bodies. Everyone shouting, disco thundering, Dan yelling for us to get out, girls screaming . . . hell on wheels. I couldn't see straight. Concussion. Caroline half carried and half dragged me out of the house and into the garden.'

'Caroline who?'

'Caroline was my girlfriend at that time. She made me sit down and put my head between my knees. Nice girl. No looker, but kept her head. I could hear the panic in her voice, but she kept it down.'

'What became of her?'

'Um? Oh. She's a professor of literature somewhere north, prestigious uni, you know. Durham? I think. I looked on Facebook once, and she was there. Married, two sprogs.'

'Good for her. So you ended up . . . where?'

'Behind one of the hedges. Some of the gang followed us into the garden, but we lay down in the shadows and kept quiet. They didn't see us. Then, every time I tried to stand up, I got dizzy and had to sit down again. The wonder of it was that Caroline stuck by me. Eventually, I'd recovered enough to stand. I'd been to the house before and knew there was a side gate on to an alley at the bottom of the garden. Caroline hoicked my arm over her shoulder, and we set off down the path. And that's when we came across them, on the lawn beside the pool. Four of them, on their knees around Vera. And she wasn't moving.'

Silence. Ellie thought about it. 'Were her eyes open?'

'She looked asleep.'

'Drugged.'

He shrugged. 'I thought so.'

'It was Dick Prentice who brought the drugs to the party, wasn't it?'

A swift glance away. 'I don't know.' Was there the slightest emphasis on the word 'know'? Probably.

Ellie said, 'You tried to stop it?'

'It was too late.' His eyes implored her to forgive him. 'Abdi had just finished, and Raff was about to . . . But yes, I did try. I disentangled myself from Caroline and lurched over to them and said something stupid like, "You can't!" and, "Leave her alone!" They laughed. I could hardly stand upright, and I was telling them to . . . Caroline grabbed my arm. She said there was nothing we could do and got me going down the path. The door to the alley was open. She said it was no good knocking on doors asking for help at that time of night. She said probably someone else would have done it, but she'd ring the police when she got home.'

He bit his lip. 'Poor Vera. She didn't deserve . . . Caroline got me home somehow, rang the bell to summon my father and handed me over. We could hear police sirens and knew help was on its way. We were so relieved. By that time I was about ready to pass out again. My father assumed I was legless from drink. He was not amused, but he helped me into bed. I was sick an hour later and, after that, every time I tried to stand upright I'd throw up again. My father rang for an ambulance and got me to hospital. And yes, I had concussion. I surfaced some days later to find that Dan was coping all right, but no one wanted to talk about what had happened. The papers said it was druggies who'd killed the doctor. Vera was nowhere to be seen, and I didn't ask.'

There was the source of his pain. He hadn't been able to stop the rape, he hadn't asked about Vera afterwards, and he hadn't gone to the police about it, either.

Ellie said, gentle-voiced, 'You couldn't have done anything

much at the time, could you? But because you didn't do anything then, you've lived with the feeling of guilt ever since. Is that right?'

A long, long sigh. 'Yes, Mrs Quicke. I've lived with it ever since. I went to see Vera some time later. She was pregnant and desperate. Her father had sold the business, and she had nowhere to go. The council put her into a hostel, but soon after she got a one-bedroomed flat. I helped her move. It was pretty awful, but she'd cleaned it up nicely, so later, when a friend of my mother's was looking for someone to help her with the housework, I told Vera, and she got the job. I ought to have done more, but I didn't. For months at a time I've managed not to think about it, and now . . .' A helpless gesture.

'You never talked to Dan about what happened to Vera? He thinks she was a willing participant in what went on.'

He flushed. 'It seemed best to let him think that. She didn't want anything to do with him afterwards, got her father to tell him it was over. Dan was bitter about it at first but, as I told him, it wasn't as if their relationship had been going anywhere. She was never going to wait for him to train as a doctor, was she?'

Jack met Ellie's eye and flinched. He said, 'You think I ought to have told him about her being raped? What good would that have done? If she'd decided not to see him again, he was better off not knowing. Look, this is just wasting time. I've decided not to give you a statement after all. And if you try to quote what I've said, I'll deny it.'

A disappointment. 'I can try your Caroline.'

A grim smile. 'I doubt if she'll help. She went off on holiday immediately after the party. And then to uni. I don't think I ever saw her after that night. Oh, in the distance, once. In the park. With someone else. I started going out with one of the nurses from the hospital. A year later we married, and now we have three children and a hefty mortgage. Story of my life.'

'Not a bad story. Not a bad life. Better than Vera's.'

'Yes . . . well. I'll see you out, shall I?'

*   *   *

Home again and, oh dear, news of fresh disasters. Rose met Ellie in the hall with a long face. 'Mikey came back half an hour ago. Playing truant. Got one of his dumb fits on him. I gave him some lunch, and he pushed it aside. Wouldn't eat.'

Now that *was* serious.

Rose shook her head. 'Then there was a courier, delivery special to Mikey, and it's one of those expensive jobs that's a phone and a computer and an I don't know what. He took it off to the Quiet Room and he's just sitting there, looking at it. So I told Thomas, and he was on the phone, so goodness knows if he took in what I said, and then I thought about phoning Vera, but she's got enough on her plate as it is, so I'm really glad you're back, even if you have forgotten to get the mince for tonight's supper.'

Ellie hadn't forgotten. She hadn't known it was needed. But there was no point worrying Rose about it. Rose was worried enough already. 'I'll deal with it.'

Ellie shed her coat and went along the corridor to their Quiet Room. This was where Thomas did most of his praying. Sometimes Ellie joined him, but she was more likely to send up an arrow prayer in the middle of doing something else, rather than set aside definite times to be with God.

Mikey was sitting on the floor, cross-legged, an expensive iPad before him. Staring at it. He looked up when she opened the door, and then looked down again. Ellie understood that he was waiting for Thomas.

Fair enough. She went along to his study at the end of the corridor to fetch him. He was busy at his computer and on the phone but, when he saw her face, he brought the conversation to a close and put his programme on hold.

'Mikey needs you. He's gone dumb and refused food.'

Thomas got up and stretched. 'Not surprising, is it?'

'Abdi has sent him an expensive present.'

'Par for the course. Did your research turn up anything helpful?'

'Complications. Neither Dan nor his friend Jack can or will give Vera an alibi. More work needed.'

He led the way to the Quiet Room and took his usual

seat. Ellie sat beside him. Mikey held up the iPad for them to see, and then dropped it, quite deliberately, on to the floor.

'Ah,' said Thomas. 'Bribery and corruption, you think? Your father showing you that all the treasures of the world can be yours, if you only agree to his terms?'

Narrowed eyes. A nod.

'The life he's offering could be an adventure. Fast cars, luxury hotels, no need to work for a living. Seventh heaven to some. You could go to Eton or Harrow. A first-class education with tutors.'

Another nod. Mikey had worked that out already.

'Beware of pride,' said Thomas. 'You know perfectly well that you have a good brain, and you understand that, with luck, you can get anywhere you wish by your own efforts. Pride, and a quick brain. You get both of those from your father.'

A face of stone.

'Then there's integrity. Courage. An equable temper. Love. You get that from your mother. But you can't measure that in terms of iPads, can you?'

A dark look.

Rose inched into the room, holding a plate of sandwiches in one hand and a glass of milk in the other. 'He ought to eat something. He didn't have any breakfast, either.'

Thomas pulled up a chair for her. 'Join us, Rose. Put the food down. He'll eat when he's sorted this out. Mikey, some people think that a person has no choice in life but to copy the traits they've inherited from their parents. If that is so, then you are going to be a battleground between arrogance and love.'

Mikey started at the word 'arrogance' and frowned.

'But,' said Thomas, 'there's another theory which says that character is formed by influences during upbringing. You've picked up all sorts of other influences since you were born. Your mother's love, of course. The teachers at your schools, who've encouraged or discouraged you. The friendships you've formed. The enemies you've made. The boys you've fought with. The kindness and the cruelty that you've observed along the way. And there you were, Mikey, with no father, conscious of having a good brain but unsure how to use it. You must have felt cramped, stifled. Then along came Edgar Pryce, your stepfather . . .'

The boy seemed to have stopped breathing, his eyes fixed on Thomas.

'A gentle soul. I think we can say "a gentle *man*". Some people wrote him off because he failed in business, ended up working as a caretaker in schools and died early of cancer. You and I know different, don't we? Edgar loved you and taught you a lot. You hadn't been exposed to an educated mind before. He opened doors for you, and for your mother. Edgar recognized your mother's good qualities. She in turn took heart from his encouragement, realizing she didn't need to stick to dead-end jobs, realizing it was not too late for her to get more education. To grow, to get a better job. She sorrowed when he died. As you did. Your mother has a big enough heart to love everyone, hasn't she? But then love doesn't weigh very heavily in the scales against a life of wealth . . . or does it?'

Another frown. Mikey had to think about that.

Thomas sighed. 'Then there's the influences that you've come under in this house. Books that you've read. Computers offering you a glimpse of the big, wide world. A school where you're being stretched. You've got yourself into scrapes and out of them. Sometimes you've been headstrong and needed help getting back to safety, but you've learned something about yourself. You've learned that justice is important to you, and that it is worth fighting for. If you'd ducked those opportunities to fight for justice, then you'd have a little worm of self-disgust crawling around at the back of your mind. Am I overstating the case? No, I don't think so. You know the difference between right and wrong – which is one thing – and you are prepared to do something about it if you perceive injustice is at work – which is another. What else have you learned here, Mikey?'

Thomas leaned back in his chair and folded his arms across his stomach.

Mikey looked at him with narrowed eyes.

Ellie wondered what he was seeing. Wisdom and comfort? Thomas had accepted Mikey's forays into the library, had helped him choose books to read, had answered his questions on everything from infant mortality to death ray guns. Thomas had taught Mikey that man could live by Christian principles. A good influence, yes. How much had Mikey understood about what had made Thomas the man he was?

Mikey turned his head to look at Ellie.

Ellie wondered what he saw when he looked at her. A bumbling sort, good-hearted but inclined to trip over her own two feet? Someone who meant well. She hoped. But not a great brain.

And Rose? What did he see when he looked at her? A tired little Jenny Wren of a woman, grey and sere, inclined to get into a muddle with the housekeeping and fall asleep with the television on in the evenings?

The door opened, and Vera stepped in. She didn't look quite as well-brushed as usual, and there were dark lines beneath her eyes. What did Mikey see when he looked at her?

He got to his feet in one swift movement and showed her the iPad. She said, 'What is this? Where did you get . . .? Oh, did Abdi send it to you? But . . .'

He pushed it at her.

She recoiled. 'No, I don't want it. I know I can't give you everything you want, but . . . What do you want me to do with it, Mikey?'

'You could sell it, Vera,' said Rose. 'On . . . what do you call it, eBay? Get yourself some decent clothes.'

Vera said, 'I don't know . . . I've never used . . . Yes, I suppose I could ask someone at college to do it for me, but . . .'

Mikey snatched it back from Vera.

Vera gaped. 'No, Mikey. You don't understand. You have to be eighteen and have a credit card—'

Mikey nodded and disappeared.

Thomas started to laugh. 'I bet he knows your credit card numbers *and* how to sell stuff on eBay. You've done a good

job bringing him up, Vera, but he's got a lot of his father
in him, too. He still thinks that rules don't necessarily apply
to him. And, in point of fact, we need people like him to
question stupid rules.'

Ellie couldn't let that pass. 'Having to be over eighteen
for eBay is not a stupid rule though, is it?'

'I take your point. But for people who know how to get
round it . . .'

'But it's *wrong*!'

Mikey made a lightning return to collect his food and
drink. He gave Rose a high five and disappeared again.

'At least he's recovered his appetite,' said Thomas.
'And now, I must get back to work.'

Wednesday evening

Vera did a big session in their kitchen once a week, cooking
and storing several meals in the freezer to be eaten when
she or Ellie couldn't get to the shops or hadn't time to cook
from scratch. Occasionally, Rose cooked a meal, but as often
as not nowadays she'd produce two apple pies and no meat
course, so Ellie and Vera worked round this to supplement
or replace whatever was on offer.

Vera and Mikey were free to eat upstairs, but usually they
would all eat round the big table in the kitchen. As they did
this evening. Vera picked at her food. Understandable, if
unlike her.

Mikey was still not talking. Also understandable, if
irritating. It was difficult to know what to say to him. Ellie
tried to put herself into his shoes and found her head going
round. Dizzy.

Thomas met Ellie's eyes and shook his head. He didn't
know, either. If *Thomas* didn't know how to deal with Mikey,
then how could Ellie manage it? Yet she must try, for Vera
was building up a head of steam. She wasn't the sort to give
up and start weeping and wailing. She was more like a
volcano getting ready to erupt.

Perhaps it would be best to attack the problem head on,
rather than leave it to fester?

Ellie put the last dirty plate in the dishwasher. 'There now. Council of war, everybody?'

'I'll make some coffee,' said Thomas, ducking responsibility.

Mikey lowered his eyes to the cat Midge, who was sitting beside him.

Ellie said, 'No coffee for me. Vera, whatever you and Mikey decide to do about Abdi, you should do so without pressure.'

Vera said, 'I am *not* going to the police. I couldn't bear it.'

Ellie sighed. 'I realize that. It would be a desperately hard thing to do, especially now, when you and Mikey are so settled here. But we've got to work out how to deal with Abdi, who says he has a witness to you killing the doctor—'

'What nonsense!' Vera flushed.

'Agreed, but to stop his nonsense, we have to get the people who were in the garden that night to help us. Do you remember Jack the Lad? He confirms what you've told us, but doesn't want to get involved with the police. However, he did give away some names—'

'Abdi was one,' said Vera. 'I guessed another, but I had no proof.'

Thomas said, 'How did you know who it might have been, if you were unconscious?'

'There was someone who might have brought drugs to the party. I didn't know. I wasn't sure. I tried a name on Abdi. He laughed, but I thought I was right. I went to see the man concerned at his home. I don't know if Abdi had warned him or not, but he threw me out, saying I was trying to blackmail him, that he'd never taken part in such a disgraceful act, and that if I repeated the slander, he'd have me arrested.'

'Was that Dick Prentice?'

Vera winced. 'How did you know?' Then, she nodded. 'Yes, it was.'

'Jack gave me his name. He also mentioned a friend of Dan's called Raff.'

An indrawn breath. Shock. 'Raff was one of them? Oh! That's awful! He was a close friend of Dan's.' She tried to absorb the news. 'I heard he died. Afghanistan, wasn't it? Got a medal for bravery.'

Ellie said, 'Dick Prentice. Abdi. Raff. Do you have a fourth name?'

Vera had her head in her hands. 'No. I don't know . . . What makes you think there were four?'

'Because Jack says one of them has too much to lose for him to name him. He said the man is standing for some kind of office. Who do you know in that position?'

Vera shook her head. 'I can't cope with this.'

'All right,' said Ellie. 'Let's try something else. Let's see if we can find out who really killed the doctor.'

EIGHT

Vera lifted her hands in a helpless gesture. 'They said he was murdered by someone after drugs.'

Ellie nodded. 'The police hauled in the gatecrashers and cleared them. In the end, they ran out of ideas and shelved the case. At least,' she said, trying to be truthful, 'I haven't checked with them yet, but that's what I've been told.'

Mikey gave her a dark look, and she sighed. 'Yes, Mikey. You are quite right. I've heard several people's versions of that night's events and haven't checked any of them. For instance, when I spoke to Dan—'

'You did *what*?' Vera pushed back her chair. 'I can't believe you'd—'

The doorbell rang. Everyone froze.

'Speak of the devil,' said Rose, inching herself to her feet. 'I'll get it, shall I?'

'I'm nearer,' said Ellie. 'It can't be him. I mean, no! Really!'

It was Dan, all right.

He'd changed into a grey and blue designer shirt over dark-grey jeans. He'd probably shaved again. He'd certainly brushed his hair. He was not nervous . . . or was he? He was, perhaps, amused at himself for taking so much trouble with his appearance. Ellie wondered if he'd had the contents of his wardrobe out and tried on several outfits before deciding on this one.

'Mrs Quicke. I hope you don't mind my dropping in. Fortunately, you are in the phone book.' A deprecating smile.

'We're in the kitchen, having a council of war.' She led the way, and he followed. She made the introductions. 'My husband, Thomas. Our housekeeper, Rose. Vera, you know. And her son, Mikey.' She swept her hand around. 'Everyone, this is an old friend of Vera's, Dan McKenzie.'

'Coffee?' Thomas held up the cafetière. 'I've just made some.'

'Thank you, but no.' Dan's eyes went past Rose to Vera, who was on her feet on the other side of the table.

Well, well! If I stood between them, would I get an electric shock? So this is what it's all about? A simple case of physical attraction between two people from different parts of town?

Dan broke the spell first. Perhaps he'd come prepared with what to say? 'Nice to see you again, Vera.' He was very much in command of the situation.

This was rotten for Vera, who'd come straight from college, whose hair was tied back at the nape of her neck, and who was wearing a creased, long-sleeved white T-shirt and black jeans. No make-up. She looked all right, but not as fantastic as she could appear when she was dolled up.

She let herself back down on to her chair. 'Dan. Long time no see. Ellie, you forgot to introduce the family's cat. Dan, our cat is called Midge, and he's sitting next to Mikey. Take care, he bites.' And from that you couldn't tell whether it was the boy or the cat who might take a bite out of the newcomer.

'Cats usually take to me,' said Dan, holding out his hand to Midge who, to everyone's amazement and, perhaps, annoyance, lifted his head to let his jaw be scratched. Dan's gaze passed on to Mikey. 'And you are the boy genius?'

Mikey narrowed his eyes. 'And you are the man who ought to have been my father?'

That got through to Dan, all right. Various expressions passed over his face. Shock first. Horror? Was he going to reject Mikey's suggestion outright? Was that amusement? Was he going to laugh at the boy, or with him? 'Yes, Mikey. That's right. Your mother and I were once very good friends, but something happened and I was told she didn't want to see me any more. Only, today I heard something which made me wonder if I'd been misinformed. I've come to find out if what I'd been told was right and to say sorry if I got it wrong.'

'Too late,' said Vera's voice. Her eyes said something different. Her eyes said she was hungry for him.

'Try me.'

A shrug. 'After . . . what happened, I was ashamed. I couldn't bring myself to ring at first. When I did ring, I spoke to your mother and left a message for you. She said you wanted nothing more to do with me.'

'I rang your father. He said much the same thing.'

Rose settled herself into her big chair. 'I remember, I had this boyfriend once. My father hated him, and there were words said. He was turned away from our door when he called, and I didn't find out for ages. By which time he was seeing someone else. Ah well. If we could only have our time back again.'

Vera lifted her chin. 'I wouldn't wish anything different. I have Mikey and good friends. I have a lovely flat and the offer of a good job when I finish at college.'

'While I,' said Dan, 'lead the usual aimless life of the middle-classes. I have a job which I enjoy but brings in no great kudos. I distract myself from the pointlessness of my life by competition cycling. I've bought an old house which needs underpinning and am living in characterless rented accommodation. Oh, and I'm divorced.'

Ellie's eyes switched from Dan to Vera and back again. As did Thomas's. As in a tennis match.

'I haven't been with a man,' said Vera. 'Since.'

Dan corrected her. 'Yet you are "Mrs Pryce", according to the newspapers.'

Vera flushed. 'He was a good man. He needed me. He was dying. He couldn't manage to . . . But I would have, if he'd been able to.'

'He left you with good connections.'

'Thankfully. And how did Daphne leave you?' A silky tone of voice.

'You've kept tally?' Amused.

A shrug. 'It was in the papers. Your mother won, after all. She always wanted you to marry Daphne.'

'It didn't last. Your father won, too. He didn't want *you* to marry *me*.'

'He's dead, and so is my mother. But your mother is still alive and living in luxury.'

Narrowed eyes. 'Now I don't think you got that information from the papers.'

Vera lifted her chin. 'One of my friends worked as a cleaner for your mother. She used to keep me up to date.' And that was rubbing his nose in the fact that cleaning had been Vera's job, too, wasn't it?

'I thought you were no longer working as a cleaner. You're at college now? And with a good job in view?'

Vera turned to Ellie. 'I was going to tell you, when all this blew up. On my way home yesterday I met the manager of the new hotel and she said their reception staff were dire, giving them lots of grief. She asked if I'd consider going in part-time as soon as I could, and if it worked out, I could take over the desk as soon as I got my degree. I said I'd be delighted.'

'Ah, that's the new Pryce Hotel, named after your husband? The one that's been in the papers so much recently? The papers had a picture of you and Mikey cutting the ribbon at the opening. Do you have shares in the family business?'

Vera set her teeth. 'Certainly not. I'm going to get the job on my merits and not on patronage.'

'As did I,' said Dan.

Vera relaxed her shoulders. With her eyes still on Dan, she said, 'Mikey, homework!'

Mikey wriggled. He pulled his schoolbag towards him but didn't take anything out.

Thomas pulled out a chair for Dan. 'Join us, do. We were discussing how to find your father's murderer before you arrived.'

Dan might not have heard. His eyes never left Vera. 'Mrs Quicke said Abdi wants something from you.'

'My son. He can't sire any more children, so he wants Mikey.'

Incredulous. 'Mrs Quicke said he threatened to get you arrested for murder if he doesn't get the boy?'

'Correct. On evidence offered by a private investigator whom he's paid to dig up dirt.'

With his eyes still on Vera, Dan said, 'And what's your reaction to that, Mikey?'

Mikey stilled. Mute.

Thomas intervened. 'Mikey will make up his own mind in due course. It's a wise child knows his own father.'

Which you could take several ways.

Ellie thought it time to start a new thread in the conversation. 'Can we clear up a small point? Was it Dick Prentice who took the rape drug to the party?'

Vera pulled a face. 'I suppose it might have been. He was desperate to get a girl, but none of us would look at him.'

Dan said, 'Slightly dodgy exam results for everything except maths. Did he cheat? Possibly. Risqué jokes. Plenty of pocket money.'

'I know he tried cannabis. He once offered me some in exchange for a kiss.' She shuddered, remembering perhaps that Dick had taken by force what she'd refused to give.

Dan looked self-conscious. 'I know I said our lot didn't use drugs, but we had all heard we could get them at the school gates. I didn't fancy playing Russian Roulette with drugs though. My father had told me enough stories about their effects . . .' His voice trailed away. 'I suppose it must have been Dick.'

Vera nodded. 'He was after Gail that last term. Probably bought it specially for the party.'

'Gail? She despised him.'

'Perhaps that was why. I know you thought he was harmless, and that I was overreacting when I said he gave me the creeps, but . . .' Vera swept her hair loose and retied it. 'Thinking about it afterwards – and I had plenty of time to think about it afterwards – my guess is that he put it in the bottle of Diet Coke and gave it to Gail after we took refuge in the hut in the garden. She passed the bottle on to me. I was thirsty and upset. I drank and passed out.'

He frowned. 'You think Gail passed you the drink, knowing what it contained? Or innocently?'

'There wasn't much that was innocent about Gail, even then. I think Spotty Dick gave her the drink, she suspected something wasn't quite right about and passed it on, not caring whether it was spiked or not. She didn't like me. Had her eye on you—'

'Did she?' Yet there was knowledge in his eyes.

Vera threw back her head. 'Don't tell me she's got you at the end of a piece of string nowadays?'

'I do see her every now and then, yes. She's moved back into town, working in a local GPs' partnership.' This line of questioning was making him uncomfortable. He'd told Ellie he was seeing someone suitable. Was it Gail?

Vera shrugged. She got to her feet. 'Mikey, homework.'

Mikey delved into his school bag. Slowly.

Vera said, 'I'll just get a loaf out of the freezer for breakfast. We're running low on cereal, as well. Remind me to put it on the next order for Tesco's.'

'Let me help you,' said Dan, on her heels as she made for the larder.

Vera said, over her shoulder, 'I can manage perfectly well by myself.'

'I know that.' She went to pull the larder door open. He put his hand up and leaned on it, keeping it shut.

Heads swivelled to watch.

Vera and Dan froze in time and space . . . eye searching for eye.

A long, long kiss.

'Aaah.' Rose breathed out. 'At last he's got the right idea.'

Mikey shot to the kitchen sink and threw up. With their arms around one another, neither Dan nor Vera noticed.

Ellie attended to Mikey. At first he tried to thrust her off. Then he gave in, sobbing.

Ellie tried to imagine what he was going through. Mikey had had his mother all to himself since he was born. Did he feel betrayed by Vera taking an interest in someone else? Yes, of course he did.

Ellie cleaned him up. He wouldn't look at her. Was on the verge of angry tears.

Ellie sat down and opened her arms. 'Are you too big to sit on my lap now?'

He snuffled a bit, managed to get on to her lap and somehow nestled into her with his head cradled under hers. She wondered if it would be all right to rock him, as you would a hurt child. He was almost a teenager and might resent it. Or not. She rocked him, gently. He didn't object. She wished she knew the right words to comfort him.

Thomas put the kettle on. 'My coffee's cold. Shall I make some tea, instead? Cup of tea, Mikey? Some spring water? Don't fret, lad. Your mother loves you more than anything in the world.'

Mikey shuddered.

Thomas said, 'Now don't let's jump to any conclusions, Mikey. You've had your mother all to yourself all these years, and what's she been through on your account, heaven only knows. You've been all in all to her. She's always put you first. Now some new possibilities have entered your lives. I doubt if she will do anything without consulting you, and I expect you to do the same.'

Muffled words. 'If she's going to go with *him*, I might as well go with Abdi.'

'Don't be so hasty. Weigh up all the pros and cons. You're a valuable commodity.'

Vera stormed back into the kitchen, hair loose around her shoulders, eyes sparking electricity. Without the bread from the freezer. 'The nerve of him! Asking me to marry him, just like that, after all this time!'

Mikey lifted his head to look at his mother.

Vera tossed her hair back. 'I told him, "No!" Honestly! Who does he think he is! Stupid man!'

'Bossy boots!' And that was Dan, following her. Also flushed. Also slightly disarranged as to hair and collar. Reverting to childhood insults.

'No!' yelled Vera. 'No, I will not marry you!'

'What she means, Dan,' said Thomas, setting mugs on the table, 'is that she won't marry you . . . yet!' He made a big pot of tea and got some milk from the fridge. 'Tea, everyone? Have we any cake, or biscuits? Carbohydrates needed, definitely.'

'A cuppa for me, yes,' said Ellie. Rose nodded, too. Vera shook her head.

Dan also shook his head. He returned to his seat, not taking his eyes off Vera. Mikey wiped his eyes, pushed himself off Ellie and went back to his own chair.

Vera reached for the biscuit tin. 'Mikey, homework.'

Mikey shifted papers about and fidgeted with a pen.

'The thing is,' said Ellie, 'that we've got to clear Vera of the murder charge before any decisions about the future can be taken. We must ask Gail and this Spotty Dick what they think. If we can only prove Vera had long gone before the doctor returned, we're home and dry.' She took a couple of chocolate digestive biscuits, clapped them together and took a bite. Mm. 'Alternatively, as I keep saying, we could find out who really did kill the doctor.'

A mobile phone rang, and everyone sought for theirs to check.

'Not mine,' said Thomas. 'Batteries low.'

'Different chime,' said Ellie.

'Mine,' said Dan. 'Ah. Would you excuse me a minute?' He took his phone away from the table. 'Gail . . .?'

Vera said, 'Ha!'

Dan ignored Vera to speak to Gail. 'You got my message? No, I know you don't like being interrupted at work, but I think you'll . . . Yes, I did get tickets for the theatre tonight, but I'm going to have to cry off, I'm afraid. Sorry about that, but something has come up and, yes, it is serious enough to warrant a change of plans. Tell you what, why don't you drop in here –' he lifted his eyebrow at Thomas, who nodded – 'and collect the tickets? Perhaps you can find someone else to go with you? . . . You'll do that? Good. I'm not at home, by the way. I'm at . . . Sorry, I've forgotten the number . . .?'

Thomas gave him the address, and Dan repeated it into

the phone. 'Did you get that, Gail? It's a friend's house. Vera Pryce lives here. You remember her?'

They all heard Gail explode. 'What!' Dan held the phone away from his ear. A scratchy voice yelled, 'Have you lost your tiny mind?'

'Possibly,' he said, returning to the phone. 'Anyway, this is where she lives now. So we'll expect you in about ten minutes.' He clicked the phone off.

Vera flushed, running her hands down her T-shirt. 'I need to change . . . No, why should I? Oh, this is ridiculous.'

Dan smiled. 'You look fine as you are.' He seated himself on the other side of Mikey. 'So, Mikey, what's the homework for tonight?'

Mikey pushed some worksheets in Dan's direction. Dan concentrated. He picked up the worksheets, scanned each one. Of course, he would know exactly what stage Mikey was at. He said, 'Ah. Taking your exams a year early, are you?'

Mikey said, 'Maybe. I have some catching up to do in English literature.'

Vera slammed dirty dishes into the dishwasher and started it up. 'You leave him alone. Mikey, we'll make a move upstairs, shall we?'

Dan said, 'No, you don't, my girl. We've wasted far too much time as it is. Let's see it out together.'

'You'll regret this tomorrow and remember what people expect of you.'

'Tomorrow never comes.'

The house phone rang, and it was for Thomas. He said, 'Oh? I'll have to look that up.' He said, 'Sorry,' to Ellie and disappeared, making for his study.

Bother! thought Ellie. She'd have preferred him at her side if they were to deal with Gail. She said, 'Shall we move into the sitting room?'

'I like it here,' said Dan. 'Any chance of a cuppa from the pot now?'

Rose inched herself to her feet. 'It'll be English Breakfast, not Earl Grey. That do you?'

'I like the strong stuff.'

The front doorbell rang. Neither Dan nor Vera moved, so Ellie went to open the door.

A well-turned-out woman in a good-looking suit and high-heeled boots stood there. In none too sweet a temper. Her hair was probably naturally red, but had been artfully and expensively streaked with blonde highlights. She had slung a caped greatcoat over her suit, and she toted a huge leather bag. 'Is this it?' she asked. Not pleasantly.

'It depends who you want,' said Ellie, not taking to the newcomer.

'Vera Pryce.' Spitting the name out.

'Vera lives here, yes. I'm Mrs Quicke, and this is my house. Do come in.' Ellie held the door wide and indicated the passage to the kitchen. 'Vera's in there, with Dan.'

'Is she, now!' In a grim tone. Gail marched through to the kitchen, took in the informal gathering, and plonked her massive bag on to the table. 'Well, Dan. This is a surprise. Hello, Vera. Long time no see. Still cleaning, nowadays? And this is your son, I suppose?' She didn't wait for a reply, but turned her shoulder on Vera, to speak to Dan. 'Dan, shall we be on our way?'

'I told you. I'm opting out of the theatre tonight.'

'You said something important had come up, but this can't—'

'Vera has been accused of murdering my father. Is that important enough for you?'

'I don't see that it has anything to do with me. Or with you. Surely you can't wish to open that can of worms again? Not after all that has passed!'

Vera said, 'I never wanted to look back, but now we're being forced to bring up the past. Gail, I never got to thank you for pulling me out of the hall that night. That was good of you. But when we got down to the changing hut in the garden, what happened?'

A lift of an upper lip. 'You got drunk. Legless. Off your face. On the grass, on your back. You don't really want the gory details, do you? Not before the child.'

Mikey stilled, but Ellie said, 'Sadly, he's heard all about it from the wrong people. It would be better if he heard the truth now.'

'That is the truth.' Gail fidgeted, looking at her watch. A pretty, expensive trifle of a watch. 'Dan, I really think we should be getting along or the curtain will have gone up and we'll have to wait for the first interval to be let in. I don't want to miss it. It's had good reviews.'

Dan said, 'And Vera's had some bad ones. How did she pass out so quickly?'

A shrug. 'How should I know?'

'I know she wasn't drinking at the party, so how come she was legless within a few minutes of leaving the house?'

'Lots of people were passing stuff around. How should I know?'

Vera said, 'You handed me what I thought was a Diet Coke. Did Spotty Dick give it to you?'

A tinge of colour in pale cheeks. 'I really can't remember. Now, if you don't mind—'

'How long did you stay out in the garden?'

'Long enough to observe your acrobatics on the lawn. I was amazed. Had never seen anything like it. I didn't want to join in. Not my scene. Clearly, the party itself was over, so I went home. End of. Now, if you're finished raking up the past, Dan, perhaps we can make a move?'

Dan said, heavily, 'Dick gave you a spiked drink. You suspected it might not be what it ought to be and passed it on to Vera, not caring what might happen to her.'

'That is ridiculous. She made a spectacle of herself and has no one but herself to blame for what followed. I refuse to spend any more time on this. Now, are you coming, or are you going to let yourself be dragged down to her level again, because I've had enough of this! What would your headmaster say if he knew you were planning to tangle with a whore who had an illegitimate son, eh? What would the parents at your school think, if they heard? Let's get moving, and we'll say no more about it.'

NINE

Would Dan go off with Gail? Ellie thought it was touch and go. Thomas hadn't returned. Evidently, his phone call had been about something serious. Rose had shrunk down in her big chair and was dozing. She was out of it, too.

Vera was looking down at her hands. Was she trying not to cry?

Dan's eyes were on Vera.

Ellie gently cleared her throat. 'Um, Mrs – er – Gail. I don't think you quite understand the position. For years it's been in everyone – except Vera's – interest to forget what happened. But now Abdi wants to—'

'What's Abdi got to do with anything? He hasn't been around for ever.'

Vera lifted her chin. 'He wants Mikey because he can't have any more children. He's employed a private detective to confirm that Mikey is his child. He says that if I don't agree to let Mikey go, then he'll produce someone to say I killed Dr McKenzie.'

'What? But that's ridiculous. You were in no state to—' Gail changed colour, flushing as red as she'd been pale before. She dropped into a chair, sitting awkwardly, no longer careful to keep up appearances. 'Well, I can't help you. I'd left before you came round.'

'Really?' Dan's eyebrows rose.

Gail's eyes switched to and fro. 'Gracious, you don't really want to drag that up again, do you? I mean, it was all quite horrible, and certainly not the sort of experience that you'd want to talk about afterwards. Or now, come to think of it. No doubt Vera will wriggle her way out of trouble. She usually does.'

'That,' said Dan, 'is not how it looks from here.'

Vera shuddered. 'I agree with Gail. Yes, I was raped. I did not go to the police, and nothing on this earth will force me to do so now. Not only for my own sake, but for Mikey's. So let's leave well alone, shall we?'

Ellie shook her head. 'I understand how you feel, Vera. But how are we to fend off Abdi, unless we can work out exactly what did happen and clear you of his monstrous claim that you killed the doctor? Gail, the time has come to name names. We have to contact the people who took part in what happened all those years ago and get their statements, in order to stop Abdi taking the matter to the police.'

'Certainly not,' said Gail. 'As Vera says, leave well alone. People have moved on and—'

'Simon,' said Vera, snapping her fingers. 'Are you thinking of your brother, who's standing for Parliament?' Her eyes widened in shock. 'You mean, he was involved, too? Simon? No! I can't believe it. I remember he was there, and drinking hard, but . . . really? Simon Trubody?'

'What nonsense!' Gail flushed a deep red.

Ellie took a worksheet from Mikey, turned it over, and wrote down the name 'Simon Trubody'.

Gail was furious. 'Of course I'm thinking of him. He was not, repeat *not* involved. An onlooker, merely. I'm thinking of the others. It won't do any good to Dick's reputation at the council, or to Jack's funny little music business, and as for you, Dan . . .!'

'I'll take my chances, if it means we finally discover who killed my father.'

'Well, Vera did! You said. Abdi's got proof.'

Dan shook his head. 'The timings don't fit. Besides, what value has the word of someone who's been paid to produce evidence? Gail, this can't be hushed up any longer. I agree we don't want the business of the rape to be taken to the police, but we do need to sort out who did what. I agree, Simon has a lot to lose. Perhaps more than the rest of us all put together, but if he did—'

'He didn't!'

'Are you sure? Would you swear on the Bible that he was

not involved? I agree with Vera. He was drinking heavily at the party, and if he did take part in the rape—'

'I tell you, he didn't!'

'We can always ask Dick Prentice. Or Abdi.'

Gail shifted on her seat. 'Well, they might lie. Simon doesn't deserve to lose his career for the sake of this . . . this tart!'

Vera reddened and looked away.

'Gail, be careful who you call names,' warned Dan. 'You and your brother and his friends between you destroyed Vera's reputation and her hopes of a university education. You left her, pregnant and homeless, to fend for herself. You started the chain of events by giving her a spiked drink, and your brother took his turn in raping her. In law—'

'In law! It's never going to come to that.'

'I hope not, for Vera's sake,' said Ellie. 'But if Abdi persists in saying that Vera killed the doctor—'

'He wouldn't take it to the police, because if he did, he'd have to admit that he himself took part in the rape.'

'That,' said Ellie, trying to be patient, 'is exactly what I've been saying. We've got to have just enough to stop Abdi, and we don't have to take it any further.'

'From what I remember of him,' said Dan, frowning, 'Abdi hasn't much regard for the law. He might well throw Vera to the wolves if he can't get his own way by other means.'

Silence.

'I've had enough of this,' said Ellie. 'If nobody else will act, I will. I have contacts at the police station, and I'll go to see them tomorrow morning. I'll give them what names I have, and they can start questioning the rest of you till they get at the truth. First on the list: Simon. What's his surname? Trubody? Really?'

'No,' said Vera. 'I can't bear it!'

'Mrs Quicke, you mustn't,' said Gail. 'You'd be ruining so many lives. Simon wouldn't be able to stand for Parliament, and I . . . I'd have to move to a practice somewhere else.'

'I suppose,' said Dan, 'that that would be tit for tat. Between you, you destroyed Vera's future, so now she can destroy yours.'

Vera complained, 'You're not listening to me. How many times do I have to say that I don't want this to go any further?'

'You've heard her,' said Gail. 'This goes no further. Vera wasn't conscious, so she can't name names. As for naming other people, that's hearsay and has no value in court. Also, it's slander. If you try to involve us, Mrs Quicke, we'll have *your* guts for garters, as well as Vera's.'

Ellie stood up. 'I'll take that as a threat, shall I? It seems to me that it's you who doesn't understand the possible consequences of Abdi's actions. He wants Mikey and is prepared to blackmail Vera to get him. If she rejects his demand, he goes to the police with his accusation. Unless you help us to fend him off, her defence will have to be that she was gang-raped and in no position to kill anyone. I don't see any other way in which she can protect herself from a murder charge. Can you?'

'She can say that Abdi alone . . . After all, he is the father of her child. She should have *him* arrested for rape.'

'Yes, she could do that. And what will his defence be? That he was drunk and invited to join in a gang rape. If he tries that, he'll have to name the other members of the group. And he will do so, won't he? He won't worry about your brother's reputation. Why should he?'

Gail worried at her lower lip, her eyes switching to and fro.

Without seeming to look at the boy, Dan held out his hand and said, 'No, Mikey. Bad idea.'

Mikey removed his hand from his school bag and placed his mobile phone on the table. Dan picked it up and switched it off.

Ellie gaped. Had Mikey been recording the conversation? If so, and Dan had noticed, then it must be true that good teachers have eyes in the back of their heads.

Gail reared up. 'Was that boy recording . . .? How dare he! You're going to confiscate his phone, right?'

'Certainly not,' said Dan. 'It's his phone. He will decide what to do with it. But I'm advising him to think carefully about recording anything while your position is still . . . fluid.'

'Fluid?' Gail thought about that. 'You mean that there's another way to get my brother off the hook?'

Ellie said, 'I suppose there might be. Someone helped Vera home. Who was it, and will they speak up for her? If so, we might not need to approach Simon at all.'

Gail considered that. 'I suppose that's worth trying. It was Sylvia, wasn't it?'

Ellie wrote down the name. 'Surname? And, how do you know it was Sylvia, if you'd left before Vera?'

'We met in the town centre one day, shortly after, and I asked if she'd had to give a statement to the police. She said she hadn't, that she'd managed to escape while the gang were rampaging through the house. She'd been in one of the bedrooms with . . . someone.'

'Who?'

Gail grimaced. 'Someone who was further into drugs than any of us. He's still around, but the drugs have destroyed him. He's nothing but a zombie, nowadays.'

'So he's not going to be any help. What about this Sylvia person?'

'I don't know, do I? All she said was that she'd found Vera flat out in the garden and helped her to get away. Not that we discussed that part of the evening in detail. We talked about the murder, mostly.'

'Surname?' insisted Ellie. 'Where can we find her?'

'I have no idea. She left to go to uni. So did I. Haven't seen her since.'

Dan said, 'I looked her up on Facebook once. She emigrated to Australia.'

Ellie said, 'Gail, we have to start somewhere. Can you tell us your movements that evening?'

A gesture of helplessness. 'We were dancing in the hall when all hell broke loose. Vera tangled with the Hulk and got knocked for six, almost brought me down, too. Dan yelled at us to get out, so I helped her through the kitchen and into the garden. We all went off in different directions, trying to get away. Raff caught up with us, said there was somewhere we could hide down by the pool. I suppose half a dozen of us landed up in the hut. We were all somewhat hysterical.

We could hear the gang hallooing for us for a while, blundering around in the dark, but they didn't find us, and after a while they went back to the house and everything went quiet. Someone said there was a way out to the road further on, and a couple of the boys went to see if they could get out that way. They didn't come back. I didn't want to walk home by myself, so I waited for Simon. Dick gave me a drink, which I didn't want, so I passed it to Vera. She collapsed. Dick dragged her out on to the grass, with . . . with someone.'

'Raff?' said Ellie.

'You know about Raff? Yes, Raff helped him. They were well away; laughing, staggering about, saying it was their birthday or some such nonsense. Dick pounced on Vera first. Raff and Abdi were egging him on.' She wet her lips. 'I was the only one left in the hut by then. I couldn't believe it was happening. Was afraid they might start on me. They were so hyped up . . . Raff was such a big lad, and Abdi . . . No one got in Abdi's way if they knew what was good for them.'

'Didn't your brother make any effort to stop them?'

'I told you; he wasn't there. But someone else tried. Jack . . . Jack the Lad, you remember? . . . loomed up out of nowhere with his girl, what was her name? Carol? He could hardly stand up straight, I suppose he was drunk, but he did try to stop them, stood there trying to fight them, windmilling, you know, enough to make a cat laugh, with Carol trying to pull him away. Raff gave him a push, and he landed in the shrubbery. After that he got the message and went off down the path with Carol.'

It wasn't Carol. It was . . . Caroline? With Jack. This confirms what Jack said.

Dan said, 'Was Simon second or third?'

'I told you, Simon wasn't there. I waited till they were all concentrating on Vera, and I slipped away. I found the gate, got out through the back alley and went home.'

Dan said, 'So your brother Simon was still on top of Vera when . . .?'

'No. Certainly not. He wasn't there. And no, I've never spoken of it to anyone since. Ever.'

She'd protested too much. Ellie didn't believe her. Gail had said she'd been waiting for Simon to walk home with her, so he *had* been there. Hadn't he?

Vera was ashen. 'Dick, Abdi, Raff. And maybe Simon. Anyone else?'

Gail shrugged. 'I have no idea. I left.'

Vera ran her fingers back through her hair. 'It *was* Sylvia who rescued me. I remember her coming down the garden from the house. There was a blue light flashing somewhere in the sky. A police car. She helped to clean me up in the hut, but she didn't see me home. You say she went to Australia?'

Gail said, 'She's well out of it. As is Simon. He didn't do anything. It's wrong to talk about him just because he was there. It could ruin him.'

'I don't want to ruin anyone,' said Vera.

'Doesn't he deserve to be ruined?' said Dan. 'Or, at least, to pay for what he did?'

'I keep telling you,' said Gail. 'He didn't do anything. Anyway, others do far worse things.'

'Serial killers? Child abusers? Rapists?'

Silence.

Gail said, 'I think this has all got out of hand.' She managed a rueful smile. 'I mean, what has Vera really got to worry about? Abdi is a bully, and she has to call his bluff. She tells him to get lost or she'll sue him for rape and, as he's already admitted that Mikey is his child, he won't have a leg to stand on. He won't dare go to the police. He'll have to pay her a hefty cheque for looking after the boy all these years. Then, if he still wants the boy, he can negotiate access. Vera will get a golden handshake, Mikey will get a prince's upbringing. Abdi has a son to show off to the world, and everything turns out for the best. I'll put you in touch with a good solicitor, if you like, Vera.' She turned her smile on Dan. 'Don't you agree, Dan?'

'Some of what you say makes sense. But it doesn't answer the question of who killed my father.'

'Oh, that. It was one of the drug dealers, of course. You're never going to get at the truth of that, now. I agree, this has all been very upsetting, but we must get over rough territory as lightly as we can. You and I should keep out of Vera's hair and let her make the best arrangement she can for her future.'

'Not so fast,' said Dan. 'I've asked her to marry me.'

'What!' Gail's complexion went from a blushing pink to a sickly white. It seemed she'd invested more than time in her friendship with Dan.

Vera snapped back: 'And I refused him. What do I want with a husband? I'm busy all hours of the day and night as it is, what with Mikey to keep on the straight and narrow, my work at college, helping Rose out with the housekeeping and looking after my flat upstairs. I need a hole in my head as much as I need taking on a man to look after, to feed and wash and clean for, to have to account for the housekeeping and consider all his little ways.'

Dan said, 'State your terms.'

'Can you promise not to drop dirty socks and pants all over the bedroom floor, or leave the cap off the toothpaste, or forget your keys, or expect me to pick up your cleaning from the shops, or find the files you've left at school or under your desk, or locate your games kit? You don't really think I'd take on someone else who needs looking after, do you?'

Mikey stared at his mother, open-mouthed.

Dan began to laugh, but quickly sobered. 'You're right. I'd be a demanding husband. And you'd hate the rented house I'm in at the moment. I didn't think about how it would look from your point of view. You've forgotten my cycling. Perhaps you didn't know about that? I joined a club and spend a couple of hours a week doing events. Or rather, I did, but that's . . . We can discuss that later. The thing is, you've always been so practical, I thought you'd be able to organize me and still have time for your own career.'

'Yes, my career is important to me.' Angry tears were in her eyes. 'I want to stand on my own two feet.'

'As I said, state your terms, and I'll agree to them.'

Vera swiped tears from her cheeks. 'Soft talk. It'll get you nowhere.'

Gail said, 'Dan . . .? Really . . .? You and Vera?'

'Yes,' said Dan. 'Whatever happens. Sorry and all that, Gail. We've had some good times together, haven't we? But you always expected more of me than I could give.'

Gail recovered, clutching and releasing the catch on her handbag. 'And *you* expected more of me than *I* could give. I have a demanding job. You can't expect me to drop everything to provide clean underpants or look for lost keys.'

'Indeed,' said Dan, shaking his head in sorrow. 'I'm afraid I need a lot of looking after.'

Mikey's mouth remained open, his eyes switching from one to the other. Was he working out that Dan was manipulating both Vera and Gail?

Vera snorted. With laughter, or outrage? But had the wit to hold her tongue.

Gail stood up and smoothed down her coat. 'Well, I'm glad we've had this little chat. Cleared the air. We part good friends, right?'

'You're a great girl, Gail,' said Dan, with a mournful smile. 'I'm not worthy of you.'

He'd overdone it. Vera hiccuped, hand over mouth. Mikey lowered his head till it was almost on his worksheet, while Ellie shot a sharp glance at Gail, to see if she'd cottoned on. But she hadn't. Too self-absorbed?

Ellie said, 'I'll see you out, Gail, shall I?'

Gail left, without a backward glance. As Ellie was in the act of shutting the front door, Vera pushed Dan before her into the hall. 'He's leaving, too.'

Dan was laughing. 'Till tomorrow?'

'I'm otherwise engaged!' At least, that's what Vera's mouth said. Her eyes said that she was looking forward to it.

He took her by her shoulders and gave her a long, sweet kiss. She didn't object.

As Ellie held the door open for him, Dan said, 'Thank you, Mrs Quicke.'

Once he'd gone, Vera let herself relax, leaning against the wall, sighing. Then pulled herself upright. 'Well, this won't get the ironing done, will it?' And swept off up the stairs.

Ellie returned to the kitchen. Rose was asleep in her chair.

Mikey was fingering his mobile phone. Ellie cleared away the tea things and wiped down the table.

Mikey said, 'Mr McKenzie. Could be a lot worse, I suppose?'

Ellie nodded.

Mikey twisted his fingers into his hair. 'He's good at getting people to do what he wants, isn't he?'

Ellie nodded again.

Mikey reflected, 'I should think he's a good teacher. Wouldn't stand any nonsense.'

'Do you want another biscuit?'

He took one, absent-mindedly. 'I'm glad she – that Gail woman – is not our doctor. He won't go back to her now, will he?'

'I wouldn't think so. Did you delete what you'd recorded?'

'Mm. Probably. She's going to get on to her brother straight away, isn't she? He'll be hopping mad.'

Ellie set the table for breakfast. 'I expect they'll all ring one another.'

'What will they decide to do?'

'I don't know.'

Mikey grimaced. 'They deserve to be punished for what they did. Don't they?'

'You must ask Thomas questions like that. And remember, your mother doesn't want to go to the police about it. I don't blame her. The victims of rape often get a rough ride in court, and then it all gets in the papers. It's tough.'

He shook his head. 'Thomas will say that if they're sorry for what they've done, you should forgive them. I don't feel like forgiving them.'

'I think Thomas would say that if they're sorry for what they've done and want to make amends, *then* you must forgive them.'

'You mean, make amends by giving us money?'

Ellie wasn't sure. 'Money doesn't always fix things, does it?'

He fiddled with his pen. 'Abdi doesn't seem to be sorry for what he did. He's not a Christian, is he?'

'I expect he's a Muslim, though I haven't asked.'

'I wonder what Muslims think about rape. They probably think Mum ought to be stoned to death.'

Ellie tried to smile. 'I should hope they're more civilized than that about it.'

'I wouldn't mind seeing Abdi stoned to death. Do you know what they do? They dig a hole and tie your arms down and put you in the hole and fill it up with sand right up to your neck and then they throw stones at you. Small ones at first, so it takes a long time for you to die.'

Ellie was silent. She didn't like the sound of that. Not at all.

Mikey sighed. 'Well, I suppose I'd better finish my homework. Double maths tomorrow.'

Later Wednesday evening

Ellie was staring into space when Thomas joined her in the sitting room. She saw at once that he was upset about something, so she made an effort to forget Vera's problem. 'Trouble?'

He threw himself into his La-Z-Boy. 'Some supposedly clever men have the brains of a . . . peahen? What's the male equivalent of a peahen?'

'A peacock. Who could be more brainless than a peahen?'

'A Venerable who doesn't know how to count.'

'Forgotten to send you his article?'

'Sent me one he was supposed to send to the *Church Times*. And they've got mine. Theirs has been proof-read already. Mine is twice the word count I have room for. I am not amused.' He held out his hand, to take hers. 'And how have you been faring with the not-so-young lover and his lass?'

Ellie produced a genuine smile. 'He's winning Mikey over, and he'll have Vera eating out of his hand within days. Mikey wants to know if he is supposed to forgive Abdi and the others. He's feeling bloodthirsty about them at the moment.'

'Justifiably. How far did you get?'

'Gail will be ringing around as we speak, alerting all and sundry to the possibility that I'm going to blow the whistle

on them in order to rescue Vera from Abdi's clutches. I
suppose it might make Abdi rethink his strategy.'

'Vera's going to have to go to the police and charge him
with rape. That's the only way to stop him.'

'She doesn't want to do that. The alternative is to find out
who really killed the doctor. That would draw Abdi's fire
and salve the hurt that Dan has suffered. He has suffered for
it, you know. He's conscientious. Probably blames himself
for everything going wrong that night, for inviting so many
people, for letting in the gatecrashers, possibly even for his
very existence. Not to mention he's now been hurt all over
again, having to admit that he misjudged Vera, that he didn't
go to her aid, that he took her father's word for it that she
didn't want to see him.'

'You like him?'

A nod. 'I do. I think that, given a fair chance, he and Vera
will make a go of it . . . though what we'd do without her
here, I don't know.'

'We'd manage.'

Ellie nodded again, thinking that she knew who'd have to
find another housekeeper who could cope with Rose's eccen-
tricities, and it wouldn't be Thomas.

Thomas's mobile phone rang, and he answered it, gritting
his teeth. He mouthed to Ellie, 'It's my Venerable Idiot again,'
and went off to his study to take the call in peace and quiet.

Ellie did a bit more thinking, and then got out her own
mobile phone to make a call. 'Lesley, is that you? I'm not
interrupting anything, am I?'

DC Lesley Milburn was not only an efficient police officer
but had also become a friend on Christian-name terms.

'Only a very boring telly programme. Everyone's taking
turns at being blown up. Then they walk away from the
explosions without so much as a bruise. I thought I'd enjoy
some blood and thunder, but it's not convincing enough to
hold my attention. I'd much rather hear what you've got
yourself involved in.'

'Who said I had?'

'I know you. What is it this time? Murder or mayhem?'

'Murder. An old one. Twelve years ago, a doctor named

McKenzie was murdered, and no one has ever been brought to book for it.'

'I was still at school then.'

'I realize that, but could you look it up for me?'

'Um, why?'

Yes, that was the question, wasn't it? Ellie had decided not to bring Vera and Abdi into it. No need to open that can of worms, as Gail had said. 'My housekeeper – you remember Vera, who's doing a college course at the moment, yes? – well, she's met up with an old boyfriend, who turns out to be Dr McKenzie's son, and he's still hung up about it, I'm afraid. So I was wondering if you could find out anything, such as whether the police really knew who it was but couldn't take action for some reason . . .?'

'I suppose I could look it up tomorrow. If Rose is baking, maybe I'll pop in at teatime, right?'

'It's my business morning tomorrow, but in the afternoon you'll be most welcome.' End of call.

There. She'd done what she could now.

Thursday afternoon

Thursday mornings were reserved for the weekly meetings of Ellie's charitable trust, after which she was accustomed to have a light lunch and follow it with an hour on her bed with a book. Not dozing, exactly. But resting. As she was expecting Lesley that day, she couldn't afford to fall asleep.

DC Lesley Milburn arrived early. Frowning. Tall and well-built, she had a pleasant, nearly handsome face and a good brain. 'Something came up. Don't bother about tea and cake.'

Ellie had been going to say she could do with a cuppa herself, but refrained. She hung Lesley's mac up and led the way into the sitting room.

Lesley said, 'You've been treading on someone's toes, Ellie. I don't know whose, but someone has got it in for you. Or maybe Thomas? Someone's said that Thomas abused a thirteen-year-old girl.'

Ellie clutched the back of the nearest chair. 'What!'

Lesley nodded. 'No, I don't believe it, either. A woman

came into the station this morning to lay a complaint against him on behalf of the daughter of a neighbour.'

'WHAT!'

'And then decided not to take the matter further. Refused to make a formal statement. Said she'd have to think it over, that she might have been too hasty.'

Ellie let herself down into her chair. 'That,' she said, 'was quick. I mean, obviously Thomas didn't . . . wouldn't!'

'No. I know that, and so do you. But if this woman had made a formal complaint—'

'And she didn't, which proves . . . Ah, let me guess. My most unfavourite police inspector has got wind of it—?'

'He sent me to "sound you out". Because "there's no smoke without fire". He wants me to "see if we can make it stick".'

'If the woman didn't make an official complaint, he hasn't anything to go on.'

'Complaint or no complaint, you know perfectly well that my boss will now do his best to make life uncomfortable for you.'

Ellie knew all right. Many years ago, Ellie had had a 'senior citizen moment' and, unable to remember the inspector's name, had referred to him as 'Ears', since those appendages of his turned bright red in moments of stress. An unpopular officer, the nickname had spread till he'd heard it himself. He'd never forgive her for it. If he could bring Ellie down, he would do so.

Lesley said, 'You said, "That was quick." You were expecting retaliation for something that I ought to know about?'

Ellie gazed out of the window at the rain. 'Now here's a dilemma. I've been asked not to draw your attention to a certain incident, because my doing so might reflect badly on certain people. Also, the victim doesn't want to go to the police. But if one of the people involved in the, er, happening has retaliated in this way, what do I do? Keep quiet, or tell you what I know?'

'Something criminal?'

'I can't say.'

'Do you know who is behind this allegation about Thomas?'

'I can guess, but I might be wrong.' It wasn't Dan McKenzie. No way. It wouldn't be Abdi. No, his mind was set on other things. Ellie didn't think it would be Jack the Lad: no, most unlikely. Raff Scott had died in Afghanistan. Not Gail, but . . . possibly either her brother Simon, the would-be Member of Parliament, or the man who worked at the council offices, whose name was Spotty Dick?

On balance, Ellie thought that Gail would have been most concerned about her brother Simon. Yes, she would have rung him, to warn him that Ellie Quicke wanted to get statements from the perpetrators of that long-ago rape.

Ellie opened her mouth to ask Lesley if the woman who'd made the complaint had worked for Simon, and shut it again. Suppose she were wrong, and it wasn't Simon who had thought up this horrible story? Granted, he'd participated in a crime twelve years ago, but he might not have been responsible for smearing Thomas's reputation. Perhaps he'd repented of his part in the rape since; would it be overreacting to destroy his future because of that one lapse? Suppose it were the other man, Spotty Dick?

She twisted her hands in her lap. 'I'll have to ask Thomas what would be the right thing to do.'

Lesley was no fool. 'This has to be connected with the murder of Dr McKenzie.'

Ellie shook herself back to attention. 'No, on balance, I don't think so.'

'It must be,' said Lesley, 'or you wouldn't have commented that retaliation had been so quick.'

Ellie lifted her hands, helplessly. 'I can see that that's what it looks like, but it doesn't necessarily follow.'

'You mean that the two incidents at the McKenzie house that night were not connected?'

Ah. Of course. The police knew there had been two incidents because they'd been called in to deal with the gatecrashers *and* the murder. But they didn't know about the rape.

Ellie decided it was all right to talk about those two things. 'Of course you're right. You looked up the death of the doctor and discovered the police had tried to link it with the invasion of the uninvited. I'm told no arrests were ever made.'

Lesley said, 'What's your interest in this, Ellie? And why now?'

'I can't tell you the whole story. I'll have to check with Thomas. Oh. I've just realized that Thomas needs to know about this alleged abuse straight away. We'll have to get our solicitors on to this, in case someone leaks the story to the press.'

Yes, that would be the next step for the man who'd thought this up. A man had arranged this . . . or a woman? No, on balance Ellie thought it was a man because she couldn't see Gail going this far . . . unless she'd completely misread her. And Sylvia, the girl who'd helped Vera after the rape, seemed to be out of the loop nowadays.

So, let's look at the unsubstantiated allegation to the police. That had been intended to send a threatening message to Ellie and Thomas. If Ellie dropped the investigation, that would be that. The woman who'd made the accusation would never surface again. If Ellie didn't drop the business, there would be another threat, and this time it would be to take the matter to the press. That would ruin Thomas's reputation quicker than anything, and there would be no need to substantiate the story with evidence. The tabloid press would lick their lips with glee, thinking that this was another story about a corrupt member of the church, a man who was still taking services, a man who was the much-respected editor of a national Christian magazine. Oh, what a field day they'd have. The shame of it!

Ellie said, 'I'm not going to panic, but I must say I do feel like it. What name did the woman give, and where does she live?'

'"Ears" didn't bother to check, but I did. False name and address. Ellie; I must ask you again. What is your connection to this old murder, and how have you got involved?'

Ellie chose her words with care. 'Once upon a time, many years ago, my lovely Vera was going out with a lad called Dan McKenzie, son of the doctor who was murdered. There was a misunderstanding after that dreadful night, and they didn't see one another for many years. Just recently they've met up again, and I think they are going to resume their relationship. Dan is still hung up about his father's death and

wants to know who did it. I understand that the police thought
the doctor was killed by someone looking for drugs and that
they looked very hard at the lads who'd gatecrashed the party
at the doctor's house earlier than night and then trashed the
place when they didn't find what they wanted. Some of
the gang were taken to court for the damage they'd done,
but no arrests were ever made for the murder, and there were
no other leads. Is that right? Dan lacks closure. That's why
I asked you to look the case up.'

A long, considering stare from Lesley.

Ellie knew she was colouring up. 'Sorry. That is the truth,
if not all of the truth.'

'You think that whoever did the murder is alarmed to hear
you're looking into it and has taken steps to neutralize you
by accusing Thomas of abuse?'

'I can't see how anyone I've spoken to about this could
have taken part in the murder. Maybe I'm looking at it from
the wrong point of view.'

'Because . . .?'

Ellie opened her mouth but, realizing that whatever she
said would lead Lesley to the rape, and away from the murder,
closed it again.

Lesley got to her feet. 'I'm missing something here.
Something obvious. What is it you're not telling me, Ellie?
I thought you trusted me.'

'I do. I would, if only . . .'

'If only. Well, all I can tell you – and I am not holding
anything back – is that the police came to the conclusion
that the murder was committed by one of the local drug-
pushers or users, but that they couldn't make it stick and had
to leave the case unsolved.'

'"*Cherchez la femme*," said Ellie, remembering the elderly
Mrs Dawes' pronouncement from her chair in the old people's
home. 'That's what one of my neighbours said about it.'

'Really?' A light laugh. 'And what grounds did she have
for saying that?'

'I don't know.'

'Well, no one's ever suggested that a woman was involved.
It was a drugs deal that went wrong. End of.'

'I'm sorry, Lesley. I'm being no help to you at all today, am I? And I haven't even a cuppa or a slice of cake to offer you. Do you fancy a cup of tea now? And maybe there's some biscuits in the tin.'

Lesley shook her head. 'No, I have to get back now I've warned you about the threat to Thomas.'

'Point taken. I'll get on to my solicitor straight away.'

Lesley collected her mac from the hall. 'Promise me one thing, Ellie. Talk to Thomas. Clear it with him so that you can tell me what's going on. I do not like to think of anyone being falsely accused of abusing a child. If this accusation got out and people talked, the damage . . .!'

Ellie winced. 'I know. I'll get back to you as soon as I can.'

She saw Lesley out and set her back to the door. Now what . . .? And who . . .?

TEN

Thursday p.m.

Ellie decided that she must speak to Thomas straight away . . . except that he'd gone out somewhere. Or had he? No, he must be back, because she could hear his voice. He must have returned while she was talking to Lesley and would now be in his study at the end of the corridor.

Yes, he was on the phone but, on seeing her, he ended the call abruptly. 'Trouble?'

'With a capital T. I've stirred things up a little too well. A woman – false name and address, but who's quibbling? – went to the police this morning, saying you'd abused a child.'

He froze, mouth agape.

Ellie forced herself to continue. 'She left without signing a statement. "Ears" wants the matter followed up. Luckily, Lesley came to me with the tale. She doesn't believe it because she knows you, but other people who don't know you . . . She's worried about it, and so am I. She wanted to know whom I'd been upsetting. She also wanted to know why I'd enquired about the doctor's murder, and whether the two events were connected. I couldn't tell her about the rape, and I couldn't give her the names of the people we believe were involved. At least, not till I'd consulted you, and them. Or at least warned them. And if Vera still refuses to go to the police, I don't know what I can say or do to help.'

She threw up her hands. 'I don't know whether I'm on my head or my heels. What duty do we owe the men who raped Vera? Surely, none. But is it up to us to take the initiative and bring them to justice? Possibly not. Yet we can't have someone going round accusing you of rape. I can understand how Gail feels about not upsetting Simon's chances at election . . . or can I? Help me, Thomas. I don't know what to think.'

He blinked. Trying to take it in.

She shook her head. 'Such evil. What are we going to do?'

'I don't know.' He sat quietly, stroking his beard, eyes hooded. 'You think it was Simon who set this story going?'

'It might be. Or it might be Spotty Dick – not that I ought to call him by that name, because he probably isn't spotty any longer.'

'Gail herself wouldn't have thought of it, would she?'

Ellie shook her head. 'Not her style. I think it's either Simon or Dick. But to accuse them both of slander is wrong, if only one of them did it. I assume. I can't think straight. Perhaps they both deserve to be exposed?'

'It's a dreadful thing to accuse someone falsely of anything.'

'I expect you'll want to pray about it. I'm so worried. The longer we wait to scotch the story, the more likely it is that it will get out. However false, some people are bound to believe it.'

'You're right.' Quietly. Steadily.

She ploughed on. 'I thought of getting our solicitor to take action. What do you think?'

He stirred. 'I am not clear in my mind what we should do. The words that come to mind are, "Judge not, lest you be judged." And, "Let him who is without sin, cast the first stone.""

'That's all very well, but that doesn't cover the problem of someone bearing false witness against you, does it?'

'No, it doesn't.' A frown.

She said, 'As I understand it, we have been given the laws of the land for our protection. These men have broken the law so, by the law of the land, they ought to be punished.'

He nodded, but she wasn't sure it was because he was agreeing with her. She could tell he'd gone a long way off inside his head, thinking, or praying, or both.

She threw up her hands. He was so unworldly! Why did she think he'd be able to sort this mess out for her, when she ought to have known he'd try to bring his Christian principles to bear, instead of reaching for handcuffs?

Or, torture weapons.

At that very moment, she'd rather like to use some red-hot pincers on someone's flesh. She would twist and squeeze and . . . well, probably not. She couldn't quite see herself as Torturer in Chief. Or even as Assistant Torturer, come to think of it, because he probably had the job of mopping up the blood afterwards. Ugh.

Now she was calming down, she couldn't see herself putting the handcuffs on anyone, either.

It was a dilemma; these men deserved to be brought to judgement for what they'd done, but she was not able to act as policewoman and judge herself. At least . . . Oh, why did life get so complicated?

How about, 'An eye for an eye, and a tooth for a tooth'? Except that she didn't want to condemn anyone to being drugged and raped just because they'd done it to someone else.

She tried to think calmly.

The problem now was that if *she* didn't blow the whistle, then who would?

Thomas yawned. How could he yawn when so much was at stake? When his whole *future* was at stake? Granted, he thought less of himself as a person than anyone else she'd ever met, but still . . .

He said, 'Have you considered that what these men have
done once, they might do again? Or even *have* done again?
They got away with it once, didn't they? So why not repeat
the crime?'

No, she hadn't considered that. She sat down in the nearest
chair with a bump. 'Oh. But how could we find out . . .? I
suppose if I asked Lesley to look into their records . . .? But
the moment I mentioned their names, it would be a dead
giveaway, wouldn't it?'

'Have you also considered that this attack on me might
come from whoever murdered the doctor, and not from one
of the rapists?'

No, she hadn't considered that, either. She frowned. 'I
haven't spoken to anyone who hung around after the party
had been broken up, except Dan. The guests had fled, and
the gatecrashers had all been rounded up. There's no one fits
the bill.' She thought about that some more. 'I suppose one
of the people we know about might have been in touch with
others, people whose names we don't even know, and they
in turn might have passed the news on that we were digging
into the past. But how would we find that out?'

'Like dropping a pebble into water. Rings spread out from
the central "plop".'

'In which case, we can't stem the rumour by giving two
names to the police. We haven't the resources to question
everybody who might have heard something.'

'This needs some thought.' He meant he'd have to do some
serious praying about it.

She thought she'd leave the praying to him and take some
action herself. Well, an arrow prayer might be in order. *Dear
Lord, help!* And after that . . . action stations.

She retreated to her own study in order to ring their family
solicitor, the eccentric but reliable Gunnar Brooks. He could
always be enticed to visit with the promise of Rose's Victoria
sponge and a glass of something mature.

'Dear lady, what is causing you alarm and despondency
today?'

'Something horrible has come up. I hardly know where to
begin.'

His tone was indulgent. 'So, tell me what tangle you've got yourself into now.'

She told him, concluding, '. . . and I don't know whether it's right to go by God's law, or the law of the land. These men have raped and got away with it. They distorted the course of Vera's life. The son she bore by one of them has been brought up without support, financial or otherwise, from his father. Is it any argument on their behalf to say that they shouldn't be brought to justice because twelve years have passed, during which time they haven't so much as put a foot wrong? Except that, having got away with it once, they might well have tried to do it again? Which I can't be sure about without checking with the police, and that's something Vera doesn't want. Worst of all, how dare they attack Thomas!'

'There is no statutory limit to rape.'

'I know that, but what if a man has been a model citizen ever since?'

'If tried and found guilty, the judge would take all circumstances into account. In certain cases, where the girl concerned had given a false impression that she was willing, or acted in predatory fashion, the sentence might be suspended. But it is wise to think carefully before crying rape. How would Vera stand up to cross-examination in court?'

'She'd do well, I think, but she doesn't want things to go that far. Also, because she was unconscious, she can't identify her assailants of her own knowledge, although we have found out who they were later. We'd have to bring in other people to prove their identity.'

'What about this man, Abdi? The one who impregnated her? Presumably, he could be subpoenaed to give evidence, since he claims to have sired the boy.'

'If he admits rape and goes down for it, won't that make matters worse, rather than better?'

'What is he like?'

'Proud. Moneyed. Intelligent. Disdainful of other people's wishes . . . He seems to think he has a right to whatever he wants.'

'If he's like that, then even if Vera doesn't get him charged with rape, you may have to get her to bring a civil suit against him, in order to obtain an equitable settlement.'

'Yes, but he's threatening her with . . .' No, Ellie decided she wouldn't bring up the witness who said he'd seen Vera kill the doctor. Alleged witness. Had Abdi invented him? She wouldn't put it past him. Anyway, that wasn't anything to do with the urgent problem of clearing Thomas. She rubbed her forehead. 'Sorry. Just trying to get things straight in my mind. I don't believe Abdi has ever considered he could be arrested for rape. His attitude is that his money, his family connections, put him out of reach of the law.'

'He doesn't have diplomatic immunity, does he? Because if so . . .'

'Not that I know of. Honestly, Gunnar, I don't think it was Abdi who's made up this story about Thomas. It's not his style. A knife in the dark,' she said, improvising, 'that's his style. And he wouldn't wield it himself, but get a servant to do it.' She tried on a laugh. 'I'd better tell Thomas to start wearing a flak jacket.'

'Dear lady! Be serious.' A long sigh. 'I'm playing bridge this evening. Suppose I drop round to see you tomorrow morning, and we can discuss the matter then.'

She put the phone down and went along the corridor to report to Thomas, but he wasn't in his study any longer. She paused outside the door to the Quiet Room and heard him murmuring words of worship and adoration. Not pleas for help.

That was all very well. Yes, she knew you were supposed to start any approach to God with prayers of worship and adoration, but this was a crisis, and action was needed as well as prayer.

Probably, she'd got it all wrong, and Thomas was doing the right thing. If she were a better woman, perhaps she would be on her knees, too. Well, not literally . . . Getting down on her knees was too painful at her age. But in times of crisis she couldn't be bothered with meditation.

Another quick prayer should do the trick. *Well, Lord. How about it? Help needed. Ideas. You wouldn't want Thomas pilloried in the press, any more than I would, because he'd*

*lose all his usefulness to you. Oh. Sorry. Not meaning to
bully you . . .*

That made her laugh. As if she could bully God!

She returned to her study and looked at the phone. The attack
on Thomas had been launched because Gail had been forced
to face up to the possible consequences of what had happened
long ago. After she left, Gail would have wanted to warn her
brother. Undoubtedly. Probably Spotty Dick as well.

What Gail had said to them had triggered the attack on Thomas.

So, let's see what Gail has to say about it now.

Ellie dialled Gail's surgery. No, said the receptionist: she
couldn't speak to Doctor Gail. No, there was no free slot
with her that day. Nor on the morrow. They were very busy.
Was Ellie a patient of theirs? Because if not . . .

'Please tell the doctor that Mrs Quicke rang and that we
need to talk urgently, about a matter affecting her brother.'
That should do it.

Ten minutes later, Gail rang back. 'Yes? What? I'm very
busy.'

'Someone you spoke to last night has started a rumour
that Thomas abused a young girl.'

'What! No! Why . . .? You cannot be serious.'

'Never more. Our only defence must be to tell the police
what—'

'No, no! You can't! Look, I'll come round as soon as . . .
I have three more patients to see and then—'

'Ring your brother and tell him to hold his horses.'

'What! Ridiculous! No, of course I won't. I mean, what
you are suggesting is absurd!'

'Or was it Spotty Dick?'

'I . . . He . . . Oh. You think . . .?'

'Ring them both.'

Heavy breathing. 'Will you promise me, will you swear
that no harm will—?'

'It's not up to me. Ring them, and ring me back when
you've got them to—'

'It wasn't Simon. I swear—'

'Don't swear. You can't be sure which of them it was, can
you?'

The phone went dead.

Mm. Well, that had gone well, hadn't it? Except it hadn't actually settled anything. She stared out of the window. It had stopped raining. Good. Time for a little stroll outside? She hadn't been out of the house all day and could do with popping round to the shops. She could check whether or not she needed anything for supper, and then perhaps . . .

She found her magnifying glass and looked up Simon Trubody in the telephone book. No entry. He'd be ex-directory, of course.

Ellie put the phone down and went to fetch her coat. If Simon wasn't available, she could always pop into the Town Hall and have a look at Spotty Dick. Well, why not?

The Town Hall had spread itself over several buildings. One had been designed by Gilbert Scott and was in monumental Victorian style, reminiscent of a baronial hall, all turrets and pinnacles. Another was in the brutalist fashion, all steel and concrete. A third was shaped like an old threepenny bit, eight sided, all windows and efficiency. Well, supposedly all efficiency, although Ellie rather doubted that a modern structure meant up-to-date practices. Only look at the muddle there'd been when she'd tried to pay their council tax in one go last year, instead of in ten instalments. Thomas usually paid the household bills, but he'd been away when they'd become due, and she'd tried . . . Oh, well. Some people have minds that can cope with bureaucracy and some haven't. Ellie had to admit that she hadn't.

Problem: in which building would she find Spotty Dick? She consulted the notes she'd made. Richard Prentice. Accountant working for the council. Divorced, no children.

When in doubt, ask. There was a reception desk, and she asked, 'Mr Prentice, Accounts?'

'Third floor.'

She took the lift up and asked again. Open-plan offices. Oh. She'd hoped Mr Prentice would have an office of his own, if he was middle management. She asked the woman at the nearest desk and was directed to the far corner.

She had to wonder at herself, marching into the lion's den,

but she felt such a surge of anger that she was capable of daring any lion that day. How dare he traduce Thomas like this? HOW DARE HE! And then, would she know the man when she saw him?

But she did. Oh, yes. At the far end there was a well-padded and unhealthy-looking man with acne scars and glasses. A slug, seated at a desk. That would be Dick Prentice; divorced.

He had a visitor, who was dressed in an expensive, silk-mixture suit. He was big and beefy, with a thickening neck, and was standing over The Slug. She hadn't thought she'd recognize him, but now she realized she'd seen his picture in the local *Gazette* many a time. He was in politics, wasn't he? Naturally, he'd turn up to all sorts of civic affairs. Simon Trubody, Gail's brother and would-be Member of Parliament. A tough nut.

Dick Prentice was on the phone but, on seeing her bearing down on him, suspended the conversation.

'What . . .?'

Ack! Jack had been right about the smell. Halitosis? Or unwashed clothes?

Ellie thumped her handbag on his desk to command his attention. Oh frabjous day, to act like a stroppy teenager for once. She looked them both over. 'Simon. Dick. Well, this saves me a journey. I'm Ellie Quicke, by the way.'

Simon stared at her with narrowed eyes.

Dick blustered, 'The devil you are! What do you think you're doing, breaking into my—?'

'Oh, please,' said Ellie. 'Let's dispense with the formalities, shall we? I'm really glad to catch you both together. Let's talk about conspiring to pervert the course of justice, shall we?' She drew up a chair and seated herself. 'Now, gentlemen. Which of you is going to start?'

The Slug ended his call with a hurried, 'Speak to you later.' He half rose from his chair and sank back again. He asked Simon, 'Shall I get security to remove her?'

Which told Ellie – as if she'd needed confirmation – that in this matter Simon was the boss and Dick the servant.

Simon shook his head. So she was right about him being Top Cat.

She treated them to a ferocious smile. At least, she hoped it was ferocious. 'Now, gentlemen – if I may so miscall you, as I don't think either of you have earned that title – which of you have broken the law recently? Or, perhaps, since I see you are so friendly, you did it together?'

Simon said nothing, but turned a narrow, laser beam of a glare on to Dick.

A film of sweat broke out on The Slug's brow. 'I swear to you that—'

She said, 'Don't swear, or I'll have to add "oath-breaker" to the other names I can call you. We all know you've broken several of the Ten Commandments, plus a few of the laws of the land, in your time. Swearing won't help.'

Simon lifted a hand to attract her attention. 'Let me deal with this. Mrs Quicke, I fail to understand why you have forced your way in here without an appointment.'

'Cloth ears, have you? Your sister warned you I was on the warpath, and you decided to pre-empt any strike I might take by making a false allegation against my husband, which, I may say, has thoroughly ticked me off. "Ticked off" is not a phrase I would normally use, but I think it is fully justified by the circumstances. Didn't Gail tell you that Vera refuses to press charges against you?'

'She . . .' Dick bleated. But, after another narrow-eyed look from Simon, he subsided. The Slug's colour, Ellie was pleased to note, was none too good.

Ellie said, 'Perhaps Gail didn't explain clearly enough. Vera. Refuses. To. Press. Charges. She never wanted to, even when it happened. She doesn't wish to do so now. You are perfectly safe from her. Of course, I don't agree with her decision. She was shamed, abused, beaten by her father, maligned to her friends, lost her chance of further education and her boyfriend, and was left alone to bring up, support and educate a child conceived in rape. Still, she doesn't wish to press charges. May I add that she's of a more forgiving disposition than I am?

'Personally, I think you should be put in the stocks in the marketplace so that everyone you know may come and pelt you with rotten eggs and tomatoes. Or, come to think of it, how about tarring and feathering? I understand that the transgressor, after being tarred and feathered, is made to ride a rail out of town, which must be most uncomfortable, if not actively dangerous to health. I am really sorry that such archaic practices have gone out of favour.'

Simon said, calm of eye and demeanour, 'She couldn't make it stick, anyway.'

'You think not? We have the names of other people who witnessed what happened, and who are now prepared to speak about it.' That was stretching a point, but so what?

Dick ran a hand up his forehead. His hair was already thinning. 'The thing is, Simon: Vera could always change her mind.'

'True,' said Ellie. 'She has at present no intention of doing so, but your actions might well force her to change her mind. Or, since you've taken pains to involve me in your affairs, I myself might force her to change her mind. This attack on my husband has made me very angry.'

Silence.

Simon turned away from her to look out of the window. Ellie waited, understanding he was the brains of the outfit. Such as it was.

Simon said, 'You can't prove the story about your husband originated with either of us.'

Ellie leaned back in her chair. 'By that, you mean that I can't prove you asked a woman to make a false declaration to the police about my husband, hoping it would stop me in my tracks. A volunteer for your political campaign, perhaps? If I took photographs of your employees and asked the police if they recognized the woman who laid the complaint, what would happen? I believe there are CCTV cameras installed at all police stations, and they would have caught her entering and leaving the building.'

Simon shrugged. So, it wasn't his idea to drag Thomas's name in the dirt? Ellie was confirmed in her guess when Simon shot a dark look at The Slug, who gulped. So it was he who had instigated the slander?

Dick squirmed. 'She didn't give her own name or address.

No official complaint can be acted upon without that.' So that proved it was he who'd set up the false witness.

'Shut. Up.' Simon knew the best defence was to say absolutely nothing when accused.

Ellie said, brightly, 'You know, you've picked the wrong target. As I said, of her own accord, Vera wouldn't wish to press charges. It is not in her best interests, as she sees it, to do so. I, on the other hand, will take on anyone who tries to make out that my husband abused a child.'

'Perhaps,' said Simon, 'an apology may be due to you?' He made that a question, still looking at Dick.

The Slug squirmed again. 'Yes, yes. A mistake. Least said, etcetera. Let bygones be bygones and all that.'

'I wish we could,' said Ellie. 'Perhaps you are not aware what has happened to reopen the rape case? It's Abdi who's stirred up this whole mess. He wants his child by Vera and is prepared to go to extreme lengths to get him. You two are amateurs by comparison. Abdi has employed a private detective, who has come up with a statement from someone who says he witnessed Vera killing Dr McKenzie. The only way we can stop him is to prove Vera was out of it at the time.'

No reaction. They'd both heard the story before. Gail had been thorough in passing on what she'd heard.

Dick said, 'Well, that's ridiculous, of course. But you must see that we can't risk our names being bandied about, and we will go to any lengths to prevent it.'

'Any lengths? Would you go so far as murder? I can't see how else you can stop it. You'd have to get rid of –' she counted them off on her fingers – 'Vera and her son, myself and my husband, Dan McKenzie, Jack the Lad and his girlfriend, Sylvia who rescued Vera after the rape, and others who have since heard all about it, such as my housekeeper Rose. Then there's Gail, your sister . . . Have I left anyone off the list? I really don't think you're set up for wholesale slaughter. No, you're going to have to live with the knowledge that other people know what you've done . . . and perhaps that's your punishment.'

Yes, she thought, suddenly realizing that that was indeed a punishment, and possibly worse than a trial and conviction.

Thomas had known that. Of course! That's why he'd wanted to pray about it, rather than take action. And here she'd gone waltzing into the lion's den to stir up consciences which were already pretty active. Or were they? Perhaps not Simon's. And Simon, she realized now, was the one she needed to convince.

Dick's phone rang. He picked it up, glanced at Simon – who shook his head – and said, 'No calls for the moment.' And put the phone down again.

Simon stroked his heavyweight chin. 'You mentioned Abdi. I haven't seen or heard of him for years. You say he's found someone who saw Vera killing Dr McKenzie?'

'So he says. It's nonsense, of course. Abdi paid someone to find a lever which would force Vera to give up the boy, and that's what this person has come up with. If he takes that accusation to the police, everything's going to come out. That's why we've got to find people who'll confirm the fact that she was raped, to get her off the hook for the murder.'

'We can't give written statements. You must see that.'

'I understand you don't wish to do so, but how otherwise are we to persuade Abdi not to use that threat—?'

Dick burst in, 'But he was the first to abuse her!'

Ellie said, 'I don't think so. *You* brought the drug to the party. *You* tried to give it to Gail, who suspected what it was and passed it to Vera. Who didn't suspect anything. *You* were the first on to her.'

Dick changed colour yet again. 'No, I . . . Abdi first, then Raff Scott . . . I didn't want to . . . The others egged me on to . . .' His voice trailed away.

Simon half-closed his eyes and turned his head away.

Ellie sighed. 'No, you were first. Then Abdi. Raff was next, and Simon was last. I suspect he was careful not to leave his seed in her.'

Simon puffed out a soundless laugh.

Someone pounded along the line of desks to interrupt them. A middle-aged woman with skinny legs and unconvincingly blonded hair. She was wearing a crimplene suit and an air of doggy-eyed devotion. 'Mr Prentice, the phone . . .'

Ellie clicked her fingers. 'Ah-ha. Is this the woman you sent to the police station to smear my husband's name?'

Dick put his head in his hands. Simon's mouth stretched into an almost smile.

The woman bristled. 'And who are you, may I ask? If you are the wife of that dreadful man Thomas, then all I can say is that you ought to be ashamed of yourself—'

Ellie was outraged. 'I hope you know that people in glass houses shouldn't throw stones?'

'What?' The woman gaped. And then, as the meaning of what Ellie had said, she turned to Dick. 'She can't mean . . .?'

'Enough,' said Simon. 'It seems the rumour was false.'

The woman stared at him, and then, recovering herself, said, 'Mr Prentice, do you want me to get security to remove this woman?'

'No, that won't be necessary, Maureen,' said Dick, flushing. 'In fact, Mrs Quicke here has been giving us proof that we were misinformed about the Reverend Thomas, that he has never, ever . . . In fact, it may be necessary for you to say as much to the police.'

A whine entered Maureen's voice. 'But you told me that—'

'I was misinformed.'

Her lower lip quivered. '"There's no smoke without fire," that's what you said.' She looked upset. Ellie's words had definitely struck home. 'Mr Prentice . . .?'

'That's all for the moment.' Dick aimed for an authoritative tone, and missed.

Maureen hesitated but departed, leaving an uttered threat behind her that there would be tears, and possibly 'words' said, later. This was not the woman who could be fobbed off easily. Possibly, she was in love with Dick? Or had had hopes in that direction? And now he'd gone and dumped her in it.

Splendid! thought Ellie. He was not going to be able to talk himself out of this easily. She allowed herself to breathe out, slowly.

Simon said, 'You see, Mrs Quicke, there's no need for you to get into such a state. Maureen will tell the police that it was a simple case of mistaken identity. No harm done.'

Ellie gathered herself together and stood up. 'I'm not so sure about no harm being done. The police don't like being "misled" and may wish to investigate further. Perhaps you should have a word with a policeman higher up the line than the inspector? Perhaps Dick should tell them that his assistant has been suffering from delusions, but that he is making sure she receives appropriate treatment.'

Dick winced. 'You can't ask me to do that.'

'Why not? That's better than being accused of wasting police time and of making false statements, isn't it? Or Maureen making an official complaint against you? Because, if I read her aright, she's not going to like it that you asked her to commit a criminal act.'

'This wouldn't have happened if you hadn't—'

'No,' said Ellie. 'Give credit where credit is due. *This* wouldn't have happened if *you* hadn't.'

Dick's phone rang again. He stared at it as if he'd never seen it before. He'd run out of arguments, hadn't he?

Simon said, 'Shall I see you out, Mrs Quicke?'

She felt herself beginning to wilt as he ushered her across the floor and over to the lift. No one else got in with them. He waited till the doors had closed to say, 'Were you recording that interview, Mrs Quicke?'

'I tried,' said Ellie, digging her phone out of her bag, 'but I'm not too clever with all this technology, and I can't be sure that I got it.'

He took the phone off her and checked. Handed it back. 'No, you didn't.'

She was too mortified to object to his high handedness, but she had one last try at working out what had happened. 'I know you think it's best to say nothing, but if I hazard a guess as to what has just occurred, you could nod or shake your head?'

He turned his eyes on her, thoughtful, considering. Then nodded.

'I suggest that Gail got on the phone to you last night and brought you up to date. And this afternoon she rang again to warn you that I was about to explode because of the slur on Thomas. You knew that *you* hadn't set Maureen off on a false trail, so you made it your business to visit Dick, probably to tell him not to be such a fool. Dick admitted to you that he'd organized her to spread the rumour. You probably wanted to kill him at that point . . .?'

He gave her a real, wide, enjoyment-filled smile. And nodded.

She said, 'Well, that's a relief. When I thought I was up against you, I got quite worried.'

He actually laughed as he ushered her out of the building. Once in the open air, he said, 'How far have you got in finding the doctor's killer?'

'Not far enough. The police still think it was someone from the drugs' world. Will you try to neutralize Abdi?'

'I'm sure you're perfectly capable of doing that. As you say, your best bet is to find the real killer. My car's nearby. May I give you a lift somewhere?'

She shook her head. That interview had taken it out of her. Her legs were going to start wobbling any moment now.

He said, 'You remind me of my mother, a formidable woman. You're going to go on searching for the killer, aren't you?'

She stiffened her knees. 'I hope so.'

'It won't do you any good. You should let sleeping dogs die.'

He ducked his head, turned and left her.

Ellie staggered along towards the nearest coffee shop. She wanted to find a dark corner and cry her eyes out. She was so ashamed of herself. Fancy gatecrashing someone's office like that! And tearing them off a strip! All right, they'd deserved it, but she could have been more tactful. More diplomatic.

She needed the loo. She needed someone to pick her up and give her a cuddle, and tell her, 'There, there! It's all right!'

It definitely was not all right.

The coffee shop was soulless, one of a chain. The loos would be clean, but the coffee would be mediocre. It was too bright for her, and the seating looked uncomfortable. She walked on.

She told herself she hadn't done any good at all by confronting Dick's accomplice. She ought to have left well alone.

Those two men had had to live with what they'd done for all these years . . . and that must be their punishment. Leave well alone, Ellie. You've only made things worse with your interference.

The second coffee shop she came to was dark and welcoming. And had a loo at the back. Hooray.

She was shaking.

She'd learned something, of course. Simon was someone to be reckoned with. He might even make a half decent Member of Parliament, from what she'd seen of him. He knew how to hold his tongue. Oh dear! She ought never to have gone to see them. Simon had said she ought to let sleeping dogs lie, and he was probably right.

She ordered a cappuccino and a large iced bun. She needed carbohydrates.

Let sleeping dogs lie.

Well, she would have done just that, if Abdi hadn't thrown a spanner in the works!

All these platitudes . . .

Hold on a minute. Simon hadn't said, 'Let sleeping dogs lie.' He'd said, 'Let sleeping dogs *die.*'

A slip of the tongue, of course. Except that men like Simon didn't make casual slips of the tongue. He'd *meant* to say 'die' and not 'lie'.

Which didn't make any sense at all.

She finished off the bun. She decided that even though it would spoil her supper, she needed chocolate. But if she bought one of those delicious-looking chocolate twists, she'd probably be unable to finish it.

ELEVEN

Thursday evening

Ellie couldn't remember what they'd planned for supper, so bought some ready-prepared meals on the way home, thinking that she was falling down on her job at home, as well as being a conspicuous failure as a detective.

It was just as well she'd thought to bring some food in, as she found Rose drifting around the kitchen with a tea towel in her hand, looking vague, and there was nothing prepared to go on or in the oven.

Rose said, 'Something's up with Vera. She came in with a big envelope stuffed with papers and told Mikey they were eating upstairs. Looked official, that envelope. Solicitors and stuff. You think Abdi's on the warpath again?'

'Hope not. Is Thomas home?'

'I think so. He asked where you were a moment ago, and I said I didn't know.'

Ellie went to find him. He was in the library, working, but turned off his computer when he saw her.

'Ah,' he said, noting her worried air, 'so what have you been up to?'

'What have *you*?'

'Praying. Sorted it out. I've handed the whole mess over to Him to deal with. No need for any further action.'

'Sometimes it's necessary to do more than just pray.'

His eyes narrowed. 'You've been up to something? I said, it's not necessary—'

'Sometimes it is.'

He exhaled. He was not pleased with her. 'What have you done?'

She wanted to cry. He had never, ever, before criticized her for trying to help someone in distress. Granted, she didn't think she'd done much good by her interference that day, but her intentions had been of the best. 'I went to see Dick Prentice, the man who spread that rumour about you. I think I scotched it. At least, it's difficult to stop a rumour like that once it's been started, but I think, I hope . . . He used a woman he knows to . . . And now she knows he used her, and I don't think that's going to go down well.'

He was still frowning. She half put out her hand to touch him. She wanted him to hug her and assure her that he loved her and approved of everything she'd done. And he wasn't going to do it.

She looked down at her fingers, lacing them together. 'Simon Trubody was visiting him. He's formidable. You won't find *him* doing something as silly as slandering you. He thinks we can deal with Abdi without any trouble, although I don't see how we can. He also said, "Let sleeping dogs die."'

'The quote is: "Let sleeping dogs *lie*."' Correcting her.

'I know that, and so does he. He said *die*. He was trying to tell me something.'

Thomas wasn't wearing that. 'I expect you misheard.'

Ellie twisted her fingers together. Thomas was angry with her. It was horrid. She sniffed, hard, for she didn't have a hanky. 'Supper in ten minutes.'

He nodded. He wouldn't be very pleased with a bought-in meal, either. Oh dear.

He got up and put his arm around her. 'My dear, I'm sorry. I wasn't being very understanding, was I? You were worried and wanted to help, as you always do when you see someone in trouble. Possibly, it wasn't the wisest thing to do, but I'm touched that you made the effort.'

He was being condescending, and that hurt almost as much as his sharper tone, earlier.

She said, 'I thought that if I confronted them with what I knew, they'd understand how stupid it was to try to get at you that way.'

'Yes, yes. I suppose it gave you a clearer picture of what I'm up against.'

'What *we're* up against.'

He huffed out a laugh. 'Yes, you're right, Ellie. What affects you, affects me. And vice versa. Supper, you said?' He really didn't think she'd done the right thing, did he?

Oh well. She'd tried.

Supper was OK-ish. Thomas ate what he was given and refrained from criticism. He made some coffee afterwards and carried it through to the sitting room, just as Vera appeared with Mikey in tow.

Vera looked wild of eye, but was dressed as neatly as ever and seemed to be in command of herself. Mikey looked bored. He seemed more interested in stroking Midge, who was strung over his shoulders, than in attending to business.

Vera said, 'Have you a minute?' She spread some papers out on a coffee table. 'This stuff came through today from Abdi's solicitor. He's giving me a deadline. Either I hand Mikey over tomorrow, or he tells the police I killed Dr McKenzie. I've talked this over with Mikey, but I don't want him to make up his mind about anything till we've consulted you, too.'

Thomas said, with caution, 'Isn't Dan coming round tonight?'

'I told him not to. This is family business.' Then she blushed and said, awkwardly, 'I promised to ring him later.' She picked up a sheet of headed paper with a cheque attached. 'From Abdi. A cheque for twenty-four thousand pounds. In consideration of the money I've spent on Mikey to date. He suggests I use it to give me "a fresh start" somewhere outside London, where house prices are lower.'

She picked up a different wodge of paper. 'A receipt for the cheque. A form which releases me from making any claims upon Mikey, or even approaching him, in future. He's given Mikey a different name, too, but we'll disregard that for the moment. In consideration of accepting the above, I am supposed to deliver Mikey to an address in Bayswater tomorrow, after which he'll be flown off to meet his grandparents and the rest of his family. Abdi writes that there is no need for Mikey to take anything with him, except the clothes he stands up in. A suite of rooms has been prepared for him, and he has been registered for a new school. A boarding school.'

She took a deep breath, dropped those forms, and picked up another. 'This is a report from Abdi's private detective, to say that he has a witness to my killing Dr McKenzie. The alleged witness statement is not included. The solicitor says that Abdi will bury the report and the witness statement provided I accept his terms. He suggests that I get the Reverend Thomas and Mrs Quicke to sign as witnesses to my signatures.' She sat back. 'I think that's it.'

Ellie looked at Thomas, who looked at Mikey. 'What do you think, Mikey? You must have wondered about your father's family?'

A shrug. 'It's all about him, isn't it? Not about me. I like me as I am.'

Thomas stroked his beard. 'He's offering you a life of ease.'

Mikey grimaced. 'He's a cheapskate.'

Ellie blinked. 'Offering twenty-four thousand?'

'I expect to earn more than that in the first year after I leave university. I've done the maths, which I suspect he hasn't. It's two thousand for every year of my life so far, and that is thirty-eight pounds and almost fifty pence per week. Peanuts. And him a millionaire.'

Ellie was intrigued. 'Is he a millionaire?'

'I googled him. The family's into oil and shipping and the manufacture of arms.'

Vera rubbed her eyes. 'I keep telling Mikey that if he wants to go, I won't try to stop him.'

'Baked beans,' said Mikey, as if that were the clincher.

Vera smiled, palely. 'He means that in the old days the money had usually run out by the end of the week, and we used to have baked beans for supper. He means that Abdi ought to have helped us then. But, as I keep saying to Mikey, he didn't know about us before, and he is trying to make up for it now. Or rather, he did know but –' she rubbed her temples – 'well . . . you understand what I mean.'

'He thinks he can buy me, and he can't,' said Mikey. 'For one thing, I'm worth more than he's offered. And we won't even discuss the blackmail because it makes me want to puke.'

'He's offering you a ready-made family.'

A shrug. 'If they're all like him . . .!'

Thomas said, 'Mikey, don't close out all your options without thinking it through. He is your father. You don't have to go to live with him, but you could spend some time with him, get to know him. Perhaps you could meet your family on neutral ground and make up your own mind about them. There could be advantages for you in the future. Holidays abroad, foreign travel, money to spend. Why not?'

'He doesn't want "to get to know me". He wants to own me. Like a racing car, or a dog or a gold ring. "This is my son." He doesn't know what I'm like. He's even given me another name. I'm *me*, and I'm staying *me*.' Mikey formed his hand into a gun and spat out, 'Bang, bang! You're dead!'

'Pride, Mikey!' warned Thomas.

'Yes, I am proud of being me,' said Mikey. 'I'm proud of Mum, too. We're not asking for handouts. We can make our own way in the world. "Conkers!" to him.'

Ellie hesitated. She wanted to cheer Mikey on but, like Thomas, she didn't think it right for him to cut his father out of his life if there were any possibility of forming a better relationship. 'If your father had come looking for you, saying he was sorry for what he'd done, and asking to make it up to you . . .?'

'He's not doing that. He doesn't understand the word "sorry". Instead, he's trying to blackmail us.'

Thomas said, 'Vera, we've heard what your son thinks. How do you view this offer?'

Vera bit her lip. 'I've tried to make myself believe Mikey would have a better life if he went to live with his father. If he wanted to go then I'd wave him goodbye and try to get on with things. Yes, Mikey's in a good school now, but maybe he could be in an even better one, and of course it's tempting to think he could have every IT gadget under the sun, and never have to worry about making his shoes last another month. It would be good for him to have the rough and tumble of a family around him, because he's developing into a loner.

'But it worries me that Abdi hasn't made any effort to understand what Mikey is like. He's my son and I love him, but he's not perfect. He thinks for himself and doesn't listen to advice, so he sometimes makes mistakes. You know what he can be like when he's crossed. He pulls the shutters down and goes his own way. He's obstinate and, well, bloody-minded sometimes. You're right: he is proud, and he can be a little so-and-so when he can't get his own way. So what would happen if Abdi caught Mikey in one of his moods? Mikey's only twelve, and he's not fully grown yet. I'm afraid Abdi might use physical force. It's no good saying you're not allowed to beat a child, because he's from a different culture, and I don't think that would weigh with him at all. If he were to beat Mikey . . . I can't bear the thought of it!'

Silence.

Mikey said, 'Cool, cool! Icy cool. My mama is my papa, too. And I've got homework to do.' He walked out of the room with the cat still across his shoulders.

Vera picked up the papers. 'All right. I'll tell Abdi to get lost. He can't really mean to carry out his threat to frame me for murder. I mean, that's so ridiculous it's unbelievable.'

Ellie wasn't so sure about that. She thought Abdi meant exactly what he said, and that if he didn't get his own way, he would go to the police with his so-called witness statement. But how to stop him? 'Leave those papers with us for the moment, will you? I'd like to show them to Gunnar tomorrow.'

'Oh? Yes. All right. I'm going to return Abdi's cheque to him tonight, with a note saying that we're not interested. I'll sleep better once I've done that.' She swept out, too.

Thomas said, 'That wasn't quite the judgement of Solomon, but very near. It was the right decision.'

'Yes, but I think I'm going to have to do some more interfering, to find out who really did kill the doctor. That is, if you don't mind, Thomas?'

He sighed and smiled, both at once. 'Can I stop you, once you've got the bit between your teeth?' A gesture of resignation. 'All right. Who are you going to attack next?'

'Not "attack". Talk to. I think we ought to go back to the beginning. I can't think that there were three totally unrelated incidents that night: the gatecrashers, the rape and the murder.'

He was surprised. 'What could possibly link them, other than that fool Prentice taking a date-rape drug to the party?'

'The police didn't find a connection. Logic says that maybe there isn't one. But I've a feeling that there is.'

'Have you heard anything to confirm your theory?'

'Well, there was a ruckus with a neighbour over a hedge or a fence or something, but it fizzled out after the doctor died. Then an old friend said I should look for the lady.

"*Cherchez la femme*." But she's drifting in and out of Alzheimer's: my friend, I mean. So I really shouldn't take any notice.'

He stared at her. '"Look for the lady"? What lady?'

'I think she meant the doctor's wife.'

'What has she got to do with anything?'

'I don't know. I just feel that something is not quite, I don't know . . . it's as if a picture has been pushed out of the straight. Skewed. I've been told different stories—'

'That's just it, Ellie. If you ask four witnesses to an accident what they've seen, you'll get four different stories. That's what's happening here. It doesn't mean that they're not telling the truth as they see it.'

'I know that. But still . . . I could bear to know a little more about Mrs McKenzie.'

He patted her knee. 'Light of my life, I fear I was less than gracious earlier when you leapt to my defence, but I do worry about you, you know. You go striding out into the badlands without any backup. I didn't know where you were today, or who you were with. Suppose you'd stirred up someone who has already killed and would have no compunction about killing again? Promise me you'll tell me where you're going and who you're going to see in future.'

'That's sensible.' She crossed her fingers in her lap. 'But, if something comes up while—'

'Then you ring me before you go off on your new tack. Promise?'

She nodded. 'Of course.' And meant it. At the time.

Later that evening, she was clearing up in the kitchen when Vera reappeared. The girl didn't possess any expensive clothes, and she hadn't made the mistake of showing too much cleavage, or wearing jeans so tight that she could hardly move. But this was a sleek version of their everyday Vera, with hair shining and smooth, loose around her shoulders. There was even a touch of rose on her cheeks and lips. From excitement or make-up?

'Dan insists on taking me round to drop that cheque in to

Abdi's place. I asked Mikey if he'd like to come, too, but he said "no". I won't be late.'

The doorbell rang. 'That'll be him.'

Ellie said, 'Hold on a mo. I want a word with Dan.'

Dan was waiting in the porch, his car in the drive. A Volvo, safe and steady, like the man himself.

Ellie said, 'Just a quickie, Dan. Could you step inside for a moment?'

He came in and closed the door behind him, his eyes asking Vera what this was all about.

Ellie said, 'Dan, is your cousin Sam still around? Do you think I might have a word with him some time?'

'Whatever for?'

Vera winced. 'Abdi's threatening, you know . . .'

Dan said, 'Abdi doesn't mean it, of course.'

There spoke the quintessential English gentleman, who would never have thought of descending to such tactics himself. Hadn't he learned anything about other people in his career as a schoolmaster? Surely, he must have done. He was seeing the world through rose-coloured spectacles at the moment, wasn't he?

'I'd like to speak to Sam, just in case,' said Ellie.

Dan shrugged. 'I don't know that he can be much help, as he was in hospital at the time my father was killed.'

'I know, but I'm trying to get a better picture of what went on that night. Sam was older than you, and he might have seen things you wouldn't have noticed. I'd really like to talk to him and to your old neighbour, Mr Scott, if I can.'

'I don't see what good it would do. But . . . well, Mr Scott's in the phone book. I haven't seen him for years, but I think I'd have heard if he'd passed away. Sam? He was with a merchant bank in the City, married into the aristocracy, nice woman, I like her. Two children. The last I heard, he'd stopped work to do some research on his family history. He's loaded, lives in Turnham Green in an architect-designed house and sits on cultural committees. Does a lot of good, unobtrusively. I don't see much of him nowadays. Perhaps once a year for a drink, that kind of thing.'

His eyes were on Vera while he talked to Ellie.

Ellie persisted. 'Do you have his phone number?'

'I suppose. Are you sure you . . .? All right. Hang on, I'll get it for you.' He accessed his smartphone. He reeled off Sam's full name, address and phone number, which Ellie repeated and carefully wrote down on the pad by the landline phone.

He was about to usher Vera out of the house, when Ellie said, 'Just one more thing, if you don't mind—'

He smiled. 'Or even if I do?'

'Sorry, I realize I'm holding you up. Dan, someone said something . . . It's probably nothing, but I wondered if . . . No, I can't say it.'

He lost his smile. 'Perhaps you'd better say it, before I begin to imagine the worst.'

Ellie was hesitant. 'I'm sure it's nothing. Someone said to look for the lady. I'm wondering if your father had perhaps been, well, looking elsewhere?'

His lips compressed. He was angry, but controlling himself. 'Who said that?'

'I'm afraid I was listening to neighbourhood gossip.'

'That's . . . hard to take. No, Mrs Quicke, nothing like that was going on.'

'Would you have known if it had been?'

He looked startled. 'I . . . No, you're right. I suppose I wouldn't have known. But I don't think, my father was always so busy . . .' His voice trailed away.

Vera took his arm. 'Your father wasn't like that. You boys might not have noticed, but us girls always knew if a man had roving hands, and he didn't. Quite definitely not.'

Dan spoke to her, and not to Ellie. 'Not for young girls. I accept that. But I'm trying to think back . . . It never occurred to me before that he might have, for an older woman, perhaps . . .? My mother was a very demanding person.'

'No,' said Vera. 'Doctors live life in a sort of spotlight. There would have been gossip—'

'Mrs Quicke says that there was gossip.'

'Yes,' said Ellie, feeling miserable. 'I don't know how reliable it is. Now I've made you doubt your memories of your family. I'm so sorry. I wish I'd never started asking questions. Perhaps you are right, and the past is best left undisturbed.'

'Yes,' said Dan, 'and no. For years I grieved because I had no closure on my father's death. For an equal number of years after that, I thought it best to forget it and move on. Now the past has come up and hit me, it's brought a lot of good with it. I was young and naive then. I couldn't imagine my parents had any life outside the doors of our house, but of course they did. They must have done. If you turn up something which might be painful for me to hear, Mrs Quicke, then don't hesitate on my account. You've brought me more happiness than I could ever have dreamed of.' He put his arm round Vera's shoulders.

Vera had tears in her eyes. 'Dan, you're going too fast for me. Which is not to say I don't like it.'

Dan laughed. With a nod to Ellie he led Vera out to his car.

Would it have been a good idea for Mikey to go with them, to have a look at Abdi's house?

Yes, probably. But, if he'd dug in his toes, then that was that. Hopefully, he would be tackling his homework rather than emailing his friends on the computer or watching the telly. Well, you could always hope.

At that point in time things became even more complicated. The phone rang, and it was Ellie's difficult daughter Diana, asking – no, demanding – yet another favour.

'Mother, you know I said I'd need you to babysit at the weekend—'

'No, you didn't, dear.'

'Yes, I did. I told you when I collected little Evan the other day. The au pair has gone down with toothache and is insisting on flying back to visit her own dentist in Germany, can you believe? I told her, I'd pay for her to go my own man, but she's determined, and when I said I didn't expect her to leave me in the lurch like this, with a business to run as well, she was, well, not to put too fine a point on it, she was extremely rude.'

Ellie thought, but didn't say, *Good for her*.

'So I've shot her out of the house and I can't get a

replacement till Monday, so I shall need cover. The simplest thing would be if you were to move in here to look after him. The au pair's room is in a bit of a mess but I'm sure you can clean it up and put clean sheets on the bed, there's plenty in the cupboard, at least there should be, although you can't trust anyone to do even the simplest things for you nowadays, can you?'

'Sorry, Diana. That is absolutely out of the question. I'm up to here in—'

'I did think you could do just this one thing for me! I don't often ask you to help me out, now, do I!'

'I'm sorry, Diana. That really is out of the question.'

A put-upon sigh. 'Then there's no help for it. I'll have to bring baby over to you first thing tomorrow on my way to work. I can pick him up at the end of the day and bring him home for the evening, but then on Saturday I'll need you to look after him again. He's got a touch of the runs, nothing serious, but please don't let him catch another cold as it tends to go to his chest and then we can never get a proper night's sleep . . .'

Ellie didn't hear the rest of her daughter's diatribe. How was she going to get to the bottom of the doctor's murder with a baby hanging round her neck? Much as she loved him. Well, of course she loved him. But at times like this she did feel a little, well, tired.

Friday morning

Little Evan was teething. And grizzly. On the plus side, he loved being with Rose, who in turn adored him.

Ellie had got up early to receive Evan and to bake her solicitor his favourite Victoria sponge. Rose could sometimes still bake the most wonderful light cakes, but every now and then she'd forget to put in the eggs or the baking powder and then she'd weep and say she was no good for anything any more. So Ellie baked while Rose amused Evan, sitting in his high chair. Now and then Rose read out bits from the local paper. Fortunately, the little boy fell asleep a few minutes before Gunnar arrived.

Ellie's solicitor was a big man with a big presence. Ellie took him into the sitting room and outlined what had been happening, indicating the pile of papers Vera had left for him to see. Gunnar picked up the first one and concentrated. His lips pinched in and out. In and out. He frowned.

Ellie offered cake. He ignored her.

He inspected the rest of the paperwork, seated himself with a huff and a shake of his head. 'Ellie, where is your friend Vera now?'

'At college, but she's letting me act for her.'

Gunnar said, 'This paperwork . . . I am not amused. Dear lady, rest easy in your mind. I have heard of this so-called solicitor, a semi-educated, foolish young man, picking up work where he can, mostly dubious claims for whiplash injuries and inflated claims for repairs to cars which have been involved in minor accidents. In short, an ambulance chaser. He parties all night and stumbles through his work all day. No doubt he met up with your Abdi at one of his all-nighters and registered pound signs in his eyes without having the intelligence to check the status of those concerned. If this matter ever comes to court, a half-decent barrister would rip his case apart. Vera did well to return his cheque.'

'Abdi can be forceful. And, perhaps, a little careless with the truth.'

Seeing Gunnar relax a trifle, Ellie offered cake and tea. This time he accepted but perused each piece of paper again, one by one.

Ellie kept quiet. *Danger, men at work.*

Gunnar held one sheet of paper at arm's length, as if he feared it might infect him. 'This threat to have Vera exposed as a murderer. It claims that someone saw a person answering to Vera's description, arguing with the doctor. The private detective's name is not given, for a start. A copy of the witness's statement is not included. His so-called "witness" has not been named, his address has not been given, the reason why he was in that street in the early hours of the morning is not stated, nor the hour at which the encounter is supposed to have taken place. Phooey.'

'But the police would be bound to follow it up if Abdi sent them that report.'

'That is so. Can Vera produce an alibi?'

'Not really. Her father had waited up for her and could have given her an alibi, but unfortunately he's dead. The only possible defence must be that of the gang rape – which would open a different but equally distressing can of worms.'

'Humph. What is your opinion of this man, Abdi?'

'He's from a moneyed background and accustomed to thinking he can have whatever he fancies. He wants the boy to back up his position in his family, not because he loves him. Mikey is like him in many ways, though neither of them have yet understood that.'

'Does this Abdi respect the law?'

'Judging from past behaviour, no. Oh, perhaps I shouldn't say that, because the rape happened twelve years ago, and he might well have matured since then. "I don't know" is the right answer.'

'Your tone betrays doubt?'

'If Abdi thought he could get away with something, I think he would do so. I imagine he has no compunction about fiddling his taxes. That is, if he pays any.'

Gunnar leaned back in his chair, which creaked under his weight. He frowned. 'There have been a number of disturbing incidents concerning the children of mixed parentage. Let us say that the court rules a child is to live with this parent or that. If the parent who's lost the case whisks the child out of the country, it is difficult if not impossible to get an international warrant in order to trace the child and get him or her returned.'

Ellie hadn't thought of that. 'Ouch. I've read about such cases. Heart-rending.'

'You understand that if Mikey were taken abroad, Vera would have little chance of seeing him again?'

'In such a case I would give her money to have him traced and brought back.'

'Somalia is not party to the Hague Convention and therefore there is no legal framework to resolve parental abduction cases. Vera would have no legal case for the return of her

child under Somali law, so if she wanted to see Mikey again
she'd have to move there herself – once she'd found him, of
course. The boy is only twelve?'

'Half-grown. Not particularly tall.'

'Has he his own passport?'

'No, there's been no money for holidays abroad. How
would Abdi manage to take him abroad, without a
passport?'

'Dear lady, let us enter the realms of conjecture. Would it
be beyond a man of Abdi's resources to acquire the passport
of a boy with a passing resemblance to Mikey? Some cousin's
passport, perhaps?'

'Mikey would fight not to go.'

'He might be made too drowsy to object.'

Ellie shivered. Gunnar meant the boy would be drugged
into acquiescence.

Gunnar nodded. 'That is the worst case scenario. Let us now
consider how we ourselves might handle the situation. You
could ask me to deal with the matter through the courts.
You could instruct me to hire a barrister to represent Vera and
the boy. The barrister would discover what the boy's wishes
were. If, as you say, the boy wishes to stay with his mother,
then the barrister would suggest a compromise. He would argue
that the father should have access to the boy for, say, holidays,
but that he continue to live with the mother for the rest of the
time. He would suggest that the father should pay the mother
a certain sum of money, backdated, etcetera, and make her an
allowance, etcetera.'

'You think that there is a very real danger that Abdi would
ignore the court's ruling and run off with the boy?'

'Don't you?'

'Not till you mentioned it, no. We're not going to have a
minute's peace from now on, are we?'

Gunnar finished his glass. 'The other way is simpler. Vera
must go to the police and have Abdi arrested for rape.'

'She doesn't want to do that. Rape victims – particularly
gang rape victims – are not treated well by the courts, and
she'd have to name the other men as well. She's reluctant to
destroy them.'

'She's more forgiving than I would be.'

'Agreed.'

He sighed. 'Charging Abdi with rape is the only foolproof way I can think of to stop him, though even then . . .' He lumbered to his feet. 'I must get on, I suppose. Tell your Vera to ring me for an appointment as soon as she likes, and we'll talk it through.'

'The bill comes to me.'

He inclined his head. 'Understood. Meanwhile, warn the boy to be on the lookout. Perhaps arm him with a pepper spray? It's illegal, and you haven't heard me mention it, but it might save him from a nasty experience.'

As Ellie showed Gunnar out, noises from the kitchen informed Ellie that little Evan was now awake and demanding attention. He always started with a faint mewing, 'pp' for very soft. They could ignore that. The next step was a sort of growling squawk. Not exactly 'p' for soft, and – for those who knew what it portended – a signal that worse was to come.

Ellie hastily made a phone call, noting that 'p' was working rapidly up through the decibels. By the time she put the phone down, Evan had progressed to a full-blown, you'd-better-pay-me-attention yell at 'f' for forte meaning 'loud'.

By the time Ellie reached the kitchen, he was at double forte, eyes fast shut, mouth open so wide that you could see his tonsils. Rose had managed to pick him up, but it was no good. Evan wanted attention, NOW!

He was also very smelly. Ugh. What had Diana said about him having the runs? Oh dear.

Ellie coped as best she could. She set about changing him while Rose tottered about trying to get a bottle to the right temperature for him. Ellie tried to master his wriggles. He was big and strong for his age, and his favourite trick was to wait till his nappy was off before squirting wee as high as he could into the air, preferably getting his unfortunate attendant in the eye. And then, as soon as he had a clean nappy on, to perform again, both ends at once.

By the time he'd been spoon-fed some of his favourite dinner and had his bottle, he had to be changed again. Both Ellie and Rose were wrecked. And so was the kitchen.

Evan was still not a happy bunny. He was winded, burped and crooned to. They took it in turns to walk him up and down while the other had a quick bite to eat. Evan quite liked the soothing movement of being walked up and down, but the moment they stopped, he squirmed and yelled.

Rose was ready to drop. She usually had a nap after lunch.

Ellie said, 'The only thing is to keep him moving. I'd walk him round the block in his pushchair if I wasn't expecting a visitor.' She put him in his buggy, strapped him in despite his protests, and jiggled it up and down till he subsided, great eyes staring up at the ceiling. The moment she stopped jiggling, his mouth opened.

Rose was fighting to stay awake. She said, 'Shall I take over?'

'You go and have your rest.'

Ellie rocked the buggy to and fro, keeping an eye on her watch. If she could only get Evan to sleep before her visitor arrived! He'd said he was going to be in the neighbourhood, something to do with a local archive that he needed to consult. Evan was almost quiet, sucking his lips on the air. A pity Diana didn't believe in dummies. Well, Ellie didn't, either. Except in emergencies. And this was an emergency.

The doorbell rang, and Evan started awake and yelled. Was he smelly again? No? Thankfully.

Ellie got the door open, continuing to jiggle the buggy with one hand.

A tall, spare, pleasant looking man with a beak of a nose stood there. 'Mrs Quicke?' His eyes went to the baby, but he was too polite to remark on his existence.

'My grandson. My daughter's busy today, and he . . . Oh dear, the moment I stop moving . . .'

He had a nice smile. 'I remember it well. My first was a contented little chap, but the little girl . . . Let me.' He took the pushchair from her and somehow – was it the male touch? – Evan directed his gaze at the newcomer and seemed to approve what he saw. He even managed a smile.

'I'm Sam, by the way. Dan's cousin. You wanted to see me, and I said I'd be in the area but I'm afraid I really haven't time to stop. I'm due in the Broadway in fifteen minutes, and I haven't the car today.'

Ellie had an inspiration. 'May I walk along with you? Evan's a little angel when he's being walked around.' Grabbing her coat and handbag, she checked that she had her keys with her. 'That is, if you don't mind?'

He was amused, rather than annoyed. 'Why not? You said it was about Dan and what happened to his father, but I don't think I can be of any assistance. I was in hospital that night, and we don't see much of one another nowadays.'

TWELVE

It wasn't raining for once. Good.

Ellie said, 'You and Dan don't see much of one another nowadays. Because of his divorce? He gave me the impression that you were like a big brother to him in the old days.' That was stretching the truth a bit, but not too much.

Sam seemed flattered. 'I suppose I was, in a way. Our mothers were sisters, and although Dan and I aren't at all alike, my sister Daphne was the spitting image of his mother. Still is, as a matter of fact. I believe they get together every now and then to discuss fashion and film stars.'

'I like Dan.'

'So do I.'

They eyed one another. How much to say? If she pressed him to speak of his relatives, would he think her impertinent? How loyal would he be to his aunt?

He smiled, crow's feet crinkling around his eyes. 'Daphne had something of a crush on Dan. I suppose it takes marriage to bring you to your senses.'

Ellie smiled back. 'They've both moved on.'

He nodded. 'Now we've got that out of the way, what is it you want to know, Mrs Quicke? You said that the case was being reopened?'

'Not exactly. A private detective has turned up with the suggestion that a friend of mine murdered the doctor, which is absurd. The best way to counter this suggestion is to get at the truth.'

'Ah, the truth. A difficult commodity. As I said, I wasn't there.'

'I know that.' They turned the corner into the road leading down to the Broadway. He looked at his watch. She told herself to be brave. 'There was a hint that your aunt might perhaps have known more about what was going on than was apparent at the time?'

'What?' He jerked to a stop. Evan started awake and opened his mouth to yell.

Ellie moved on, and Evan subsided. Sam stopped short, and then caught up with Ellie. 'What was that? Who has suggested . . .? What a ridiculous idea.' Then, he frowned. Was that a flash of knowledge in his eyes? No, not knowledge but . . . surmise? An unpleasant thought had struck him. If so, it had quickly been dismissed. He wasn't looking where he was going, and he narrowly avoided bumping into a small boy on a scooter.

'Mrs Quicke, that is an outrageous suggestion. I'm surprised that you should . . . Who has had the temerity to . . .?' His lips twitched with annoyance. 'That is not remotely . . . It's slander.'

He was blustering. Protesting too much? 'It hadn't occurred to you before?'

'No! Of course not! It's so ridiculous that—'

'Now it's been brought to your attention, do you think that there could be anything in it?'

'No, of course not.' He hastened his step, looking at his watch. 'I'm afraid I must leave you, or I'll be late for my appointment.'

'You'll give the matter some thought?'

He turned to face her, and she brought the buggy to a halt. 'If I hear that you have repeated the slander, I shall contact my solicitor.'

'Surely it's Dan's place to contact a solicitor, not yours?'

'I . . . Mrs Quicke, I don't know what to say, except that if I'd known what you were going to say, I'd never have agreed to meet you. Please don't try to contact me again.'

Ellie had stopped walking, so Evan opened his mouth to scream. Ellie hastily began to jog the buggy again. She said, in her meekest voice, 'I'm sorry to have upset you. An old friend suggested that your aunt might have known more about what went on that night than you, but I agree, it must be most upsetting to hear such things said of a near relative.'

'Yes. Well. Apology accepted. I take it you won't be repeating the slander . . .?'

Ellie made her eyes wide. 'I am so anxious to clear my friend of a murder charge.'

'Well, not by slandering everyone in sight.'

'No, no. Only asking.'

He snatched at his temper, gabbled something about being late, and almost ran away from her down the road.

Ellie jiggled the buggy, thinking that Sam was a decent man, and she was sorry to have upset him. But he'd known, or guessed, something about his aunt, hadn't he? And the more he thought about it, the more worried he was going to get. That is, if there were any truth in the gossip . . . And it rather looked as if there might be something . . . Nothing too obvious, or Dan and Vera would have known about it, but . . . something. Yes, something.

She reflected that this business of asking awkward questions was rather like planting a time bomb. You couldn't be quite sure when detonation would take place. On the other hand, the time bomb might turn out to be a damp squib. She wondered if Sam would get back to her that night, or on the morrow?

She looked at her own watch, which was still stopped. She really must find time to get it seen to.

It was a Friday afternoon. Mikey's school let the children out early on a Friday afternoon. She said to Evan, 'Well, little one, it's nearly time for the schools to be out. Now we're nearly there, shall we wait for Mikey and walk back home with him?'

As she strolled along towards the school, she saw that boys were already beginning to leave. Some were piling on to a bus which had stopped nearby. It was quite possible that Mikey would fail to see her and do the same. He would feel safe enough, in the company of his friends. A selection of cars had drawn up at the roadside to collect boys who lived at a distance. Small cars, medium sized and giant four-by-fours. She'd never been able to understand why townspeople who never ventured into the countryside needed to drive around in a Range Rover or equivalent.

'Mikey!' She waved her arm, catching sight of him, blazer open, bag hanging from one shoulder, in the company of a couple of his friends.

He waved back and started towards her. 'What's the matter? Is everything all right?'

'Evan was fractious. Walking him around was the only way to keep him quiet.'

For some extraordinary reason, Mikey liked Evan, and Evan liked Mikey. Mikey swung off his bag to undo the harness which kept Evan in the buggy, and to lift him out. 'Pooh! You smell!'

'What, again?' Ellie turned the buggy round and . . .

Saw Mikey lifted into the air . . .

She abandoned the buggy to grab at him . . .

Was lifted off her feet and thrust into the back of a large car with tinted windows . . .

A man's voice said, 'Shut it!'

'What . . .!'

The buggy and Mikey's school bag were thrown in on top of her feet, and they were off!

She was tossed backwards on to a seat.

Evan squalled.

Mikey cried out.

Something was thrown over her head, something heavy and black. She fought to breathe, fought to get her arms free, was afraid she was going to suffocate.

They'd been kidnapped!

'Quiet!' said a muffled, heavily accented voice above her. 'Or the granny gets it!'

Had he been listening to too many American films?

Another voice, a different one, said something in a foreign language. Objecting, aggrieved. Probably, he was saying they were only supposed to lift the boy.

The other replied. It sounded as if he were the boss. Slightly uneasy but forceful. On the lines of, 'Well, we've got him, haven't we?'

Someone plucked Ellie off the seat and dumped her on the floor, still shrouded in the blanket, or whatever it was. The one with the heavy accent said, 'You! Keep quiet! Don't move or the baby gets it.'

Ellie couldn't breathe properly. She told herself not to hyperventilate or she really would pass out. It was terribly uncomfortable, down on the floor. Her skirt had risen up; she could feel carpet under her legs. Someone – one of the men who'd kidnapped them – was folding up the buggy; it had a distinctive squeak and grind.

Kidnapped. They'd been kidnapped? She could hardly believe it. In broad daylight!

Ah, that was better, she'd made room somehow around her head. She could breathe better. She wriggled into a more comfortable position. Was Mikey all right? And Evan?

She listened, hard.

No sound from Mikey. Had he been muffled up as well? Could he breathe?

What about little Evan? Ah, but he liked riding in cars, didn't he?

The car changed gear, soundlessly. They had moved on to a faster road. Where was it that Abdi lived? Somewhere in Belgravia? If so . . . let us pray. Hard. *Dear Lord, dear Lord, dear Lord . . .*

No one knows where I am. The last thing Thomas said to me was always to let him know where I was going. Rose knew I was meeting Sam, but Sam had left us before these men drove up in the car. They'd have taken Mikey, whoever was with him. Surely someone in the road would have noticed us being kidnapped and alerted the police?

Possibly not. It all happened so quickly. One minute I was waving to Mikey, the next he'd picked up Evan, and then . . . we were in the car.

Thomas! He'll go spare when he hears I'm missing. But it may be some hours before anyone realizes that we're not around. Vera won't be back from college till about six.

It was about three when I met Mikey. Rose won't know anything.

What will Thomas do? Does he know where Abdi lives? It will be on the papers I gave Gunnar, but will Thomas think of that? He will ring the police . . . and say what? Does he have enough information to get the police moving? Gunnar might help. But it's the weekend, and everything slows down on Friday night. Would Gunnar be available? Probably not. Would the police act? Y-yes. Eventually. Vera will be frantic.

There's at least two men in the back of this car plus a driver. I didn't get a proper look at any of them.

Abdi is not one of them. No. These are hired men. And stupid, because they've taken three people instead of one. Abdi's not going to be pleased to find me with Mikey, is he? I suppose he may have plans to whip the boy off to Somalia or wherever this evening. Yes, but what is he going to do with a middle-aged lady who is getting cramp, crouched in an uncomfortable position on the floor of this car? And the baby? Thankfully, Evan seems to be enjoying the ride. But, oh, when Diana hears about this!

Abdi won't kill me. No.

Surely not.

No, surely not!

He'll take the boy off and . . . what? Dump me and Evan somewhere, to be found after he's left the country? He wouldn't try to take me with them, would he? No, no. Of course not.

The man seated above her was complaining. 'Urgh!'

Mikey's voice, small but unafraid. 'It's the baby. He's not well. He needs changing.'

Another man laughed. A taunting comment, which one could translate as, 'Wait till the master hears . . .'

The car slowed and stopped. Traffic lights?

Ellie felt around her. Could she find the door, and a handle?

'Don't even think it, boy,' said the one who spoke American. There were two men in the back. There would be one on either side of Mikey.

The car moved off again. Ellie tried to find a more comfortable position. She was up against someone's legs. Honestly!

Couldn't they take pity on her grey hairs? Someone cursed, but allowed her a little more room to stretch out.

Evan was crooning to himself. Lucky Evan.

Ellie dozed . . . and jerked awake as the car bumped and jolted down a slope and came to a standstill.

'You! Out!'

Could she make a break for it from the roadside, attract the attention of passers-by before being hustled into the house?

She was lifted and dragged to her feet, and the coat, or whatever it was, removed from her head. She blinked, accustoming her eyes to the light. They were in a dimly lit concrete chamber. They were not in the street, but in a private, underground garage. Oh.

Mikey was brought out next. He was still clutching little Evan, who seemed to have fallen asleep, hurray!

'Mikey. You all right?' Her tongue was stiff.

He nodded.

She said, 'Let me take Evan. He's heavy.'

Mikey handed him over. 'I think he's leaking.'

Oh. Whiffy, definitely. And yes, leaking. There was a tell-tale brown stain down Mikey's shirt. But at least Evan was asleep, praise the Lord.

One of the kidnappers had his smartphone out, reporting their arrival.

The buggy and Mikey's school bag were thrown out of the car. Ellie tugged her clothes straight with the hand that wasn't clutching the baby. Amazingly, she still had her handbag over her arm.

'I'll take that,' said the man with the bad accent. He was tall, dark and handsome. Another Somalian by the look of him. He yanked her bag from her arm, took her mobile phone and stowed it in his own pocket. He rifled through the bag, didn't find anything else of interest and thrust it back at her.

Mikey went to pick up his school bag. The man took it off him, retrieved Mikey's mobile and flung the bag into the shadows. Mikey said nothing. Neither did Ellie. What good would it do?

Ellie looked around. There was parking for at least four

cars in this garage. There was a fine-looking Mercedes, a sports car, and some kind of people carrier. All expensive. All looking pretty new.

'Move.' They were being shunted towards a lift. In they got. Mikey was wide-eyed, apprehensive but not fearful.

Ellie put one arm around him in the lift, hefting the baby to keep him on her shoulder. Oh dear, he really was whiffy, wasn't he? Would he leak on to her coat?

Up and up. Second floor or third?

Sunlight. Bright, too bright.

Lots of gilded furniture. Lots of green. Flashes of light as sunlight struck the bevel of mirrors.

'Move!'

They were shepherded through a large landing into a room which was also filled with sunlight. A well-appointed sitting room with a bedroom and a bathroom off it. Furniture by Harrods out of the repro department, all tapestry seats and backs, and spindly legs. Occasional tables with carved legs. Settees that didn't look as if they'd be very welcoming if you sat on them. Not at all suitable for a boy of twelve.

And there was Abdi.

Abdi was in full spate. Furious!

Ellie might not understand every word he said, but could translate nevertheless.

'Fools! Imbeciles! Brains of a frog! Offspring of . . .!' Well, she got the picture.

Abdi put his hands on Mikey's shoulders. 'This is not the welcome I dreamed of for you, my son—' And then, recoiling: 'What . . .?'

Mikey said, 'It's the baby. He's not well. I was carrying him. He needs changing.'

Abdi turned on his men. 'You idiots!' Or words to that effect.

Ellie felt her knees give way under her and found a chair, transferring Evan to her lap. 'Yes, the baby needs changing and some food. Can you find me some nappies? I need to clean him up. A dummy – you know, a pacifier – would be helpful, and a bottle of milk, and oh, some puréed carrots or whatever you can find in the kitchen. And then, if you please, you may call me a taxi to take me home.'

Abdi clapped both hands to his head. More temper. He stamped around, shooting out orders in – whatever language it was. Somali, presumably.

His men slid out of the room.

Abdi towered over Ellie. 'Why did you have to poke your nose in, eh? Only see what you've done, now. I hadn't taken your interference into account. You can't go home till we're safely away. You must see that.'

Mikey looked around him. 'Is this your house?'

Abdi mopped his forehead. 'Of course. And yours, now.'

Mikey shook his head. 'This is not my home. You wanted me to see it, and now that I have, I wish to return to my mother.'

'You can forget all that. Your future is with me, and not with the woman who bore you. In a few hours' time we'll be on our way, and you need never see her again.'

Mikey sighed. 'I'll make you regret it, if you don't send me home straight away.'

An indulgent smile from Abdi. 'Yes, yes, of course you are a little bit upset. I will have some food sent up for you, and a change of clothes. Now, I will leave you while I make the final arrangements for our journey. Be ready to leave in two hours' time.'

'And me?' said Ellie. 'My husband will call the police if I don't return by supper time.'

'Who cares about him? Anyway, he won't have a clue where you are. I'll phone when we reach our destination, and my men will release you then. What a nuisance you are, woman!'

Mikey caught Ellie's eye. Did he really wink at her?

She kept her face straight.

Abdi made as if to embrace Mikey, caught the stench of the baby and recoiled. With a handkerchief over his mouth, he left the room as one of his men arrived with a pile of soft hand towels and some safety-pins. 'Bathroom . . .' he indicated, and fled.

Mikey went to the door, opened it, and closed it again. 'Mrs Quicke, would you like to use the bathroom while I explore?'

Ellie hoisted up the sleeping baby and took him through the bedroom into the bathroom. Everything glittered. She wondered if the taps really were made of gold. No, they'd be gold-plated, wouldn't they? She washed Evan down and, in lieu of proper nappies, pinned some soft hand-towels around him. He woke up, yawning. Eyes bright, moving around. He liked the gold of the taps.

Ellie used the facilities herself. She took off her coat and sponged down the brown stain the baby had made, before taking him back into the sitting room. Some clothing had been delivered for Mikey. Good quality. It looked as if it was the right size, too. Abdi had probably arranged for a complete wardrobe to be made ready for him.

Ellie looked, but there was no landline phone in sight. How on earth were they going to escape?

Mikey was wandering around the room, twitching back curtains, clicking side lamps on and off. She opened her mouth to speak, and he hushed her. He was up to something, definitely.

Ellie shushed. She damped down panic. She told herself that Mikey wasn't panicking, so she mustn't, either. It would do absolutely no good to start screaming and shouting to be let out. Mikey was expecting her to be calm. After all, he might be able to think of something. He'd certainly learned a lot about electricity and plumbing last year when a neighbouring house had been undergoing conversion to a hotel. He'd forever been over there when he should have been doing his homework.

Besides which, if she gave way to hysteria, Evan would get upset and start screaming, and that would not be a good idea. Not at all.

She walked the baby around the room. There were two long windows overlooking the street. She took Evan to look out of the nearest one, parting the net curtains so that he could look out. They were on the third floor in a terrace of beautiful houses. Four storeys? Five? The drop outside this window went down and down into a basement. She spent a moment or two wondering how she'd manage to climb down a rope from that window – that is, always supposing she had a rope, which she hadn't – and especially with Evan in her arms. She concluded that, as she'd never been much of a gymnast, Abdi was correct in thinking she'd not be able to get out that way.

There were trees in the street and topiary in tubs outside the porticoed front doors. She let the net curtains drop and fingered the heavy brocaded inner curtains which were of silk damask and looked expensive. They were double-lined and looped up with tasselled cords. Each window was alarmed. What was the time now? Her watch was still stopped. She really must get it seen to. How soon would Thomas or Vera realize they were missing, and what would they do about it?

Mikey went into the bathroom, but didn't take any of his new clothes in with him.

Someone – a woman who looked to be a servant – arrived with a tray holding tea things; tea, milk, ice cream, cakes and sandwiches. Also some small bowls containing gooey-looking foodstuffs. Ellie helped herself to a cuppa and a sandwich. Evan looked interested, so she let him have half a sandwich. Mikey returned, closing the bathroom door behind him. He refused sustenance with a shake of his head.

'Can I help?' asked Ellie.

'I can manage. There's no one outside our door. I suppose they think it's not necessary since we can't escape through the windows, and there's so many of them downstairs. There's no fire extinguishers on the landing, but I expect they've got some somewhere. I had hoped there'd be some kind of Internet connection here so that we could phone out for help, but there isn't one. I expect they've got Wi-Fi, but even if I can find a computer somewhere I don't know the code, so I can't use that. I'll have to try something else.'

He removed the brightest of the side lamps from a side table and plugged it into a socket beside one of the windows. He switched it on and placed scrunched-up toilet paper over the bulb. Then he draped one of the net curtains over all. And waited.

Ellie fed Evan sips of milk and tried out the contents of the little dishes by dipping her finger in and tasting

– whatever it was. This one was honey. Or very like it. Honey and yogurt? Evan could have some of that. 'Yum yum,' she said to the baby, who smacked his lips and opened his mouth for more.

'Ah,' said Mikey, pleased with himself. A spiral of smoke arose from the lamp, and then came a flicker of fire, darting up the net curtain.

'Clever old you,' said Ellie, looking round for her coat and handbag.

'This should set off the sprinkler system. I think we should try to vacate this room as soon as possible, don't you? Where's your coat?'

'I think I left it in the bathroom.'

'I'll fetch it.'

When Mikey returned with her coat, he was careful to shut the bathroom door after himself. She noticed that the carpet around the door to the bathroom had turned black. Good. Now, where had she put her handbag? One really did not wish to be caught in a fire, did one? Cue for a hasty exit. She said, 'I don't know what happened to the baby buggy, do you?'

'It's still down in the basement, with my school bag. Let me hold Evan while you get your coat on.'

She handed the baby over and got into her coat. 'I wish they'd managed to find him a dummy.'

The fire was licking its lips as it ran up the net and started on the heavy curtains.

Mikey eyed the window which he'd not set fire to. 'Suppose we set the house alarms off before we go?' Grinning, he picked up a spindly-legged chair and took a run at the window, only to rebound. Bang!

'Is it toughened glass?' said Ellie. 'It doesn't look like it. Try again.' Evan didn't like sudden, loud noises. He stiffened and began to wail.

'Ha!' Mikey smashed the chair against the window again. This time he succeeded in breaking the glass, and the house alarm went off.

'Well done, you!' said Ellie, just as the sprinkler system went into action. 'Help! We're going to get wet!'

Ducking their heads, they ran for the door.

Ellie hoisted Evan to her shoulder, hoping he wouldn't be sick when he burped. He didn't like being bumped about like this. He was going to start yelling any minute. He was fighting to get off her. It was difficult to hold him fast. She mustn't drop him. Whatever would Diana say . . .?

Mikey held the door open on to the landing for her, and left it open. 'To help the fire along . . .'

There was no one in sight on the landing, and the yammering of the alarm covered their retreat. Mikey peered over the banister. He shouted in her ear, 'We'll have to take the stairs. The alarm might stop the lift working.'

'Three storeys. Or is it four?' Ellie groaned, shifted Evan to a more comfortable position, and gave her handbag to Mikey to carry so that she had a hand free for the banister as they descended. Evan had had enough. Just as he was starting on a nice meal, he'd been roughly carried away. He added his voice to the din.

The yammering of the alarm continued. Panicky shouts came from below. They'd be running around downstairs, trying to locate the source of the alarm. The fuse box should tell them which floor was in trouble. Would the sprinkler system also say which room was affected?

Third floor, or was it the second? Ellie shifted Evan from left to right shoulder. They should have realized that trying to cage Mikey was like trying to cage the wind.

Was that someone pounding up the stairs? Yes. Oh dear . . .

Mikey had heard, too. He opened the first door they came to and beckoned her to follow him inside. The room was empty. It was an expensively furnished sitting room, complete with a huge television set, stereo equipment . . . and a laptop.

As Mikey closed the door someone ran past them, going up the stairs. Shouting.

Mikey grinned. 'Bang, bang: you're dead!' He darted across to the laptop, picked it up, held it high over his head, and brought it down with a crash on the edge of the table.

Ellie gasped. Evan jerked in her arms and howled.

Mikey did it again. There was a rattling sound. Mikey threw the ruined laptop on the floor.

Ellie opened the door a crack, to see a second man running up the stairs past them, eyes wild, shouting to someone upstairs . . . who shouted back down. They'd found the fire and the broken window, then? Had they also discovered that their prisoners had escaped? She shut the door, breathing hard. Would they search this floor next or assume they'd gone out of the window?

Mikey said, 'Hold on a mo.' He opened drawers in the desk, searching for something. He took out a tube of . . . superglue? And squeezed it into the power plug points and over the remote control for the television. Then threw the tube under the desk.

Ellie had the jitters. If Abdi caught them now . . .? 'Hurry up!'

'One more window, then!' This time he used the broken laptop to smash the window. Yet another alarm went off. Evan had quietened down momentarily, but this set him off again.

Ellie was on tenterhooks. 'Come on!'

Mikey nodded. He cracked the door open an inch to look out, and signalled OK. They could hear shouts from above. The lift whined, passing them, going upwards. Dealing with the fire, or searching for the escapees?

They left the shelter of the room to descend the next flight of stairs. With caution, keeping to the wall so that they wouldn't be easily seen if someone glanced over the banister. More shouting from the top floor. They heard the lift descending. Someone had gone down for fire extinguishers? Or looking for the prisoners?

So, the fire hadn't put the lift out of service.

How long was it going to take before Abdi realized they were still in the building? Windows had been broken on two floors, and he might well suppose they'd gone out that way, if they'd found a rope – or tied bedclothes together . . . although Ellie had never thought that method of escape would be as easy as it sounded.

Down and down to the next landing. More shouting from below, echoed and answered from above. Which floor would they search next?

Ellie paused to catch her breath. Evan was unhappy, wriggling like mad, yelling in her ear. She shifted him to her other shoulder. He was making almost as much noise as the alarm.

Mikey gave her a look, assessing her strength, hiding impatience. If he'd been on his own, he'd probably have been out of the building before now. She knew she was holding him up. But he was a good lad. He realized she wasn't as nimble as he was, and he wasn't going to urge her to go faster, but she knew – and he knew – that at any minute . . .

The yammering continued. Ellie told herself that it couldn't be too difficult to isolate the fuse dealing with two different circuits and take them out of action . . . Or was it? She'd heard that you could have your alarms linked to the mains, which foiled burglars who thought they could cut off the alarm by removing a fuse or two. If this was so, what would it take to shut off the alarm? They'd have to shut off the electricity to the whole house. Would they know where the master switch might be? Perhaps that was what they were searching for, down below?

Down, down. Slowly. With care. The shouting continued. No one could hear what they said. The lift went up again.

If only Abdi didn't appear to block their retreat! More screaming from above. More advice shouted up from below. Surely, Abdi would come rushing up the stairs in a minute, to direct operations!

Mikey held up a hand at the top of the stairs leading down to the ground floor. A woman was screaming, down in the hall. Was she the one who'd brought up the refreshments? A man; no, a couple of men were shouting up the stairs, and others were answering back from above. Whatever language it was, it appeared they were not happy about the situation. Where was Abdi? Wrestling with circuit breakers or fuses or whatever?

Out in the street, searching for some indication of an escape?

Mikey signed for Ellie to stay put. She stayed. Mikey opened doors, one after the other. The noise was appalling. Evan didn't like it. He screwed up his eyes and threw himself around. Ellie tried to cover his ears with her free hand. She tried putting his head under her coat. That didn't work, either.

Mikey beckoned. He'd found a door leading to some back stairs. A time switch was on the wall. Would it still work? Mikey punched it and, hooray, they had light. Which meant Abdi hadn't yet found the master switch for the house.

They made their way down and down . . . how many steps down? Surely they were on the ground floor now?

Ah. A door, opening out . . . into the garage space in the basement. Good.

No one there. Even better. They were probably all faffing around upstairs.

The heavy door closed behind them. Relief! Down here you couldn't hear the alarm bells. How wonderful silence could be!

Four cars. Well, they couldn't drive out in any of them. No keys. Anyway, Ellie had never learned how to drive. Mikey went to the garage doors and tried them. 'I can't shift them. They're electrically operated.' He thumped one in frustration.

How were they to leave the house through those substantial, electronically operated doors?

Ellie was tired of holding Evan, who was grizzling but not in full voice at the moment. Ah, there was his buggy. Thank goodness! She strapped him in, and jiggled. She'd give anything to sit down and rest herself, but there wasn't a chair or a bench in sight. She tried the door of the Mercedes to see if she could rest there a while, but it was locked.

Bother. Even if she listened hard, she couldn't hear the alarms from where they were. Well, that was good. She wondered what would happen if Abdi failed to halt the spread of the flames. Would the fire spread to another room? How long could the sprinklers keep going? Were they linked to the mains? She envisaged a blackened, sodden room. And smiled.

Evan calmed down. His eyes switched right and left, up and down. He liked the shine on the door of the car, and he tried to grasp it with one podgy little hand. Evan liked cars.

Ellie wondered how to disable a car. They were always

disabling cars in books. Removing some tender part of them. But which part, and what would it look like? There was also something, if she remembered rightly, about pouring sugar into the petrol tank. Only, she hadn't any sugar on her. Pity. And no keys to get into them, anyway.

Ellie looked around. Would a house like this have CCTV? Probably. Where would the cameras be? Probably covering the front door . . . and the garage doors, too. How on earth were they to get out of here? Even if they could open the garage doors, they'd be visible the moment they left the house. *If* they could find a way of getting out.

Mikey made a helpless gesture. 'Got any ideas?'

Ellie gestured to a tool rack at the back. And there – eureka! – was a tyre iron. 'Fancy a jemmy?'

Mikey grinned. 'Wow, yes! But first, let's set off some more alarms!' He took the jemmy and smashed it against the side of the Mercedes, which reacted like an offended dowager. Whoopee! Another alarm. Evan screamed. The sports car next. Nice big dents in the side panels, which would need the attentions of a body specialist and then a repaint job. Then the people carrier. It was quite possible that the people in the house wouldn't hear the noise. Or would they?

Finally, Mikey turned his attention to the garage doors.

He put the tyre iron under the bottom of one door and tried to lift it. It wouldn't budge. But yet another alarm went off. Now that one would sound up above, wouldn't it?

Mikey sank to the floor. He hadn't the strength to lever the door up. He let the tyre iron drop from his hand.

Defeated.

Mm. Ellie really couldn't stand the noise any longer. She wondered if the lift were still working. She didn't fancy manoeuvring the buggy up those nasty back stairs. She pressed the button to summon the lift, and – hurray – it arrived.

Perhaps it was on a different electrical circuit from the one governing the alarm system? Perhaps they'd got the electrics sorted out above? Well, it was better to risk it than stay there to be discovered. 'Come along,' she said. 'Don't forget your school bag. You'll need it on Monday.'

He picked it up, moving slowly, dragging his feet. She got the buggy into the lift and pulled Mikey in after her. He didn't want to go. He'd overtaxed his strength and was as limp as could be.

Up they went to the ground floor. And the doors opened just as they should. Bravo.

Ellie's limited knowledge of burglar alarms informed her that some, especially those attached to expensive properties, had a direct line to the local police station. She hoped that Abdi's house had just such a line. On being alerted to a problem, the police might first ring the house to see what had set the alarms off, but hopefully in this case they would have assumed the worst and sent someone across in double quick time to enquire who was breaking into one of their most prestigious establishments.

So, let's hope.

Ah, as she had anticipated, there was a knot of policemen, as well as Abdi and several of the servants, in the entrance hall. All explaining, shouting, expostulating. The front door was open. The alarm upstairs was off, but for the garage door it was still all systems go.

Everyone fell silent as Ellie and Mikey appeared and walked straight past them to the front door.

'Hey!' said one of the policemen.

Think fast, Ellie. You can't yell 'kidnap' or you'd have to explain about Vera, and that's the last thing we want to do. Can you spare a moment, Lord . . .?

'You are needed downstairs,' said Ellie. 'Some poor man, perhaps a druggy looking for somewhere to kip down, seems to have got in and has been creating mayhem. You might still catch him if you're quick.'

'But who are—?'

'A neighbour,' said Ellie. 'A visitor, now going home. Isn't that right, Abdi?'

Abdi gaped. And recognized defeat. He held up his hands. 'That's right. A neighbour, now going home.'

'And one of your people took our mobile phones to top them up for us. Perhaps you'd let us have them back now?'

'Of course.' Abdi shot a look at one of his men, who handed them over as if they'd stung him.

Ellie said, 'Thank you so much. So thoughtful of you. I won't trouble you for a lift home. Is there a taxi rank on the corner?'

'Yes, yes.' In a hurry to oblige. 'Would you like someone to go with you, see you safely home?'

'No, thank you,' said Ellie. 'We're fine on our own. Come on, Mikey. Time for tea. Your mother will be worried if she gets home before we do.'

THIRTEEN

Friday evening

'Well, I never!' said Rose, when she heard what had been happening. 'Why didn't Mikey call the police on his mobile?'

'They took our mobiles off us in the garage,' said Ellie. 'And there was no phone in the room where we were held.'

'Couldn't he have emailed us on his little thingamajig?'

Mikey grinned. 'It's called a netbook, Rose. No, I couldn't unless I knew how to get into their Wi-Fi. I did think about emailing someone on the laptop we found in one of the rooms, but we'd already set the alarms off, and I didn't have time. Besides, I would have had to explain the threat that Abdi was holding over us, and Mum doesn't want that. When I saw the police had arrived downstairs, I nearly died, but Mrs Quicke talked us out of the house without giving anything away *and* got us our mobiles back.'

It was supper time. Diana had left a message for Ellie to say she wouldn't be able to collect Evan till late, and would she see that he wasn't offered anything green to eat, as he didn't like it. So he was still with them.

Thomas often cooked on a Friday evening, and this time he'd produced a huge pie containing several different varieties of fish, including prawns. Plus greens. Thomas liked cooking and usually served up more than could be eaten at any one meal. But that was all right, because Dan had appeared at the table, having collected Vera from college. Nobody said anything about Dan being there. His presence had become both natural and inevitable.

Vera had alternatively hugged and scolded Mikey when he arrived back with Ellie and the baby. Now she sat as close to him as possible, ladling food on to his plate as fast as he cleared it. Mikey was wide-eyed with fatigue and didn't object to his mother fussing over him. Suddenly, he drooped, leaning against her. And yawned.

Vera supported him with her arm around his shoulders. 'Well, that's done it. I'm going to the police tomorrow to charge Abdi with everything under the sun, no matter what it costs me.'

'Don't be so hasty,' said Ellie. 'I think we can get through this business without you having to do that. First, I want a look at this statement he says he's got, of someone seeing you argue with the doctor. It wasn't in that bundle of papers he sent you, and we need a sight of it.'

'We all know he's got someone to make it up. And now I can charge him with kidnapping Mikey. How dare he! Mikey's only twelve, when all's said and done.'

'Some twelve year old!' said Ellie. 'You should have seen him at work. Abdi's going to rue the day.'

Mikey grinned, shook himself awake and looked to see what else there was on offer to eat. The cat Midge sat next to him, as usual.

Ellie noticed that Rose was spooning puréed spinach into Evan. Ellie opened her mouth to say that he wasn't supposed to like spinach, and closed it again. Rose had no opinion of Diana's ability as a mother and had ignored the instruction. Evan smacked his lips in appreciation and then, worn out with all the alarms and excursions of the day, fell asleep in his high chair. Good.

Ellie reminded herself to change Evan before Diana spotted that he'd been wrapped in Abdi's towels.

Ellie said, 'Gunnar did warn me that Abdi might try to

snatch Mikey and take him out of the country, but it never occurred to me that he would act so quickly. Gunnar even advised getting him a pepper spray. Where does one get a pepper spray, if they're illegal?'

Dan grinned. 'All sorts of things get confiscated at school. I have something in my desk which Mikey might like to try out some time. It will only be a toy, of course.'

Mikey took the offer into consideration and accepted it with a nod.

Ellie said, 'What is the world coming to? If Mikey hadn't been so clever, he'd have been on his way out of the country at this very minute.'

Vera shuddered.

Ellie counted his deeds off on her fingers. 'He started a fire by the net curtains, which set off the sprinkler system. He did something in the bathroom, though I'm not sure what. He broke windows, which set off the burglar alarms. He destroyed Abdi's laptop and put some superglue into the power point and on the remote for the television. That'll do it a lot of no good. As for the cars in the garage, they'll all have to go to the body repair shop. The damage he did was considerable.'

Mikey said, 'What's for afters?'

Thomas stirred some goo in a saucepan. 'Ice cream with my special sauce; Mars bars melted with condensed milk. Heart attack city. But for a celebration . . .'

Mikey said, 'Yummy.'

Ellie dished out ice cream, and Thomas poured the syrupy mixture over it.

Vera was struggling between horror at the destructions and delight in her offspring's cleverness. 'What Mikey did . . . Abdi will be so angry!'

'Probably,' said Thomas. 'But he'll think twice before tackling Mikey again.'

Mikey yawned. His eyes closed, and he slid sideways. This time he came to rest against Dan.

Vera rose from her seat. 'Oh, poor lamb. He's worn out. I'd better get him up to bed.'

Dan shook Mikey, gently. 'Would you allow me to carry you up to bed, Mikey?'

Everyone froze. Ah, that was a question indeed. Would Mikey accept Dan's help?

Mikey half opened his eyes. Nodded, pushed the cat away from him. Closed his eyes and relaxed.

Everyone started breathing again. Dan smiled across to Vera who, with some reluctance, perhaps, smiled back.

'Show me where.' Dan lifted Mikey, who settled into his arms with a yawn that cracked his face in half.

'Back in a minute,' said Vera, leading the way out of the kitchen.

Ellie scraped her bowl clean. 'To echo Mikey . . . Yum.'

Rose stirred in her doze and dropped the spoon she'd been feeding Evan with on to the floor. Evan started, then collapsed back into sleep.

Ellie cleared a space on the table so that she could change Evan. His improvised nappy was clean and dry. Hurray. She put him into his buggy. Still he didn't wake. He lay there with his arms above his head. Both Rose and Evan snored, lightly.

Thomas put his arms around Ellie from behind. 'You went off without saying where you were going. Rose didn't know. You didn't leave a message. I was worried.'

'I remembered when I was halfway down the road. It was stupid of me.'

He kissed her neck. 'It might have led to a tragedy.'

'Oh, yes. I suppose. I had confidence that Mikey would get us out of it. And it gave me an opportunity to talk to Sam . . . Dan's cousin, you know? The one who was supposed to control everything at the party? Only, I upset him by suggesting that his aunt might have had something to do with the doctor's murder. He was not amused.'

Thomas was not amused, either. Perhaps he hadn't forgiven Ellie for her 'interference' earlier that day? He was certainly not trusting her judgement as he usually did.

'It's this "*cherchez la femme*" business that's got into you, isn't it? Have you thought that it might have been the good doctor who was playing away?'

'It is a definite line of enquiry.'

'After what Mikey's done – and I'm not saying that I don't understand his desire for revenge – I think the best thing we can do is to keep quiet. Let sleeping dogs die. No, it's *lie,* not *die.*' He released her to throw up his hands. 'Now you've got me at it.'

Ellie nodded. She started to clear the table. She wondered if Vera would be returning to the kitchen after Dan had put Mikey to bed, or whether she and Dan might take the opportunity to have an hour or two to themselves. One thing might lead to another and . . . No, here they came, treading softly, looking grim.

Dan said, 'Vera is determined to go to the police and file charges of rape and kidnapping against Abdi. She knows this will mean the case will be in the newspapers, and she's prepared for that.'

Vera looked defiant. 'We'll survive. Mikey and I, we are survivors. I realize I might have to find somewhere else for us to live, another school for Mikey, another college for me—'

'Don't be ridiculous!' Yes, Thomas was definitely not his usual calm self. 'You stay here as long as you want.'

Ellie said, 'Vera, don't be so hasty. There are more ways than one of dealing with Abdi. I hope it won't be necessary for you to bring the police into it, but if it is, then of course you stay here. It's your home. And I don't think the school will want to turn Mikey away. Yes, there may be some temporary unpleasantness but, as you say, we can work through that.'

'And,' said Dan, 'your real friends will stand by you.'

There were tears in Vera's eyes as she looked up at Dan. 'I never used to be able to look up to you, when we were at school. I remember I had to wear shoes without a heel, because I was taller than you then. You've shot up since.'

'You certainly haven't shrunk.' He looked down at her well-filled T-shirt.

Vera started to laugh, and if there was a note of hysteria in her laughter, nobody mentioned it. Dan kissed her, hard. Then sat her down and looked at Thomas. 'Coffee on the way, sir? Can I make it for you?'

Thomas clattered mugs on to the table. 'Coming up.' Narrow-eyed, he looked at Ellie. 'My wife here has a theory she'd like to try out on you, Dan. Ellie . . .?'

Ellie reddened. 'Oh dear. Dan, this is terribly awkward. I

know I've asked you before, and you said "no", but I really
do need you to think back. Someone who knew your father
in the old days said that we ought to look for the lady in the
case. Now, I know you were at school and it might never
have crossed your mind then, but a good doctor often attracts
a fan club of women who think he's the bee's knees. Sometimes
this becomes a family joke. Were you ever aware of that sort
of thing going on?'

'You're not serious?' Dan looked at Vera, who frowned and
shrugged.

'Yes, I know it sounds ridiculous,' said Ellie. 'But if you
two could step out of the past, when you were just schoolboy
and schoolgirl, and think about it for a minute. Did you perhaps
overhear something which didn't make much sense at the time,
but might mean something now? I asked your cousin Sam,
and he . . . I'm pretty sure something occurred to him, but he
didn't want to tell me. So he got angry and stalked off.'

'Sam? You asked Sam if my father . . .?'

Ellie winced. 'I know. It wasn't very tactful of me, was it?
I'm afraid I upset him.'

Vera put her hand on Dan's arm. 'Wait a minute. There was
that receptionist of his . . .?'

Dan burst out laughing. 'Oh, you mean old Miss Whatever?
Adored him.' He shared the joke with Ellie. 'She must have been
sixty if she was a day. Terribly refined. Bit of a laughing-stock.
But didn't she retire around that time? Yes, I think so. Before my
party. Went to look after her mother in a bungalow somewhere
down on the South Coast.'

Vera said, 'I remember that she was terribly protective of
him. Then he got that big, fat, jolly woman . . . What was her
name? Married to some handsome oaf or other, used to keep
his photo taped to her computer, remember? And there was
someone else—'

Dan thumped the table. 'Old Mrs G, who left him her
budgerigar and some money—'

'And her daughter-in-law was going to take him to court,
claiming undue influence, only—'

They were both laughing so hard, they could hardly get
the words out. 'Only,' said Dan, trying to keep a straight face,

'it turned out she, the daughter-in-law, had been feeding the old dear with some weird and wonderful herbal concoction which might have hastened Mrs G's death . . . and it all came out in the end, and she had to admit what she'd done, but she was just stupid, not malicious, so the police didn't take any action.'

They laughed so much that Vera ended up with her head on his shoulder. Then they were quiet. His arm went around her.

'You know,' said Vera, 'I used to think your father liked me.'

'He did,' said Dan. 'He told me so.' He smiled at Ellie. 'Sorry, I can't think of anyone else.'

Ellie saw that he spoke the truth as far as he knew it, but persisted. 'He was a good doctor and much loved by his patients. At home, if I understand correctly, your mother ruled the roost. He loved her, I'm sure, and perhaps gave in to her more than she gave in to him. Am I right?'

Thomas said, 'Surely that's enough, Ellie. Here's the coffee. Shall we go in the other room?'

Ellie was silent. She wouldn't go against Thomas's wishes. Well, not in public, anyway.

But once they were seated in the other room – Dan and Vera on the settee together, and Thomas on his La-Z-Boy – Dan took the initiative. 'I can see where you're going with this, Mrs Quicke, and I'll try to be objective. The French used to say that there is always one who kisses, and one who turns the cheek. My father adored my mother and did his best to please her in every way. She loved him in return. She was always caressing and kissing him, and making much of him when she was in a good mood, and she never snapped or argued with him. But it's true that she wasn't always like that. She wasn't really interested in his work, she didn't want to hear about a difficult patient, or if he were worried about someone's health. She would cut off such topics before they started. She got her own way by withdrawing herself from him, if he displeased her. Yes, I observed that, and I thought –' he frowned – 'at the time I thought that I wouldn't lie down and let a woman walk all over me as he did.' He gave Vera a quick smile. 'But maybe I would. Maybe it's in the genes.'

Vera, sitting next to him, smiled back and shook her head.

Dan said, 'So I do understand why you're asking about him, Mrs Quicke. You wonder if he had a sympathetic woman friend, perhaps someone of his own age, that he could visit now and then, and talk to as a friend or colleague. I don't think I'd have blamed him if he had done so, but all I can say is that I never got the slightest hint of it. No name cropped up in conversation that shouldn't have. He never made excuses to miss out on family occasions. Sometimes he'd withdraw to his study and say he needed to listen to some serious music. Jazz, mostly. My mother didn't like serious music, and she couldn't stand jazz.' He considered what he'd said. 'Who was it who thought he might have had a lady friend?'

Ellie sighed. 'An elderly lady who used to be a patient of his. But she's now in a nursing home. Alzheimer's.'

Dan twitched a smile. 'Oh well. That explains it. I suppose there's always gossip about people in the public eye.'

'Yes, I'm sure that's all it is,' said Thomas, with a sideways look at Ellie.

Vera was also looking at Ellie. But Vera knew Ellie better than Dan, and Vera knew Ellie didn't give up easily.

Ellie thought she'd probably got as far as she could go that evening and said, 'Thank you for being so frank, Dan. That helps a lot.'

Then Diana arrived, and woke up Rose and Evan, who howled when he saw his mother. Diana was livid that her expensive baby buggy had somehow acquired some dents and scrapes, and that Evan had not been given his evening bath and put into his pyjamas. Ellie admitted they'd been out for a walk that afternoon, and she apologized for not having woken the baby after supper to give him his bath. No one said anything about kidnappers or improvised nappies. Fortunately, perhaps, Evan hadn't the words to betray them. Diana left with a flurry of instructions for the morrow, from which it appeared that she wouldn't trust Ellie with her precious boy if she could think of anyone else who might be able to look after him, but as it was, she sincerely hoped . . . Etcetera. Ellie waved her off, hoping that she'd feel better able to cope with Evan after a good night's sleep.

Dan took Vera off to view his temporary accommodation which, he assured her, she was going to hate.

Rose grumbled herself off to bed, and the house fell quiet.

Thomas took his time undressing. He sat with one shoe on and one off, gazing into space. There was something on his mind.

Ellie hadn't seen him like this before, and it bothered her. He hadn't ever criticized her before, either. It left a nasty black hole in her stomach. Well, not a real hole, obviously. But that's what it felt like. She climbed into bed and waited for him to speak.

He didn't.

Finally, she said, 'What is it, Thomas?'

He opened his mouth, closed it again. 'Hostage to fortune.'

'Mm?'

'You.' He took the other shoe off and wriggled out of his socks. 'I've been telling myself not to panic, and it's not working. I know you lead a charmed life, and that nothing and no one is going to get you down, but I must admit that when I discovered you'd gone out without leaving a message this afternoon, I was fit to be tied! I pictured you in dire straits, being chased by villains, run over by cars with tinted windows, imprisoned in dark cellars . . .'

'Oh, Thomas!'

'I ransacked your office, to see if you'd left a message there. I knew Rose wouldn't have remembered even if you had told her something. I made a list of people I could ring; Vera, friends, Diana, people you work with. I was going to give it another half hour, and then I would have rung the police to report you missing.'

'Yes, at one time I did imagine you might have to do that. On the other hand, I had every confidence that Mikey could get us out of there.'

'It shouldn't have been necessary for you to rely on a twelve-year-old boy. I should have been there with you.'

Ellie suppressed the thought that Mikey's anarchic streak had probably served them better than Thomas's mild, law-abiding nature would have done. 'I wish you had been.'

'Don't try to soft soap me, Ellie Quicke. If I had been with you, I don't suppose I'd have been able to do much against those . . . those thugs! But Mikey is, I suppose, one of them in spirit if not in years.'

'You prayed for me? I was relying on that.'

He said, 'I prayed till I was exhausted. You're very precious to me, Ellie. I understand that you feel called to go out and fight the powers of darkness, and I honour that in you, but—'

'I was in no danger.'

'Permit me to contradict you. You were kidnapped. Locked up. Told you couldn't leave.'

She said, 'You're asking me to stop trying to find out who killed the doctor?'

A long sigh. 'I'd very much like to do just that. But no, I'm not. You've got a special talent for helping the distressed, especially those who don't have the power or know the words to defend themselves against aggression. This is the path you have to take, and I ought to be cheering you on, not holding you back with my selfish fears.'

'I've tackled problems in the past, and it didn't worry you.'

'I don't know why this one has got me so stirred up.'

'The attack on your integrity? The idea that you would have abused a young girl?'

'I thought I was immune to such lies. I thought I rested secure in God's love. And now I discover I'm as fearful as anyone else. It's a salutary lesson.'

'I can't abandon Vera.'

'No. We can't abandon her.'

Silence.

Ellie said, 'Give us a cuddle.'

One thing led to another, and that was that for the evening.

Saturday morning

Thomas sang in the shower, 'Morning has broken . . .'

A nice, bright morning. Ellie hummed along with Thomas.

Breakfast for three; Thomas, Ellie and Rose. No school for Mikey, no college for Vera. They were probably having a good lie-in. It was nice and peaceful.

The front doorbell. Diana with Evan. Diana was frowning, impatient, wanting to get on with the day's tasks. Evan was grizzling. Oh dear.

Diana hauled in a bag of his toys. 'And please, Mother, don't take him out in his buggy again. I don't know what you did with it yesterday, but I'd be ashamed to be seen out with it now. It looks like something that's been used to carry the coal home in. I'll have to get a new one, as soon as I have a minute.'

And she was gone.

Ellie looked at Evan, and Evan looked back. He lifted his arms towards her and smiled. The dear little thing! She picked him up and walked around with him in her arms. Now if only she could work out how to get him a dummy without Diana knowing . . .

She couldn't ask Thomas to get a pacifier as he'd gone straight to his study and proposed to work all morning. She herself couldn't leave the house unless she took the baby with her – which Diana had forbidden her to do. Rose hadn't been out of the house for months. Vera and Mikey . . .? If they weren't too busy about their own affairs this weekend?

The phone rang, and she answered it, not bothering to put Evan back in his buggy.

'Ellie? Lesley Milburn here.' Her friend, the policewoman.

'You have news for us? Is Thomas supposed to have been raping half the congregation?'

'No.' Half a laugh. 'I know it's Saturday. Are you going to be in? Can I drop round in a little while?'

'It will be a pleasure, especially if you can buy a couple of nice juicy-looking dummies for me. My grandson is here, and there's times I can't do anything with him, but my daughter doesn't want him to have a dummy.'

Lesley was acquainted with Diana. 'Of course. Do they come in different sizes? I'll ask. See you about ten?'

Ellie wanted to say, 'Can you give me hint what this is about?' But Lesley had cut the connection.

The doorbell rang.

Abdi. Coldly furious. 'Where are they? I wish to speak to them, now!'

'Of course.' Ellie was meekness itself. Mikey had recently hung a cowbell outside the door to their flat, connected by a cord to a tassel dangling in the hall near the telephone.

Ellie tugged on this and, when the door to the flat above opened, called up that Abdi was here to see them.

Perhaps they were expecting him? They certainly came down promptly.

By this time, Abdi was striding around the sitting room, stoking up his temper.

'Coffee?' asked Ellie. She seated herself in her high-backed chair and settled Evan on her knee. She wondered if they'd need Thomas, but decided not to disturb him unless it became absolutely essential to do so.

Abdi spat out something which Ellie interpreted as: 'Grrr!'

Vera and Mikey sat on the settee. Vera had made no particular concessions to femininity that morning. She had her hair tied back and was wearing a white blouse over jeans. She looked what she was: a healthy, strong woman who, with a little care and attention, could blossom into beauty.

Mikey was wearing a clean white shirt over dark school trousers. He looked meek, mild and about six years of age.

Ellie invited Abdi to speak. 'Do begin.'

Almost, he was thrown off his stride, but quickly remembered the speech he'd been preparing. 'I have never been so insulted in my life! Here I am, prepared to welcome my son into our family, to shower him with gifts, to remove him from an unsuitable environment and give him a first-class education, and what happens? All my generosity is thrown back in my face.' He paused to take breath.

Neither Vera nor Mikey appeared particularly impressed.

Abdi pointed, not at Mikey, but at Ellie. 'As for you . . . I am holding you personally responsible for the damage you caused to my house!'

FOURTEEN

'**M**e?' Ellie tried not to laugh. 'You think I wrecked your house?'

'Who else?'

Mikey put up his hand, as if in class. 'It was me, sir.'

'What! Nonsense. A boy of your age? No, it is clear to me that it was Mrs Quicke, and—'

'Well, I was there,' said Ellie, 'so I suppose that makes me partly responsible. But you really can't go round kidnapping people and locking them up without expecting them to retaliate.'

'I was taking charge of my son, who doesn't seem to realize who he's dealing with.'

Mikey seemed to shrink in his seat. Vera put her arm about his shoulders.

Abdi flung himself into a chair and wiped his brow. 'The fire damage! The sprinkler system! The windows! The alarms! The explanations to the police, and to my father! It's actually his house, or rather, it used to be, and he's furious, says he's flying in to—'

Ellie said, 'Did the police find a stranger on the premises?'

'What! There was no stranger, and you know it. My cars . . . they'll all have to go for body shop repairs, the cost . . .! I've had to hire another car to take me around. I couldn't be seen in something which looks as if it's been involved in an accident. And the garage doors need realigning. What did you use on them, Mrs Quicke?'

Ellie shook her head and smiled. Evan was gurgling something, trying to put his fist in his mouth. The little love!

Mikey said, in a small voice, 'Has the ceiling come down yet?'

'What!'

'Oh,' said Mikey, casting down his eyes. 'It hasn't, then.'

'What ceiling?' He turned on Ellie. 'What's he talking about?'

Mikey said, 'You made me mad. I did warn you.'

'What!!?'

Mikey explained. 'I put the plugs in the bath and washbasin and turned on the taps. Once the water saturates the floor, it will seep through to the ceiling of the room below and bring it down.'

Ellie smiled. So that's what he'd been up to in the bathroom! She said, 'Abdi, I suggest you phone one of your men and get them to investigate.'

'What!!!?'

'You'll have a stroke, if you're not careful,' said Ellie. 'You kidnapped us. We asked nicely if we might go, and you refused. Mikey warned you he'd retaliate. Why are you so surprised?'

'He's a child! Children don't go around wrecking houses.' But he got out his mobile and jabbed at buttons. 'Hello? Hello . . .?' He broke into a torrent of language, cut off the person he'd been speaking to, and shut off his phone. For once he appeared uncertain of himself.

'Mikey's twelve years old,' said Ellie, 'and more than a match for you.'

Abdi changed tactics. 'You keep out of this, old woman. This is between me and her,' he said, indicating Vera. He inched his chair towards the settee. Damping down his anger, he spoke directly to Vera. 'I have tried to do this the civilized way. If you can't see that, then—'

Vera said, 'I understand what you want, and the answer is "no".'

With an effort, he said, 'No, you don't understand. A woman of your limited education! The law is on my side, and if you refuse to cooperate, then I'll have you dragged through the mud in every tabloid in the country, because you are clearly unfit to look after a child.'

'If you do that,' said Vera, pale but firm, 'then I'll have to have you charged with rape and kidnapping.'

'What rape? Ridiculous! You were lying there, waiting for us . . .'

'Not so,' said Vera, flinching. 'I was drugged and raped. There are witnesses.'

'The drug-dealers? That trash?' He snorted.

'A doctor and her brother. A man who works for the council and a respected retailer. Yes, they would prefer the events of that night not to be brought up now, but they will testify, all right.'

Ellie crossed her fingers and hoped that Vera was crossing hers, too.

Abdi stared at Vera in amazement. 'You can't be serious!'

'Very.'

Mikey sighed. 'Look, it's quite simple. I've made up my mind that I don't want to go and live with you, and that's that.'

Abdi gaped. 'You're only a child. You'll learn to like it quickly enough.'

Ellie said, 'You've underestimated the boy all along. You're very alike, you two, although neither of you may wish to admit it. A softer approach to Mikey might have worked, Abdi, although I'm not sure that it would. But he could never bear to be imprisoned, as you—'

'Imprisoned?' Abdi yelped. 'Didn't I tell the servants to let you have whatever you asked for?'

'Except for freedom? I wonder how you imagined you'd carry a boy on to a plane if he didn't want to go?'

'He's only a child! He doesn't realize—'

'Yes, I do,' said Mikey. 'It was I who set the fire and started the alarms. I who made the water overflow in the bathroom, and it was I who destroyed your laptop and glued up the power points—'

'What, what!' Agitated. Evidently, Abdi hadn't discovered the power points had been tampered with. He drew out his mobile phone again, but didn't use it.

'It was me,' repeated Mikey. 'Go away and leave us alone.'

Vera smiled. 'Abdi, if you're thinking of charging him with malicious damage, I don't think you'd succeed. After all, as you say, he's only a child.'

Abdi gave a strangled shriek. He threw up his arms and stamped around the room. Finally, breathing hard, he stood over Vera. 'I didn't want to do this, but you give me no alternative. Tomorrow morning I'm going to let the police have a witness statement identifying you as the doctor's killer. And when you've been locked up for life, I'll take the boy.' He paused, waiting for a reaction.

Vera shrugged. 'If you try to do that I will retaliate, charging you with rape.'

Mikey stood up. 'I'm bored. I'm going back upstairs.' The cat met him in the doorway, and they went off together.

'Come back here!' Abdi might as well have whispered, for all the notice Mikey took.

'Badly behaved . . .! I'll teach him to ignore me . . .!'

Ellie put Evan over her shoulder. 'Well, Abdi, if you'd like to come back in about an hour's time, I have a detective constable coming to see me. Perhaps you'd like to give your statement to her? It might save you a trip.'

'What? I don't believe you. I'm calling your bluff, right now!'

'No bluff,' said Vera. 'It's true I didn't want the rape to come out in court, but if it's a question of Mikey's future, then of course I'll do it. And, by the way, Mrs Quicke asked her solicitor about your approach to me and, if you take us to court, he's prepared to fight you all the way.'

'I'm going to make you pay for this!'

Vera shrugged. 'It's a free country. Except for rapists and kidnappers. Shall I see you out?'

Later on Saturday morning

The doorbell rang. Ellie picked up Evan and hastened to let DC Lesley Milburn in. She'd rocked Evan for what seemed like hours. She'd walked him around the house in the buggy. She'd changed him twice, she'd offered him food and drink, but still he would not settle. He was clearly worn out, but still wailing in misery. Was he teething? She'd rubbed the recommended tincture on his gums, so far to no avail.

Lesley stepped into the hall, holding out a chemist's packet.

'You managed to get a dummy? Oh, thank goodness. He's such an unhappy little boy today.'

Between them, they fought the dummy out of its plastic packaging. Lesley said, 'They call them "binkies" in the States. I couldn't think what my American friends were on about. I don't approve of them, mind you.'

'Neither do I,' said Ellie, thrusting it into Evan's mouth. 'In principle, I think one should try to do without.' She spoke in hushed tones.

As did Lesley. 'Bad for his new teeth. They may grow in crooked.'

'I absolutely agree with you. It is not good for them. I see this one says it's orthodontically correct. Or whatever.'

Evan sucked the dummy. Spat it out.

Ellie darted into the kitchen, smeared some juice on to the dummy, and presented it to Evan again. This time, he sucked. Frowned. Sucked some more. Relaxed.

Hardly daring to hope the dummy was producing the desired effect, Ellie laid him down in his buggy and strapped him in. He continued to suck. His arms went above his head.

'I think he's supposed to sleep on his side or his front,' said Ellie, 'but whatever way you put him down, he turns till he's asleep on his back.'

Lesley, too, spoke in hushed tones. 'It's done the trick.'

Greatly relieved, Ellie straightened up. 'Coffee? And you have some news for me?'

Lesley grinned. 'Pain before pleasure. I have a picture to show you.'

Ellie pushed Evan in his buggy into the sitting room. His mouth moved rhythmically around the dummy. He wasn't asleep, but at least he was not screaming his head off. 'Show me.'

Lesley said, 'Because my boss was so anxious for me to follow up on the non-story that Thomas had been abusing a young girl, I was positively encouraged to access the security footage from the camera at the front of the police station.' She produced a printout. 'Ta-da! Is this the face of someone who has cause to be annoyed with Thomas?'

Ellie looked. A frizzled perm, a pudgy face, a shapeless cardigan over a flowered top. 'Oh, yes. Well, it's no more

than I suspected. What a silly creature he is. No, not "silly",
but positively evil. He deserves whatever is coming to him.'

Lesley was amused. 'Yes? Who do you . . .?'

'Hush a minute,' said Ellie. 'I'm trying to think. If he did
this, and that followed . . . It's like trying to do a jigsaw
with some bits fitting and others not. I wonder if . . .? That
would make sense, which it didn't before.'

Lesley clicked her fingers. 'Ellie Quicke, come back to
me. You know this woman?'

'Yes. Well, not to say *know*. I've met her and I know who
she is, though I can't for the moment recall her surname.
No, I don't think he used it. Poor creature, she believed
everything he said, and she was distressed to find him a liar.
Well, she'll know better in future. He's divorced, isn't he?'

'Ellie?'

'She's called Maureen and works for him in the accounts
department at the council.'

'Maureen what?'

'Dunno. He didn't use her surname.' She stared into space.

'Ellie!'

'Oh, sorry. Yes. Lesley, I'm going to have to start a long
way back. In fact, when I talked to Dan first, I said I wanted
him to start at the beginning and he said . . . Oh!' She stared
off into the distance again.

'Ellie!'

Ellie shook herself back to the present. 'Just speculating.
I'll have to give that a lot more thought, although I suppose
Sam might—'

'Who is "Sam"?'

'Ah. Yes. Well, he's Dan McKenzie's cousin, and he doesn't
want to be involved in any of this, and I can't really blame
him; can you?'

'Ellie . . .!'

'Right. Of course. To start somewhere in the middle, and
without going into unnecessary detail, which I assure you
we don't have to talk about now, unless of course Abdi does
fulfil his promise and gets Vera charged with murder—'

Lesley leaned over and put her hand on Ellie's arm. 'Pretend
I'm an alien and you're explaining how to make a cup of tea.'

'I have to decide how much to tell you, and it's difficult. I don't think I need to protect this particular man . . . No, I don't. He deserves whatever he gets. Lesley, all that you need to know now is that that woman works for the council in the accounts department. She's some kind of assistant or perhaps a colleague of a middle-ranking man called Dick Prentice. Richard Prentice. He looks rather like a slug and leaves a slimy trail wherever he goes. He told this woman that Thomas was a bad man and asked her to get the police suspicious of him. She believed him and did exactly what he asked her to do. I told him to make her retract her allegations, though I don't know whether he will or not. At this very moment, I don't suppose she knows who or what to believe. If you got to her before he's had another "go" at her, she might well tell you all about it. I don't know her surname, but if you show this picture at the reception desk, I expect they can tell you.'

'Richard Prentice? The name doesn't ring a bell. Why should he have it in for Thomas?'

'Ah, well. He doesn't. He's got it in for me, because I've been enquiring into the doctor's death.'

'And what did he have to do with that?'

'Nothing. As far as I know. At least . . . no, that's what I've got to think a bit more about. Dick Prentice was at the party at the doctor's house that evening, and I believe he was the one who started the train of events which ended with murder.' Ellie wasn't going to bring Vera into this unless she had to.

'You mean, because of the gatecrashers?'

'It bothered me that the gang had chosen to gatecrash that particular party. I mean, why choose that house and that night out of all the houses in Ealing? But now, it's obvious. Someone who'd been invited to the party had his eye on a particular girl who wouldn't give him the time of day. He decided to buy a date-rape drug to take with him. Apparently, everyone at that school knew where drugs were to be found, though none of those I've interviewed were taking them. At least, that's what they've told me.'

'You think that this Dick Prentice went to buy the drug, and in doing so let slip that he was going to a party at a doctor's house?'

'Someone, somewhere told me that the gatecrashers claimed to have been invited to the party. Did Dick Prentice pay for the drug with an invitation to attend the party? Whether he did actually invite them or not, I think he gave them the information that the party was in a doctor's house. So, he's the link, yes.'

'He made use of the drug?'

'Yes, but not on the girl he'd had his eye on at first.'

Lesley paced the room. 'Was this before or after the gate-crashers arrived?'

'After. The guests fled in different directions. Some took refuge in a shed in the garden. While they were there, the girl he fancied was offered the drugged drink. She passed it on to someone else, who took it in all innocence.'

'Did it take effect? Did she pass out . . . and what happened then? You mean . . . Don't tell me she was raped! Is that what you're trying to say? Why weren't the police informed?'

Oh dear. Ellie hadn't wanted to talk about the drug at all. Now look what she'd done!

She said, with care, 'It took a while before the police were contacted and arrived. They found that the hosts had been assaulted and knocked out, and that a gang of gatecrashers were wrecking the house looking for drugs or anything they could sell to buy drugs with. It took time to clear that mess up, to send the injured parties off to hospital, to take statements from the host and the DJ, and to try to round up the interlopers. By which time, what happened in the garden was well and truly over and everyone involved had gone. Including the victim of the rape, the rapists and the witnesses to the event. None of them wanted to talk about what happened then, and they've kept quiet about it all these years . . . until now.'

'Why now?'

Ellie realized she was making a right mess of this. But, remembering Abdi's threats, she took a deep breath and went on. 'One of the rapists is a high-born man of African descent. He's found he can't have any more children, so wants to pay off –' Ellie hesitated – 'his victim and adopt the boy he sired on that night. He—'

'Mikey,' said Lesley, clapping her hands. 'Vera and Mikey.

He was conceived that night, when she was raped? She should have reported what happened.'

'She was too ashamed. Her parents were unhelpful. There was a misunderstanding between her and her then boyfriend. She tried to get Mikey's father to help her. He refused. She's brought up the boy by herself. She doesn't want to report it even now, and she won't unless Mikey's father tries to make out she killed the doctor.'

'What! But . . . she couldn't have done so, could she?'

'No. I've spoken to several people who witnessed the rape and its aftermath. She was out of it. She got out of the garden through a gate at the bottom and staggered home in a terrible state. Upon which her father beat her up. He's dead now and can't confirm the time she reached home, but I believe her.'

'Witnesses? Give me names.'

'Unless Vera is pushed into charging the man with rape, she won't testify. You can't mount a case without her coop-eration, so I won't give you any more names.'

Lesley made a noise like a scalded cat. 'Wait a minute. Dick Prentice was one? He provided the drug, and it was used. I can get him for that alone—'

'Not unless Vera testifies.'

Lesley slapped her forehead. 'There must be some way I can get him. Ah. The false accusation against Thomas. Has he admitted it?'

'Sort of. But Maureen will talk if you lean on her. I'm giving you his name because he was behind everything that happened before midnight, say, on the night of the murder. When I started asking questions about the rape, I suppose he got scared the truth would come out and, instead of admitting it, he attacked me through Thomas.'

'Dick Prentice bought the drug. *He* gave the gang the information about the party. *He* gave the drug to someone who passed it to Vera. Did he rape her, as well?'

Ellie nodded.

'But he didn't cause the doctor to be murdered? Or did he?'

'Unfortunately, no. It would be helpful if he had, but he'd long gone by then, and I don't see any reason why he should have done that.'

Lesley threw up her hands. 'I get really upset when rape victims won't testify. Don't they realize that if a man has done it once, he might well do it again to some other poor creature? You said there were witnesses? Will they testify?'

'No, they won't, unless Vera is forced into making the rape public . . . which she profoundly hopes she won't have to do.'

'I can put the fear of God into Dick Prentice, though. I can visit him in his workplace at the Town Hall, so that everyone will know he's being investigated. But first, I'll speak to Maureen, perhaps take her down to the station. I can charge her for making false statements . . . No, I can't, can I? She didn't sign anything. I can have her for wasting police time. I'll get her to talk, and then I'll have him . . . for the same thing. And I'll be oh so careful, and I promise to spread alarm and despondency and blacken his name without so much as hinting—'

'Take care. He has at least one powerful ally.'

'Who?'

Ellie put on her most innocent face. 'Did I say something?'

Lesley started. 'Ah. Yes, that's the way to handle it. Drop a hint, and then backtrack. Sow suspicion and deny you'd been thinking along those lines. As for her, if she's got as much as an unpaid parking ticket—'

'In a way, I feel sorry for her. She believed what Dick Prentice told her. She thought she was doing him a favour when she went to the police with her accusations. She isn't the real villain of the piece.'

Lesley's eyes narrowed. 'Are you trying to tell me that Dick Prentice isn't really the villain of the piece, either?'

'Oh, no. He's a nasty piece of work and deserves to be prosecuted for this and that, especially the rape. All I'm saying is that he's been working for the council for ages, and presumably does a good job for them. If he's kept his nose clean all this time, won't the courts go easy on him?'

'But Ellie: we have to have punishment for those who commit crimes.'

'I know that. I've been thinking a lot about what

punishment might be appropriate for men who have committed one terrible deed and regretted it ever since. If they are of an introspective turn of mind, would their fear of exposure be sufficient punishment in itself? Dick Prentice seems to me to be a weak sort of creature, who might well have lived with fear. Of course –' and here she smiled – 'if you could have a look to see if he's done it again . . .?'

'Ah,' said Lesley. 'Definitely. I'll do that. What about the others? Mikey's father, for instance?'

'I don't suppose he thought anything of helping himself to a white girl who'd passed out at a party. He still can't get his head round the fact that Mikey doesn't want anything to do with him, and that Vera won't play the game his way. It's against everything he's been brought up to believe about men being top dog and women second-class citizens. As for children, in his culture they behave or get punished. If you tried to charge him with rape – and I rather hope it won't come to that for Vera's sake – you'd have to lift his passport or he'd be out of the country in five minutes. Even if you did lift it, he'd still find a way to leave the country. Sorry, but that's the way he is. Money and power have made him arrogant beyond belief.'

'He's committed a crime though. He's subject to the law!'

'Sure. I'm going to get him another way. He's already offered to pay Vera off. A derisory sum, in my opinion, but there you are. A substantial fine might hurt his pocket and make him think twice about doing it again.' Plus, Ellie thought, the damage Mikey's done to his house is considerable. And here, she smiled.

Lesley subsided into a chair. 'How many people were involved in the rape?'

'No more information. Unless and until Vera's hand is forced.'

Lesley made a noise like a scalded cat again. 'All right. Well, what about the murder?'

'I don't know. I need to do some more digging. At least I'm starting from the knowledge that it wasn't Vera, and I think the police would agree it wasn't someone from the gang.'

'That's so. I looked up the case.'

'How was the doctor killed?'

'Blunt-force trauma to the back of his head. The pathologist thinks there was some kind of fight, or tussle. The doctor was pushed backwards and hit his head on something as he fell. Probably part of his own car. They found blood and hairs on the offside headlight. His skull wasn't as thick as some. A blow which might have stunned another man, killed him.'

'It might have been manslaughter, then?'

'It might.'

'Had he been drinking?'

'Not enough to register. He'd been at some function or other at the golf club but had only had one glass of wine. Apparently, he was scared of being had up for drink driving. His wife didn't drive. The police did try to find the culprit, you know. They tried very hard indeed, but . . .' A gesture of frustration. 'I do see that it must have been difficult for the family to accept the fact that we couldn't find the murderer.'

She consulted her watch, stood up, and stretched. 'You know, I'm not inclined to wait till Monday morning to have a go at this Maureen. It's not too late to find someone on duty at the Town Hall who can give me her surname and address. I think I'll pop round there now and see what I can do to rattle her cage.'

FIFTEEN

Saturday afternoon

Ellie tried to do some paperwork while keeping an eye on Evan. She had put a thick rug down on the floor for him to lie on and laid out his toys around him. Only, he wouldn't stay put. He didn't seem to understand how to crawl, although now and again he got his legs under him and made valiant efforts to huff and puff himself forward. Then came the breakthrough. While lying on his back, he discovered that throwing his arms over in one direction turned him on to his side . . . and then on to his tummy. Eureka!

Ellie applauded. She turned back to her work, only to be woken by Evan's cry of alarm.

She looked down. He was no longer on the rug. Where was he? He'd rolled right over to a low chair and got himself stuck under it. And yelled for help. She picked him up, soothed him, and set him back on to the middle of the rug.

He gave her a delighted grin. Waited till she was back on the computer, and set off again. This time he ended up against the wainscoting. And yelled for rescue. Ellie abandoned her work and watched him.

She mourned the demise of the old-fashioned play cot, in which you could put a baby and know that he would be safe from becoming trapped under a chair or from rolling into the edge of the door. Diana didn't believe in confining her son in any way. But then, Diana didn't have to look after him during the day.

Diana didn't know about the dummy, either. This was currently resting in Ellie's pocket, wrapped in a bit of cling-film to keep it clean.

The doorbell rang. Ellie scooped Evan up and made for the hall. Evan had been aiming for freedom when he'd been so rudely interrupted, and he resented being picked up without warning. He twisted and wriggled and yelled.

It was Dan's cousin Sam at the door, looking diffident. 'Is this a bad time?'

'No, no. Come in.' She returned Evan to his rug, and since he appeared to be settling in for a good roar, handed him his dummy. Instant peace.

Sam eyed the dummy. 'My wife didn't agree with those.'

'Neither do I. But sanity dictates.'

A wintry smile. 'I must admit, that's how I felt about them, too. Though my children are way past all that now.'

Ellie indicated that he take a seat. 'You've been thinking about what I said?'

'"Look for the lady." It wasn't him.'

'I know. I worked it out; it must have been her. Your aunt.'

'How did you come to that conclusion?'

'I heard so much about Daphne, your sister, and how she was the spitting image of your aunt. I thought that if so, aunt and niece probably treated their men the same way.'

'Don't get me wrong. My little sister has had a tough time. She married Dan far too young.'

'She was pregnant.' Ellie didn't make it a question.

Sam fidgeted. 'I didn't count.'

'I expect your aunt did.'

'My aunt was all for the marriage. She'd always dreamed of our two families getting closer together.'

'It didn't worry her that Dan and Daphne were first cousins?'

'That's such an old-fashioned point of view.'

'Besides which, she could count and knew Dan was not the father.'

He frowned. He looked around the room. Seeking distraction? 'Dan was delighted to be a father.'

'Poor Dan. What happened to the real father?'

'Dan was the father.'

Ellie waited. Evan huffed and puffed, his mouth working overtime on the dummy. He let the dummy fall out of his mouth and turned over on to his tummy, drawing his legs up under him, and then shooting them out again. Trying to crawl.

Red tinged Sam's cheeks. 'You really shouldn't say such things.'

Ellie shrugged. 'Dan is a good man. He must have realized eventually what Daphne was like but, so far as I know, he's not said a word against her.'

'Neither should he. I admit I thought Daphne was too young to marry, but she had her heart set on it. She was besotted with Dan. She wanted a big white wedding and six bridesmaids. I admit I was concerned what would happen when the romance wore off and the reality of marriage to a teacher struck home, but she assured me that it was exactly what she'd always wanted out of life. I knew Dan would never let her down.'

'And then, her bright little bubble burst.'

'She grew up and realized that she'd committed herself to a man without ambition.'

'As her aunt had done?'

Sam crossed and recrossed his legs. 'I wouldn't have put it like that, but yes . . . I suppose so.'

'Your aunt stayed married, but Daphne opted out. She found someone else, someone who would whisk her away into the sunset on the back of a white horse?'

A shadow of a smile. 'It's true, he did have a white sports car. And she is a beautiful woman.'

'Was this new man prepared to take on someone else's child? Or was it his own?'

The smile faded. No reply.

Ellie sighed. 'It was his own child?'

'I have no idea. He adopted her as his. That's all I know, or want to know.'

'Poor Dan. He loved the child, even if he suspected she wasn't his.'

A wide gesture. 'What would you . . .? Daphne needed wider horizons.'

She wanted a bigger income. 'Is she content with her lot now?'

'Well –' a slight but distinct stiffening of his shoulders – 'as I said, she is a very beautiful and charming woman.'

Silence, while Ellie digested the idea that Daphne was not content with her second husband and was probably on the lookout for a third. Ellie wondered what would happen to the child in the case of a second divorce.

Sam looked at his watch. 'I can't stay long.' He didn't make any move to depart.

Ellie said, 'Getting back to the tragedy. It was your aunt who was playing away, not your uncle?'

'I have no idea.' He met her eye with a steady gaze. 'Until you mentioned it, the possibility had never crossed my mind. I'm shocked, I really am.'

'I dare say. But, now you have allowed the thought to cross your mind, you are remembering little incidents here and there . . .?'

He looked away from her. 'We-ell. She did used to

complain that my uncle neglected her. Not as if she were serious, but laughing about it, you know? Saying things like, "If I can only catch his attention long enough, I'd like to—"' He broke off, and then added, 'He'd have done anything for her. She was such a pretty woman, had such charm! He used to say she was a honey pot and that when they were at parties, he had to fight other men off.'

'She flirted with other men.' A statement, not a question.

An uneasy movement. 'I don't know that I'd go so far as to say that. She didn't mean anything by it. It was her charm that did it.'

'She would, perhaps, play someone else off against her husband? Say that if he didn't do this or that to please her, she would get someone else to do it for her?'

'You're making her out to be . . . I don't know. I suppose she might have . . . But you are putting an interpretation on it that I'm sure she didn't mean. You must realize that I really didn't see that much of them while I was going through university. Then there was the party, and he was killed. After that, she wanted to make a fresh start. She sold up, went to live in Knightsbridge. I mean, I hardly come across her nowadays.'

'She didn't marry again . . . as Daphne has done?'

'No. I think . . .' A long hesitation. 'I'm not sure, but I think there may have been a clause in my uncle's will that there would be no need to fund her lifestyle if she married again. But don't quote me. I might easily have misheard.'

That made sense. 'Can you give me any names?'

'I beg your pardon?'

'She may or may not have wanted to marry again, but you can't tell me she wasn't exercising her charms on other men in her circle at the time of the murder.'

'I don't know! Honestly, I don't. People at the golf club, I suppose. People she played bridge with? How should I know? Ask Dan.'

'Dan was too young at the time to take an unbiased look at his parents, and he couldn't think of anything but going to university, and Vera. He must have been rather young for his age, don't you think? The murder and the loss of Vera knocked him for six, and he wasn't mature enough to fend off Daphne's advances. He didn't see or hear any evil, because that's the way he was.'

'Does he see people for what they are now?' A bitter note in his voice.

'Yes. He hasn't made Deputy Head of a big secondary school without insight into what makes people tick. And now he's got Vera back . . .'

He frowned. 'Is that the girl he was going around with in the old days? Some shop girl or other? Totally unsuitable.'

Ellie subdued anger. 'They were pretty good together then, and now they've met up again, I imagine they'll make it permanent.'

A shrug. 'What a pity. She'll drag him down in his career. What sort of wife will she make to a headmaster?'

Ellie had a vivid picture in her mind of Vera coping with a stroppy parent and coming off best in the encounter. She smiled. 'I think she'd manage pretty well. She's a fine, strong woman, who's done a brilliant job in bringing up a boy who's not exactly easy. She'll carve her own way out of life, and she'll never let him down.'

He grimaced, understanding that she was referring to Daphne, who had indeed let Dan down.

He looked at his watch. Before he could make an excuse to leave, Ellie said, 'You knew that Vera was raped at the party?'

'What!' He stared, wide-eyed. 'No!' He hadn't known.

'Did you never hear about it?'

'No, I . . . I was in hospital for a while and went straight home after that. Daphne never mentioned . . . No, you must be joking.'

'Far from it.'

'That's terrible. Is that why they broke up? I knew Dan had stopped seeing her, but he never spoke about it to me, and I'd no idea. Are you sure?'

'Oh yes. I'm sure.'

He thought about it. 'She was the only one of his friends who had the nerve to tackle the gang when they burst in. I suppose they took it out on her, afterwards?'

'No, it was some of Dan's so-called friends who raped her, thinking she was trailer trash and could be misused with impunity.'

He was distressed. 'I'm sorry. That's awful. Why did I never hear about it?'

'Shame. And misdirection. Neither set of parents wanted the match and were prepared to stop the lovers communicating. Dan himself didn't know until very recently.'

'I'm heartily sorry. It shouldn't happen to anyone, never mind . . . You mean, it was actually some of Dan's friends who . . .? I can hardly believe it.' Yes, he was definitely upset by the revelation.

They sat, watching Evan trying to crawl and not getting anywhere. The boy had lost his dummy, but didn't seem to need it for the moment. Ellie expected Sam to make his excuses and leave, but he made no move to do so.

He said, 'They either crawl or they roll. I had one of each. Does this one roll?' He flipped Evan on to his back, and resumed his seat.

Evan looked up at Sam in horror, then transferred his gaze to Ellie, perhaps in a plea for protection? Ellie nodded and smiled at the baby.

Evan looked back at Sam, who was smiling down at him. Sam said, 'I like babies.'

So he did. Good for Sam.

Sam tickled Evan's tummy. Evan convulsed with laughter.

Sam looked across at Ellie. Ellie stared back at him. She thought . . . he knows! Or he's suspected something. No, he doesn't *know*, but he's working it out.

Don't even breathe, Ellie.

A flurry of movement. Evan had rolled off the rug again.

'Ouch!' Sam bent down to extract Evan from under a chair. Evan yelled, in fright and frustration.

Ellie produced the dummy and stuck it in his mouth. 'Give him to me.'

Sam put Evan on Ellie's knee and stood over her. Not speaking.

Ellie said, 'You've worked it out?'

A long sigh. 'If I'm right, and I can't be sure . . . What

good would it do to bring it all out into the open now, so long after . . .?'

Ellie rocked the baby. 'I know. I've been thinking along those lines, too.'

'I mean, there wouldn't be any point in trying to bring a prosecution after all these years, would there?'

So he'd guessed who it might be? Ellie tried to make him name a name. 'Perhaps it might depend on whether they'd ever broken the law on another occasion?'

He reared back. She'd guessed wrongly. 'That's ridiculous. I can see that you don't know anything, Mrs Quicke.'

Ah. She was following his reasoning, if at some distance. 'I thought, like you, that if someone had been keeping out of trouble ever since, there might be some merit in not charging him with rape—'

He turned away with a dismissive gesture. 'Is that the time? I really must be on my way.' He retreated into the hall.

She was annoyed with herself. She guessed – too late – that he'd been thinking about the murder, and she'd been talking about the rape. She followed him into the hall, carrying the baby with her. 'Must you go so soon?'

'I really must.' He let himself out of the house and shut the front door firmly behind him.

'I bodged that,' Ellie said. 'Stupid me!'

She looked at the phone. Following on her earlier train of thought, it seemed to her that if the rapists had kept out of trouble ever since, there was a case to be made for leaving them in peace . . . that is, provided she could get Abdi to calm down. But, if one or more of them had tried it on again, then it would be a different matter and they'd deserve to be pilloried, prosecuted, and probably imprisoned.

But. She didn't know how to check on their careers subsequent to the party. She could ring Lesley and ask if any of the surviving rapists had been in trouble since – but that would mean giving away their identities. Well, apart from Dick Prentice, and he deserved whatever was coming to him.

She walked the baby up and down in her arms, jiggling him to keep him quiet.

The evenings were drawing in, and she must put on some

lights soon. The conservatory window was still a crack open. It had been a fine day, but the temperature dropped sharply at night. She took Evan into the conservatory and managed to close the window, even though he nearly threw himself out of her arms in an effort to reach Midge, the cat, who had been lying there, minding his own business. Midge squawked, Evan yelled, a flower pot crashed on to the floor. A fine azalea, just about to come into flower. Bother.

She ought to have strapped Evan back into his buggy before trying to do two things at once. Babies first. Plants second.

It was something of a miracle that the pot hadn't broken. One handed, she replaced the azalea on the staging.

Sometimes, just for half a second, she imagined she could see the figure of her aunt in the corner of the conservatory. Miss Quicke had passed on some time ago, but just occasionally, out of the corner of her eye, Ellie thought she caught a glimpse of her. Which was odd because Miss Quicke had never been interested in plants. Rose often reported that she'd seen her old employer in there too. All very odd.

Dear Lord, grant her peace.

Actually, the conservatory *was* a very peaceful place, full of colour practically all the year round.

Dear Lord, grant us your protection.

Indeed, thought Ellie, smiling. I certainly need it, and so does Thomas.

Let the wicked be confounded, and grant peace to the righteous.

Vera needs a spot of peace. And Dan. And little Evan, who *will* try to kill himself by throwing himself around at inappropriate moments . . . and . . . and everyone. Especially Rose.

You're on the right lines . . .

She strapped Evan back into his buggy, pushed the dummy into his mouth, and went to see about supper. Vera usually cooked for herself and Mikey at weekends. She might even be cooking for three that day.

Ellie now knew who had killed the doctor. Or rather, she guessed that it had been one of two people. But which one?

Like Sam, she wasn't sure that it would be a good idea to probe further . . . and yet . . . and yet. Justice could be a cold tool, perhaps doing more damage to people's lives than might seem appropriate. She needed more information. Perhaps Vera could supply it?

Saturday evening

Diana collected Evan after supper. In a whirlwind, as usual. 'I don't know why you can't change him into something clean after he's eaten.'

Ellie had managed to pocket the dummy as Diana strode in. Fortunately, her action went unobserved. Ellie defended herself. 'We've got through three outfits already today.'

Diana wasn't listening. 'My husband wants us to go out somewhere tomorrow. I may have to bring the baby round again. All right?' Off she went, without waiting for an answer.

Ellie shrugged and pulled on the cord which connected to the bell outside Vera's door. When the girl answered, Ellie said, 'Vera, is it convenient to have a word?'

Vera said, 'Yes, do come up.' So up Ellie went, to find Vera scrubbing the sink in her kitchen while Dan taught Mikey the rudiments of chess in the sitting room. Vera was still wearing a T-shirt and jeans, but she'd loosened her hair around her ears and, yes, she'd used a touch of mascara on her eyelashes.

Vera said, 'They ought to be attending to their school work, both of them. But will they?' Her tone was one of indulgence. 'Like a cuppa?'

Ellie accepted and sat at the kitchen table. No need to ask questions. Vera was only too anxious to talk.

'Did I tell you that Dan took me round to see his house? Not the one he's living in now which, honestly, there's hardly room to swing a cat in and the kitchen is a joke, not that I'd quibble about that if I had to live there, though it would be a tight squeeze for the three of us, each of us, being realistic, needing somewhere to spread out papers. My main concern is that it would be difficult to make it a comfortable place in which to live.'

'You've agreed to marry him, then?'

'No.' She flushed. 'I've said "no" and he understands that I mean it. I won't have him dragged into the mud if Abdi carries out his threat.'

'I might know a way around that.'

'Mm? Really? Well, we've waited so long . . .' She relaxed, leaning against the sink, head bowed. 'Will Thomas bless our marriage when . . . If . . .?'

'Do you doubt it? Of course he will. Would Dan like to move in here?'

'Same thing applies. He needs space. So does Mikey, and so do I.'

Ellie grimaced. 'You mean, Dan wants his own front door, and he wouldn't like traipsing up through two flights of stairs in someone else's house. If only we could have got the council to agree to our having a separate entrance to the flat!'

'It might have made a difference, yes.' Vera busied herself wringing out the washing-up cloth and hanging it up. 'I said I couldn't imagine myself as a headmaster's wife. He said he thought I'd be tremendous, that I'd keep all the cranky parents in check if need be.' She laughed, colour rising in her cheeks. 'He said I was just what he needed, that I'd push him up the ladder, and that if ever I got out of line he'd give me a look, sort of sideways, and I'd get the message and maybe rethink, which is what we used to do when . . . in another life.' She filled the kettle and switched it on.

Ellie thought that sounded like an excellent way of going on. She speculated that Dan might well have made headmaster by now, if he'd married Vera instead of Daphne.

Vera moved around the kitchen, clattering pots and pans away. 'Mikey and Dan respect one another, thank goodness. I realize I've centred too much of my life around Mikey, because he's only going to be with me for maybe five or six more years. He'll want to fly away one day, he'll be off to university, perhaps a year early . . .'

Ellie smiled to herself. Dan knew how to get round Vera, didn't he?

Vera hesitated. 'Dan wants more children.'

'And you?'

'After what happened? I can't make up my mind. One minute I think yes, that would be wonderful. But it would mean I couldn't carry on working . . . or could I? And the next minute I want to run away and hide.' She collapsed on to a chair. 'Did you say you wanted a cuppa? Hark at me. Early Alzheimer's. Can't remember what day of the week it is.'

'Saturday.'

'Saturday? So it is. We went to see his own house. It smells of mice, and he's got the builders in. It's old and inconvenient. The kitchen's a disgrace, and there's only one bathroom. It fits him like a glove. Mikey loved it, too. He wants the attic rooms. Dan showed me a small room next to the main bedroom and said he wondered if I could think of a use for it. Talk about transparent! He wants a daughter. And Mikey turned round and said he'd like a little sister, and they both *looked* at me, all wounded like, as if I were refusing them the thing they wanted most out of life. I said, "Suppose I want another son?" But we didn't quarrel about it. Just . . . moved away from the subject for the time being.

'He said I could design the kitchen the way I wanted it. As if! It would cost thousands! And the garden's overgrown. Not that I know anything about gardens, and neither does he. He had the nerve to say that he thought you might help us design and restock it!'

'Clever,' said Ellie, smiling.

'Oh, he's clever all right. I'd forgotten how good he was at getting his own way. I'd seen his racing bikes and asked how much time he gave to his hobby, and he went all sad-looking on me and said he thought I'd make him give it up, and he'd do that for me . . . which was all very well, but I'd seen some stuff from his headmaster on his desk about giving up his bike to start a new club at school on Saturdays, which he'd already agreed to do, so he'd decided to give it up before we got together again.'

She met Ellie's eye, and they both started to laugh.

'Well,' said Vera, 'it's a good thing I can see through him. I suppose. But what he wants with that monstrosity of a house, I don't know. Yes, I do. It's got good-sized rooms, with high ceilings and old fireplaces. I can just see him reading his papers, working at that old desk of his, looking at me over the top of his glasses when I go in to ask if he wants a cuppa. Not that he wears specs yet, of course. I'm rambling. None of this is going to happen.'

'It might. Vera, there might be light at the end of the tunnel—'

'So long as it's not the light of the oncoming train. Besides, I can't leave you and Thomas and Rose in the lurch.'

'We'd find someone else. Vera, I wanted to ask you about some of the guests Dan invited to the party. I've met and talked to some of them, but I'd like to have your opinion on them, too. Dick Prentice, for instance.'

Vera shuddered. 'Yuk. Used to make my skin crawl.'

'You went to see him, and he threw you out, threatened you with this and that. Have you seen him since?'

She shook her head. 'Wouldn't want to, either.'

'Dr Gail. What did you think of her?'

A shrug. 'Secure in herself. Anxious that her precious brother isn't dragged into this.'

'Simon. What did you think of him in the old days?'

'Kept himself to himself. Looked down his nose at me. Polite enough . . . After all, he wouldn't want to offend someone who might be asked to vote for him in the future.' A sarcastic tone. Then, a frown. 'I went to hear him speak at the Town Hall once. He's a good speaker but, like all politicians, he takes ten minutes to say one thing. He's on his way up, they say, might even get in at the next General Election. I suppose he'll be a reasonable enough Member of Parliament. I seem to remember he married well; money and long legs.'

They both grinned at the image Vera had conjured up.

Ellie said, 'Abdi never took any notice of you before that dreadful night?'

'He liked pretty little blondes. I wasn't his cuppa at all. Cuppa coming up.' She busied herself making a couple of mugs of tea.

'What about Raff Scott?'

'I haven't thought of him for years.' A shake of her head. 'Naughty boy, Raff. He thought his good looks would excuse him everything. Tried to get into the knickers of every girl in the class. Succeeded with some, I believe.'

'Not with you?'

'Nah. Not my type. Mind you, I had to slap him down once when he got me pinned up against a cupboard.'

'You kneed him?'

Vera grinned. 'One of his mates came in and saw! Was his face red. He didn't try it again.'

Oh, but he had, hadn't he? And she didn't know that he'd raped her? No, she didn't. 'He's not still around, is he? Someone said—'

'Killed on active service. He'd always wanted to be a soldier. Was he in the Territorials before he left school? I think he might have been. He had – what do you call it? – a lust for life. It's odd to think of him being dead. You'd have thought he'd have come through, no matter what.'

'Who else do you remember from those days? What about Sylvia? She helped you get away after the rape, didn't she?'

'Sylvia. I haven't seen her for ever. Didn't Dan say she'd gone to Australia, working in TV or something?'

'Jack the Lad?'

Vera's face cleared. 'Jack's a good man. He helped me move into the council place that I had for a while. Got me my first cleaning job. I met him again down by the river a couple of years back. I was with Mikey. Jack asked if Mikey wanted guitar lessons and said he'd teach him, if he liked, but Mikey's never been interested, so it came to nothing. You remember things like that, don't you?'

She pulled out the ironing board and the steam iron. 'For years I didn't know who had done what to me. Except that, obviously, I realized Abdi was involved when Mikey was born. I suspected it was Dick Prentice, too. But I didn't really want to know. I didn't want to think about it. Now . . . some of the time I think I ought to know and the rest of the time my mind veers away from the subject. Too painful. You've been finding out, haven't you? These questions of yours. Were they about onlookers, or did they all rape me?'

'You're right. You need to know. There were four men involved. Dick Prentice brought the drug to the party, handed it to Gail, who handed it to you. He was first on top of you. Abdi was next. Then Raff, who was probably revenging himself on you for turning him down earlier. And lastly, Simon Trubody.'

Vera clung to the ironing board, assimilating the news. At the last name, she looked tired. Really tired. And shook her head. 'I'll never understand men.'

There was a huge basket of clean clothes waiting for her attention. Vera picked up the first white shirt and shook it out with hands that trembled. It was a man's shirt.

Ellie paused with her mug halfway to her lips. 'Doesn't Dan usually do his own ironing?'

'He said I'd do it so much better.'

'So today you shopped and cooked for the two men in your life. Then washed up. And now you're going to do their ironing, while they enjoy a game of chess.'

'I don't suppose I'd be much good at chess.'

'My first husband used to say I hadn't the brains of a gnat, that I couldn't possibly learn to drive a car, operate a computer or manage a bank account.'

Vera frowned. 'He was wrong about that.'

'Except about learning to drive a car. Maybe it was too late for me to learn, or maybe he was right and I'd never have been any good at it. You'll have to learn to drive soon.'

'Yes, so Dan says. He's going to teach me.' Vera picked up the steam iron to test it was working, and now laid it down again. 'You're saying that I'm letting the men confine me to the kitchen? You're right, of course.' She switched off the iron, dumped the shirt back into the basket, and marched off to confront the men.

Ellie grinned. Her money was on Vera. She finished her mug of tea, rinsed it out and left it on the draining board before making her way down the stairs. The phone was ringing. She was only just in time to pick up the phone before it switched to voicemail.

SIXTEEN

'How did you know?' Lesley Milburn, in police mode. 'You are always so circumspect about giving me names, so I knew it meant something when you fingered Dick Prentice—'

'Ah. He's been in trouble before?'

'You betcha. I've got Maureen's address. She was out when I called earlier, but a neighbour says she'll be back soon, so I'll try to catch up with her later. In the meantime, I've been checking to see what your Mr Prentice has been up to. Starting when he was nineteen. Caught in possession of drugs. Twice. Got a slap on his wrist: don't do it again, boy! Caught a third time, the following year. He was probably dealing but he got away with it that time, too.

'Now for the more serious stuff. Eight years ago it is alleged that he assaulted a teenage girl in the park. He swore he was innocent and that she'd made all the running. The girl was dressed to provoke, had been taking photos of herself and a friend in the almost-altogether before she started chatting up Dick Prentice . . . or he started chatting her up. Whichever. She exhibited some nice bruises and swore he'd dragged her into the bushes, which he may well have done, but the girl didn't impress the policewoman who took the call so Prentice got off with a caution, which he accepted while declaring his innocence to all and sundry.'

'A something and a nothing?'

'Mm. Next item. More serious. A young woman fell asleep in a quiet corner of the park and woke up to find him with his hands up her skirt. She screamed, he ran off but was caught by a couple walking their dog, who called the police. This should have gone to court, but the woman wouldn't press charges, newly married, husband would have been upset, etcetera. So he walked away from that, too.'

Ellie said, 'How many times has he got away with it?'

'Not sure. We've only got the times the police were involved. Third time. Domestic violence. The police were called out to the marital home. The wife displayed evidence of abuse, bruises, a black eye, but again wouldn't press charges. Apparently, she'd thrown him out of the house, whereupon dear Dickie had got back in by smashing a window. A neighbour called the police, but no charges were laid.'

Ellie said, 'And then she divorced him. Well, he's been lucky. Can nothing be done to bring him to court now?'

'I'm hoping that Maureen will give us something to act on. If she'll only say he was the instigator of her attempt to frame Thomas for abuse, we'll have him. But I must warn you that if he elects for trial by jury and no one knows of his previous, he'll probably get off. And don't forget, Thomas's name would be dragged through the mud, even though the allegation was proved to be false.'

'Ouch. No, we really don't want that.'

'Looking on the bright side, knowing that the police were investigating his background might frighten him into good behaviour for a while.'

'It doesn't seem to have worked well in the past. He's attacked women on, how many, three or four different occasions? Given his record, wouldn't you say he'll do it again?'

'Probably. And the pattern is that the violence will escalate.'

Silence, while they both thought about this.

Lesley said, 'Any other names you'd like to give me?'

Ellie said, 'I held back from giving you Dick's until he turned on Thomas, and it transpires that he's a serial offender. Maybe, if he'd been exposed to the light of day when he started on drugs, he'd not have had the opportunity to cause so much upset and distress to the women he's met on the way. I gave him the benefit of the doubt. There are three other names—'

'Three! Ellie, you can't be serious!'

'Yes, I am. I'm feeling miserable about it. I haven't a clue whether I'm doing right or wrong by withholding other names from you. One man died in Afghanistan. There doesn't seem to me any point in giving you his name.'

'I suppose not.'

'One, as far as I can make out, has dual nationality and is not permanently domiciled in this country. We're trying to deal with him on his own terms. If that goes wrong, then yes, I'll give you his name, but I don't think you'd get very far with him. It's a complicated matter. I'll tell you all about it one day, perhaps.'

'And the fourth?'

'I'd be inclined to think he's led a blameless life from that day to this. It's Simon Trubody.'

Muffled squawks from Lesley, and a tumbling noise. Then, 'Ellie, you still there? I dropped the phone. Did you say . . .?'

'Yes. Have you ever heard anything to his discredit?'

'No. He's reputed to be a toughie. Ellie, are you sure? I mean, he's standing for parliament. He has the backing of many important people. Our commissioner, and the outgoing Member of Parliament, and all the local bigwigs, and the mayor and, well . . .'

'That's why I didn't say anything. I think he's clean. I think his one slip, twelve years ago, is atypical. I've met him. Vera can't of her own knowledge accuse him of anything. There were witnesses, yes. And perhaps some of them might be persuaded to speak up. But I'm not sure it would be right to—'

'It would be a national scandal.'

'And ruin his prospects for a parliamentary career. I'm not sure he deserves that. I mean, he did rape her; yes. And for that he ought to be punished. Question; has it been on his conscience all this while, because if so, maybe that's enough punishment for anyone? He's an intelligent man. I suppose he may be ruthless in business, but I don't think he's entirely without morals. I wish I knew what to do.'

'Same here. Ellie, you've handed me a grenade with the pin pulled out. The moment I start asking about him, alarm bells are going to go off all over the place, and either he'll scream harassment, or start slapping writs for slander around. He can afford a good solicitor, can't he?'

'I'm telling you,' said Ellie, 'in case anything untoward should happen to me in the next few days.'

'Ellie, no!'

'Just joking.' Ellie put the phone down. Did she believe what she'd just said? Perhaps she did. Although she had an uneasy feeling that if Simon Trubody did make a move, it would be one she hadn't anticipated, and it would be a knockout.

Sunday morning

Hustle and bustle. Thomas had been called on at the last minute to take a service for someone who'd been stricken with arthritis, while Diana had dropped off Evan with no extra changes of clothing and an admonition not to take him out into the cold as there was a brisk wind blowing. Rose feared she was going down with a cold, so Ellie made her some honey and lemon mixture. Rose gave some to Evan, who loved it and wanted more. And more.

Dan called round to bring a half leg of lamb he said he'd had in his freezer which needed to be eaten . . . though as it smelt fresh and didn't look as if it had ever been frozen, he'd probably bought it for the occasion. He offered to take Vera and Mikey out for the day. Vera came downstairs to give him a kiss and say they needed to catch up on their homework . . . but he might join them for supper if he wished.

No sooner had the door closed behind Dan, than the front doorbell rang again.

It wasn't Diana's usual peremptory ring. Vera hovered, halfway up and halfway down.

'Yes,' said Ellie. 'I think it will be for you.' And it was.

Simon Trubody. Encased in a tailored silk and mohair navy-blue overcoat, hair immaculate, nicely shaven, expensively gloved. He had a smile which spoke of private dentistry and the confidence born of wealth and power.

'Apologies for intruding on a Sunday, Mrs Quicke. Would it be possible to speak to Mrs Pryce?' At least he was tactful enough to use Vera's married name.

He saw Vera on the stairs and spoke direct to her. 'Would you be so kind as to spare me a few minutes of your time?'

Vera shook her head. 'Not without a witness.'

She didn't wish to be left alone with Simon?

Ellie thought of a solution. 'Shall we all go into the sitting room?'

Vera hesitated, nodded and joined them in the sitting room. Thomas had left the Sunday papers in heaps around his chair. Ellie tidied them up while Vera seated herself on the settee, watchful eyes on their guest.

Ellie considered offering coffee. Decided against it.

Simon unbuttoned his coat and seated himself. 'I won't bite, Vera. I would prefer to speak to you alone.'

Vera shook her head. Her eyes checked with Ellie, begging her to stay with them.

'Quite a pleasant day,' observed Ellie, seating herself in her high-backed chair.

'Very well.' He cleared his throat. He was, perhaps, not quite as sure of himself as he would like to be. 'Mrs Quicke has a formidable reputation for uncovering long-buried sins. Including mine.' He tried on a smile till he saw it didn't have any effect, then returned to being businesslike. 'Yes, I've come to apologize. Twelve years too late. I know. I've been thinking what to do for, well, for some time now. How to make recompense . . . Not that there is anything that can wipe out . . . I am aware of that.'

Silence. Vera watched him with a frown.

Ellie said, 'So, as you think the news is about to hit the dailies, you're trying to limit the damage to your reputation?'

'Something like that, yes. I can't explain why I . . . Why any of us . . . We were young and foolish, we were drunk on beer and excitement. And no, I know that doesn't excuse what we did. What I did.'

Ellie said, 'So, you are throwing yourself on Vera's mercy, asking her forgiveness?'

'Yes.' Through gritted teeth.

'You are going to plead with her not to ruin your career?'

He leapt to his feet. 'For heaven's sake!' And then, quietly, controlling himself, 'Yes. I know I don't deserve forgiveness, but I am truly sorry for what I did. Also –' he got the words out with difficulty – 'I know I ought to have tried to stop it happening. I knew Dick and Raff were high on something, and Abdi – well, he's always been a law to himself, but I should have been able to . . . And instead, I . . . To my shame.'

Was he for real? That was the question.

Vera was looking down at her hands. She didn't seem to be listening.

He went to stand at the window, looking out on to the garden but sending quick glances back at Vera. 'Looking back, I see things from a different point of view from the one I had then. We were all so young, thought only of ourselves and how to enjoy life. Vera, I did hear that you'd had a child and that you'd tried to make Abdi honour his obligations. And that he'd refused. In my callow youth, I thought then that I'd had a lucky escape, that it might have been me saddled with a paternity suit. Jack the Lad told me you'd found some sort of council accommodation. He asked me if I'd like to help you out, financially. I told him it wasn't my baby. I'm ashamed of that, too. In my defence, I could say that I'd only just gone to university and was on a strict budget. I couldn't have helped without applying to my parents for money, and I didn't feel that I could tell them. Yes, I realize now that I should have done. But at the time I thought . . . I'm sorry. There are no excuses for what I did, are there?'

He turned to face Vera, but her attention was still on her hands.

He said, 'I always fancied you, you know.'

Vera shook her head. 'You fancied Jack's girlfriend, but she wasn't having any.'

He reddened. 'Perhaps you're right. It's all a long time ago. Afterwards, it seemed like a dream. I tried to convince myself that nothing much had happened. I wiped it out of my mind. Sometimes I've been able to forget about it for months at a time. Then someone would say that they'd seen you about the place, and that you'd got married and were tied up in some way with the Pryce family and the new hotel. I was pleased to hear that. It salved my conscience.'

Still no response from Vera.

He straightened his back. 'Last night I told my wife

everything. Every little detail. She was horrified. I was afraid she'd leave me and take the children. I could see my whole life imploding . . . and yes, as she pointed out, I'd helped to destroy yours. Eventually, she agreed to let bygones be bygones, if I made what amends to you that I could. I won't say that she has forgiven me, exactly, and she certainly won't forget in a hurry. But here I am. At your mercy.'

Ellie thought, This is a very clever man. He's taking a risk, but if it comes off, he's home and dry. If he fails, he'll be able to say that he is full of remorse for what he did. Does he genuinely feel some remorse? Perhaps not as much as he'd like us to believe, but yes, I do think he regrets what he did. The question is; what will Vera say?

Vera said nothing. Nothing at all.

Perhaps it was the most disconcerting thing she could have done.

He stretched out his hand to Vera. 'Please.'

Ellie's eyebrows rose. Ham acting? No, maybe he did feel some remorse.

Vera turned to Ellie. 'Did you switch the recording unit on?'

No, of course she hadn't. But Ellie nodded.

Simon blanched. 'You've recorded this conversation?' He sank into a chair, drawing his hand across his eyes. 'Well, I suppose I deserved that. Now you've got my confession on tape, you can take it to the police and . . . I must warn my wife.' He stared into a future which looked grey. 'I just hope she won't leave me. We've been married for . . . And the children are . . .' He pulled himself together. 'I'm sorry. You don't need to hear all that. The truth will have to come out. I don't think I'll lose my position in the firm, and in time, maybe . . .'

He stood up, gathering his coat around him. 'May I just say, Vera, that I am truly sorry for what I did, and I am doing, have done, everything I can to make amends.'

Vera inclined her head, but did not speak.

He took a slip of paper out of his breast pocket and laid it on the coffee table. 'I should have done this years ago. I know you needed it more, then. It's come too late, and

I know it's not enough. I'm asking you to accept it, nevertheless.'

Ellie leaned forward to see how much he'd made the cheque out for. Ten thousand pounds. Decent but not overgenerous. It would fit out Vera's kitchen at the new house.

Vera didn't even look at the cheque. She said, 'I forgive you. And, unless my hand is forced, I won't be placing charges. You can tell your wife that I appreciate your honesty. And I hope you do well at election time.'

His face changed. 'Really?' He put out his hand, as if to shake hers.

She shook her head and walked out of the room.

He looked taken aback. Ellie thought he wasn't used to being treated with disdain. He recovered himself quickly enough, though his colour had risen. He bowed his head to Ellie. 'Thank you for agreeing to see me.'

'That's all right,' she said. Though it wasn't really all right, was it? She showed him out. Was it raining again? Oh dear.

Then she heard Evan squalling and hurried to his side. Rose had been trying to get him out of, or into, his buggy and had got stuck. Both were in tears. Where had Ellie put his dummy?

Sunday lunchtime

'Well,' said Ellie, reporting to Thomas at lunchtime, 'that's one down and three to go. Vera wouldn't touch the cheque Simon left for her, so I've put it in a safe place in my study. What are the odds on Dick Prentice doing the same?'

She fed Evan a crust of bread. He spat it out. She scooped it up and fed it back to him. He looked at her and she looked back, daring him to spit it out again. He lowered his eyelids and accepted the crust. Good.

Rose was dozing in her chair. She was dropping off to sleep more often, nowadays.

Thomas was supposed to be on a diet. He chewed through a salad, without enthusiasm. 'You really think Dick Prentice will try to buy her off, too?'

'He might. He seems to be in touch with Simon, who will

no doubt suggest that it would be a good idea. Dick's a nasty piece of work. I don't think I'd want to touch any money he offered, but perhaps Vera is of a more forgiving nature.'

'You wouldn't touch his money because he tried to get me into trouble?' She could tell Thomas was still worried about that, even though she'd told him that Lesley was going to deal with the man.

Ellie sighed. 'If he came visiting with a cheque in his hand, what do you think she'd do?'

Thomas tried to lighten up. 'Knee him?'

Ellie grinned. 'I wouldn't want to soil my knee by getting so close to him. It's a nice thought, all the same.'

The front doorbell rang. An insistent peal.

Thomas said, 'Dick Prentice? I won't be answerable for the consequences if it's him. I'll cope with Evan, if you want to speak to him.'

It wasn't Dick Prentice.

It was an official visitation in a cream-coloured stretch limousine.

First came the chauffeur . . . One of the kidnappers from the other day? Then came a manservant . . . kidnapper number two? . . . who was almost hidden behind an enormous basket of fruit. A bouquet of rare flowers dangled from his wrist.

Next came Abdi, rubbing his neck and looking anxious.

Finally, out of the back of the car stepped a dapper little old man with sharp black eyes which were hooded, rather like a tortoise. He used an ivory-handled cane to indicate that Abdi was standing in his way. The godfather? No, the grandfather.

Ellie wanted to laugh. Or cry. She wasn't sure which. She backed into the hall and rang the bell to summon Vera.

Abdi's father bent his head in greeting. 'Mrs Quicke? What a very pleasant neighbourhood this is. I trust you will allow me to present you with a few flowers and some fruit in view of the fact that my son has caused you so much inconvenience.'

Total charm offensive. Oxford-educated? Intelligence personified. A slight sibilance? He gestured with his cane, and the offerings were tenderly placed on the hall floor.

Subduing a slightly hysterical impulse to laugh, she said, 'Do come in. Vera will be down in a minute. Coffee, tea?'

'Thank you, so kind. But no. I fear we have trespassed on your good nature too much already. A few minutes of your time, perhaps?' He twitched his cane again, and the servant returned to the car.

'Won't you come in?' said Ellie. Absurdly, as he was already in, and making for the sitting room . . . where he seated himself in her high-backed chair. Of course.

He looked around, assessing her and the room. With another inclination of his head, he said, 'I regret that my son seems temporarily to have lost his voice and failed to introduce us. My name is Abdi, the same as his. So confusing. But I trust you will be able to tell us apart?'

'Yes, I should think I would.' This man was a force to be reckoned with.

'Pray, be seated,' he said, as if he were the host. Ellie sat, half amused and half indignant.

Vera appeared in the doorway, her hand on Mikey's shoulder, eyes wide, taking in the situation.

Abdi the younger hovered. He was diminished by his father's presence. And flustered. He said, 'Father, this is—'

'Indeed.' The older man turned his whole body round in the chair to see Vera and Mikey better. Had he a stiff neck? Arthritis? He bent his head. 'Welcome, Mrs Pryce. And Mikey, too. For once I can understand the direction my son's heart has taken, even if his methods of wooing lack discretion. Do, pray, take a seat.'

Wide-eyed, they did so.

Flatterer! Was Vera impressed? Apparently not. Wooing? Ah-ha. This man was indeed a force to be reckoned with.

'Father . . .'

The cane twitched, and Abdi the younger fell silent.

The cane twitched again. 'You may be seated, my son.'

Everyone waited while the younger Abdi looked around for a chair and sat. Ill at ease.

The elder Abdi turned his attention back to Vera. 'Mrs Pryce, my son's impetuosity has from time to time led him into situations from which I have had to rescue him. I apologize on his behalf, and I trust, gracious lady that you are, you may find it in your heart to forgive him.'

Vera stared at him, frowning. Silent.

The old man said, 'I am a wealthy man with interests in oil and shipping. I have factories in India and China. I have four children, eight grandchildren and I believe will shortly be presented with my first great grandchild. None of them, I regret to say, have the backbone of a shrimp –' a twitch of the cane here prevented his son from bursting into speech – 'and I have been at a loss as to who might take over the reins when I am eventually forced by ill health or old age into retirement. I am absolutely delighted to hear that the merging of my bloodline with some good Anglo-Saxon genes has produced a descendant worthy of my name.'

He beckoned with his cane, and Mikey left his mother's side to stand in front of the old man. Were they going to stare one another down? And if so, who would win?

SEVENTEEN

Mikey said, 'I apologize for wrecking your son's house, sir.'

A narrowed glance. 'I am told it will cost half a million to make good the damage.'

A grin. 'He must have insurance?'

The old man smiled. He leaned forward and patted Mikey's cheek. 'Well said. But we won't compound the problem by making a false claim against the insurance company. My son will foot the bill.'

Abdi Junior grimaced, but didn't look too distressed, so he could probably afford it.

'So, Mikey,' said Abdi senior, 'will you come to work for me when you are finished with university?'

'I might.' Mikey looked back at his mother, who moved to stand at his shoulder, saying nothing, but reminding everyone that he was her son.

Abdi senior rested both hands on his cane. 'Mrs Pryce, you have been greatly wronged. It is difficult to see how we can make restitution, but one method did occur to me. My fool of a son could go through a form of marriage with you. This would legitimize Mikey in the eyes of the British law and make it easier for him to find his proper place in my organization when he is grown up. I do not suggest that you live with my son as man and wife. That would be asking too much of you. After a few weeks of this marriage in name only, you would file for divorce on the grounds of his unreasonable behaviour—'

Ellie couldn't let him get away with that. 'I'm afraid under British law they'd have to be married for much longer than that before they could go in for a divorce. Two years? More?'

'That is true,' said the old man. 'But it might be done on a visit to my country where the laws are, er, more flexible. A stay in a hotel in a beautiful resort, all expenses paid? My son would not contest the divorce, but the subsequent money settlement would mean that you, Mrs Pryce, need never work again. I would bear all the costs, of course.'

Young Abdi said, 'It's a good offer, Vera. Take it, do.'

Vera shook her head. 'One minute you're threatening to have me charged with murder and—'

'What!' The old man shot a rapier-like glance at his son.

Abdi Junior mumbled, 'The man I paid to find out about Vera, he said he'd found someone answering her description who'd been arguing with the doctor that night. Shouting at him.'

'I assure you it wasn't me,' said Vera.

Abdi Junior grimaced. 'I know that now. I went to see the so-called witness. It was dark, he was on night shift, had been walking his dog before he went to bed. He saw someone in dark clothes with fair hair arguing with a man in front of his garage. He couldn't even swear to it being a man or a woman. That's all he saw. I didn't know Vera had left by that time, and I thought it was her.'

'A man on night shift? Indeed!' said Ellie. 'In that neighbourhood? Wishful thinking. A burglar looking for an easy entry, more like. No wonder he hadn't come forward before.'

'Well, yes. I suppose. But I thought that if I said it was, she'd agree to my terms.'

His father was outraged. 'You *thought*! On such slender grounds, you tried to blackmail the mother of your only son?'

'Yes, well. It turns out it couldn't have been her. I've said I'm sorry. I'll pay the man off, tear up his statement. I promise.'

Ellie said, 'That won't do. However little your witness observed, I suppose he did see something, and the police ought to be informed.' Especially if he had been a burglar on the prowl.

'Agreed,' said Vera. 'Have you got the statement with you?'

'Well, I . . . er . . .'

His father twitched his cane, and Abdi Junior pulled a couple of sheets of paper out of his breast pocket and handed them over to Ellie. 'You can't tell much from this.'

Ellie said, 'Thank you. I'll see it gets to the right people.'

The cane twitched again, and Abdi Junior said, 'I'm sorry. I really am.' He revived, like a ball bouncing back into play. 'So, Vera; what about it? We could fly to Somalia and do the deed next week.'

'You're joking. You're already married.'

'Yes, but she . . . Now that she is aware I can't . . . I can assure you that there will be no problem.'

'You mean that she's already filed for divorce?'

'She is happy to fall in with our plans, knowing how much it means to me.'

'You're paying her off.' A statement, not a question.

A shrug.

Vera said, 'Thank you, but no. Two wrongs don't make a right. I am not going to enter into a fake marriage for the sake of money, no matter how cleverly you word your offer. It would be like selling myself. As for legitimizing Mikey, people don't judge as harshly nowadays as they used to do. He will get by on his merits.'

'I anticipated your reaction,' said the old man, 'and if I may say so, I honour you for it. I did think of promising that if Mikey entered my organization he would be well protected, but that, also, I will not do. If he comes, he comes under his own name and fights for his own place in the sun.'

'Yes,' said Mikey, 'that's how I'd like it to be.'

The old man nodded. 'I thought you'd say that. And –' turning to Vera – 'I think you were wise to turn down my son's offer of marriage. You deserve something better. Shall I introduce you to a more suitable match?'

It was Vera's turn to blush. 'Thank you, but "no".'

Abdi Junior rushed into speech: 'Mikey could join us on the yacht for a holiday.'

Both Mikey and the old man shook their heads. 'You go too fast, my son. Mikey has had one experience of your so-called hospitality, and I don't want him wrecking the yacht as well.'

Mikey grinned. 'I wouldn't wreck anything of yours, sir. I wouldn't need to, would I?'

'You may call me grandfather. That is, when you feel ready to do so.'

Vera said, 'I won't object if Mikey wishes to see his father now and then, but I don't think he should leave the country. Not yet.'

The old man bowed his head. 'Agreed.'

She went on, 'I don't know if this makes any difference to your way of thinking, but I have received an offer of marriage from another man. He and I would have been married long ago if it hadn't been for the events of the night on which Mikey was conceived. After that, we drifted apart and have only recently made contact again. This man wishes to adopt Mikey and give him his own name.'

Mikey fidgeted, eyes down. Which meant . . . what? That he didn't want to take Dan's name? Understandable, perhaps.

The old man looked at Vera from under his eyebrows. 'Perhaps he can decide what he wants to be called when he's had time to think about it.'

Mikey nodded. He put out his hand and rested it on top of his grandfather's. A fleeting caress. The old man bent forward and kissed Mikey on his cheek. 'Grandson.'

Mikey's eyes were shiny with tears. 'Grandfather. May I come to visit you whenever you're staying in London?'

'I hoped you'd say that. I'm here for a week or so, perhaps six times a year.' The old man looked around. 'Bring up a stool, Mikey. Sit beside me. I want to hear in detail exactly how you managed to do so much damage. Did Mrs Quicke tell you what to do?'

'Oh, no,' said Mikey, happily sitting down beside his grandfather. 'I learned a lot about how to start fires and what water can do when I was helping the workmen at the hotel in the next road.'

'You worked on a building site?'

'Unofficially, yes. It was fun. Anyway, I learned what water can do, and electrics, and stuff like that. I turned the taps on in the bathroom to saturate the carpet, knowing that if it wasn't discovered for a while, it would damage the floor and the ceiling beneath. I started the fire with the lamp because I'd seen how easily an unattended lamp can set paper on fire. I smashed the windows because they were fitted with alarms and I thought that might bring the police in, and then I saw the laptop and broke that, and I glued up the power points and the remote for the television. But Mrs Quicke did help me when we got down to the garage, by pointing out where the tyre lever was. I couldn't have wrecked the cars, otherwise. I had thought I might introduce a virus into the computer system, but I didn't have enough time to work out the password.'

'For this relief, much thanks,' said the old man, smiling. 'Remind me to let you have the passwords for all our systems when you come to visit. That way you won't have to destroy everything in sight.'

'Oh, I wouldn't. Not now.'

'No, I don't suppose you would.' He gestured to his son. 'Now that we've cleared the air, perhaps you would like to shake hands with Mikey. You would both make better friends than enemies.'

'I don't mind,' said Mikey, looking at his father from under his brows, 'if he doesn't.'

Abdi Junior scowled and then grinned. 'Isn't it terribly British, shaking hands?'

They shook hands, tentatively. Then Mikey was pulled into

his father's arms and given a hug. The look on Mikey's face was part horror and part pleasure.

The old man had the last word. 'My blessing on both of you.'

Ellie thought, The old man wins, hands down. 'Coffee?' she asked.

'Out of a jar? I think not.'

'Made in a cafetière. No? Tea and cake, then?'

'That would be delightful.'

Vera said, 'I'll help.' She left the room with Ellie. As they reached the hall, Vera started to hyperventilate. Ellie helped her to a chair and held her tightly till she'd recovered.

Vera blew her nose. 'Sorry about that.'

'Game, set and match to the old gentleman. Do you mind very much?'

'I don't know what I think. I'm pleased for Mikey, in a way. In lots of ways. I think his grandfather is to be trusted, isn't he?'

'I think so. I don't suppose the son will bother you much in future.'

'I couldn't marry him. I couldn't.'

'Quite right. Imagine what Dan would have said, if you'd tried. And Thomas would have been outraged.'

Vera managed to laugh at that. She pulled herself together. 'Tea and cake, then. Have we any, or shall I throw some scones together?'

Ellie said, 'What on earth are we going to do with all that fruit and that huge bunch of flowers?'

'We'll cope with them later.' Vera made for the kitchen, but Ellie was held back by the phone ringing.

It was Lesley. No preamble. 'Dick Prentice's dead.'

'What!'

'Suicide.'

Ellie felt for the chair and slid on to it. 'Are you sure? No, that's silly. You wouldn't say it if it wasn't true. But . . . how? What brought this on? Did you manage to catch up with Maureen? She might have . . . No, she wouldn't go so far as to kill him, would she?'

'Ellie, calm down. It's suicide, not murder. Yes, I did track

Maureen down yesterday evening and had a word with her about spreading rumours. She was, I am happy to say, both furious and tearful that Dick Prentice should have put her in such a false position. I used words such as libel and slander and quoted the prison terms for people convicted of either, which frightened her considerably. I had to make her a cup of tea and provide her with a tissue before she could talk rationally, and at that point she was only too happy to give me a statement to the effect that her boss had taken advantage of her good nature, etcetera. She said how disappointed she was in Mr Prentice who, now she came to think about it, had used her abominably, and it was just like her mother had always told her, that men are brutes at heart.'

'I can imagine,' said Ellie, amused.

'Indeed,' said Lesley. 'After a while she stopped being frightened and turned to righteous indignation. How dare he, etcetera. She said she was going to have it out with him, that she was going to inform their line manager about his conduct, that that would put a stop to his progress up the ladder, and serve him right. I've no doubt she meant what she said, but I can't see her storming into his house and demanding that he commit suicide, can you?'

'Well, no. But if she phoned him and told him she intended to report him, and that she'd informed the police of how badly he'd misled her . . .? I'm just trying to work out the timescale. Let's say she did ring him last night and threaten to take action. Would that be enough to push him into committing suicide? Before he's even been interviewed by the police?'

'"Ours not to reason why." Let's be thankful that he did.'

'Yes,' said Ellie. Her mind had fastened on to the memory of a man saying that he'd do what he could to avenge Vera. She tried to recall Simon's exact words. He'd said something like, 'I am doing, have done, everything I can to make amends.'

Now what had he meant by that? It wasn't just telling Dick to retract the story about Thomas, or giving Vera a cheque, was it? Or was it?

She said, 'Suppose someone else also put pressure on him.

Someone who said they could bring a witness to Dick's
raping of Vera?'

'One of the people you've talked to, you mean? Ye-es. But
which one, and why today?'

Ellie had Simon's name on the tip of her tongue, but was
not sure about saying it aloud. 'Did Spotty Dick leave a
note?'

'Yes. To Whom It May Concern. Citing depression.'

'I suppose that's as good a name for it as any. You wouldn't
really expect him to confess to rape, to taking drugs and to
trying to rape several women. And he certainly would feel
depressed if he knew he were facing a prison sentence. How
did he do it?'

'A neighbour of his heard a car engine running inside
Prentice's garage and called the police. They found him
sitting at the wheel, dead. There was no mention of Thomas
or Vera in his note.'

'Or of Maureen,' said Ellie, trying to work it out. 'I bet
if you got hold of Dick Prentice's phone records, you'd
find that Maureen did either go to see him or phoned him
last night, in order to warn him that the police were after
him.'

'Would that be enough to make him commit suicide?'

'It might,' said Ellie, crossing her fingers. She didn't know
whether or not Maureen had done anything to force the issue,
but she had a strong suspicion that Simon had done exactly
that. If it was Simon, there would be no trace of the phone
call. He'd have been wily enough to have bought a disposable
phone, used it, and got rid of it.

'Well,' said Lesley, 'I'm happy with the outcome as it is.
I wouldn't dream of suggesting that we look into anyone's
telephone records. The official position will be that
Mr Prentice was depressed and committed suicide. I've scared
his accomplice into clearing Thomas, and that will be the
end of that. Right?'

'Thank you. Yes, I suppose that is the best possible
solution,' said Ellie.

What a pity that someone else had to die . . . but also,
what a relief. It was, she had to admit, a merciful conclusion

to the investigation into the rape, at least for all those left alive.

She put the phone down, wondering if she herself had any responsibility for Dick Prentice's death. If she hadn't interfered, if she hadn't given Lesley those names and told her about Maureen . . . what would have happened?

She'd acted with the best of intentions, but . . . No, no. She shook herself back into a sensible state of mind.

Let God be the judge. Justice has been done. Praise be.

Sunday teatime

After the deputation had departed, Ellie found herself unable to settle.

One minute she was amusing Evan, and the next she was gazing out of the window. It was a bright afternoon, and she rather fancied a breath of fresh air. 'Is it going to rain, do you think? I thought I'd take Evan for a walk around the block. I know Diana said not, but he's fractious and likes being wheeled along. Do you want to come?'

Thomas yawned. He'd taken a service that morning at short notice, had had a nice long nap in his La-Z-Boy chair, and looked forward to cooking the evening meal. 'That leg of lamb that Dan brought. An hour and a half in the oven, do you think? With roast potatoes, parsnips and whatever greens we've got in the larder? You're only going round the block, Ellie? You're not going to do anything silly?'

Anything silly? He shouldn't have said that. Wasn't she capable of deciding such things for herself? What *was* the matter with the man? She'd got him cleared of the abuse charge, hadn't she? 'I might call on a neighbour, if he's in. I'll ring first, to make sure, and I promise to leave a note of the address if he asks me over there for a cuppa.'

Thomas yawned again and went off to rummage in the larder.

Ellie paused in the hall, listening. Sometimes, if Vera forgot to close the door to the top floor properly, you could hear what was going on up there. Dan wasn't due for a while.

There were faint telly noises upstairs. Nobody was shouting or crying. Three of the clock, and all's well.

She dithered. Did she really want to go out?

Everything had been cleared up beautifully. Dick Prentice was dead, and his assistant had been dealt with by Lesley. Simon had seemed repentant. He'd made the right noises, and his cheque would help Vera to her dream kitchen. Mikey had established a relationship with his grandfather, and his father's threats against Vera had been neutralized.

All was hunky dory. Except that the man who'd murdered Dan's father had never been brought to justice.

She made a phone call. The person who picked up the receiver at the other end wasn't surprised to hear from her, which told her everything she needed to know. Yes, if she'd like to drop around sometime that afternoon, that would be good.

Ellie left a note for Thomas, tucked an extra blanket around the sleeping form of Evan, who was . . . oh dear, just beginning to wake from his nap. Time to get his wheels a-rolling, or he'd start screaming. She checked that she had an umbrella in her handbag and pulled on a mac, just in case.

She let herself out of the house, closing the front door gently to behind her.

It was one of two people. She'd known that for a while. One was dead. One lived two roads over. Dead or alive? Take your pick.

Simon had known. *Let sleeping dogs die.*

Simon had implied it was the young one. Maybe it had been. But when Ellie had been told to look for a woman, her old friend hadn't been talking about a lippy girl from the chippy, but about a mature, manipulative woman, who could charm the birds off the trees . . . or seduce an old family friend into comforting her after a shock. Comforting her into her bed? Mm. Possibly not. Though the suggestion might have hovered in the air, so to speak.

On the night of the murder, Dan had needed help in the aftermath of the party. His cousins had been whipped off to hospital. The house had been ransacked. His guests had gone. He was alone and needed help.

So what had he done? He'd rung an old family friend. Mr Scott had driven over with his son, who'd been at the party earlier but who had got home safely. Raff stayed on in the house while Mr Scott drove Dan to the hospital. Mr Scott had then returned to look after the house and to be there to explain to Dr and Mrs McKenzie, when they returned, what had happened. Mrs McKenzie had gone inside alone, while the doctor had stayed outside to garage their car.

Mrs McKenzie had been met by Mr Scott. He was their old family friend, solicitous and helpful. Charming, fragile Mrs McKenzie would have been distraught at seeing what had happened to her beautiful home. Mr Scott had calmed her down. Mr Scott had gone up to her bedroom with her and made sure there weren't any nasty burglars still lurking under the bed or in the cupboard. He'd looked behind the shower curtain and soothed her until she was able to cope and see herself to bed. Mr Scott had then gone back downstairs and taken a seat, waiting for the doctor to return . . . and fallen asleep. He said.

What had Raff been doing all that time?

Ellie was about to find out.

EIGHTEEN

Mr Scott lived in a large, detached house, circa 1910, red brick, a turret on one corner. It wasn't as huge a house as some, but it had been built for someone who intended to employ servants to look after it. Ellie would have taken a bet that there'd be a billiard room or a conservatory at the back and that the kitchen would be large and inconvenient. She manoeuvred Evan in his buggy into the porch and rang the bell. One bell only. The house was still occupied by one family, and it had not been divided into flats.

Evan had been turning his head from side to side to look up at the trees as Ellie pushed him along. Now his view was limited to the inside of a large, dark porch, and he screwed up his face, ready to yell out an objection.

The door was opened by an imp of the feminine gender. 'Grandpa says he's out in the back.' She clung to the door, balancing herself on roller skates. Her feet went every which way until she regained her balance, when she shot off across the hall and down a short passage into the back garden.

Ellie pulled the buggy into the hall and shut the front door. There were clashing sounds nearby. Someone washing up the lunch dishes? A slight odour of dog. A clutter of coats of all sizes and colours, a hat stand containing umbrellas, sticks and a kite. Yes, a kite.

The imp had been about Mikey's age. She had fair, tightly curled hair. Both the colour and the curls were natural.

Raff's child?

An ancient dog of indeterminate breed appeared, enquiring who the visitor might be. Too old and rheumy to be a threat. 'Good dog,' said Ellie, who knew more about cats than dogs. Apparently, that was the right thing to say, for he turned himself round with an effort and padded off back down the passage to the garden. Ellie followed.

A couple of steps at the back led up to a pleasant but nondescript garden, bounded by brick walls. There was a lawn with shrubs around the perimeter and, full in the sunshine, a plastic table surrounded by chairs. Scattered around the long lawn were a trampoline, a barbecue under wraps, a climbing frame, a half sized football net, and a paved path on which the girl with the curly hair was trying out her roller skates.

A white-haired man in his sixties was sawing away at an overgrown lilac bush, half of which had been brought down by the wind and was lying on the lawn. He stopped when he saw Ellie and laid down his saw. 'Did Hedda see you come in?' He gestured to the chairs. 'Are they dry enough to sit on, do you think? Will you be warm enough out here?'

Ellie manoeuvred the buggy up the steps and put the brake on. 'They look fine. My grandson likes the great outdoors.'

'Such as it is. I'm afraid I'm no gardener. It's as much as I can do to keep the place tidy. Tea or coffee?'

'Thank you, but I've just had some. Apologies for breaking in on your Sunday.'

The dog laid himself out on the paving stones beside the chairs, placed his head on his paws and closed his eyes.

The girl sang out, 'Grandpa, watch what I can do!' She tripped, recovered herself and tore on up the path.

He sang back, 'I'm watching you!'

'Raff's child?' said Ellie.

A long sigh. 'Yes. So, it's over at last.'

'You knew you'd be called to account some day?'

A nod. 'I've made provision for Hedda and the child. My wife passed away long ago. You want me to go to the police with you? I'd rather they didn't come here. I don't want the child to see me taken off . . . although I suppose it can't be kept from her much longer.'

Evan was grizzling. Ellie adjusted the angle of the buggy so that he could see around him. He chewed on his fist. He was definitely teething again. Where, oh where, had she put his dummy?

Ellie said, 'Could you bear to tell me about it, Mr Scott?'

A long sigh. 'Where to begin? We'd known the McKenzies for years, ever since they moved into the area. He was our doctor, we dined with them and they with us. We made up parties to go to the theatre, even went on holiday with them once. Our sons went to the same school. They were not best buddies, but if we had a barbecue evening, they came to us and vice versa. Raff loved their pool and wanted one, too, but as you can see, we haven't enough room. Then my wife began to ail and became so painfully thin – cancer, untreatable – that she didn't want to go out, though she encouraged me to do so. Marcella – Mrs McKenzie – was wonderful. She insisted on including me in all their social activities. She said I mustn't mope because it would do my wife no good. She recommended that we had an au pair. That's how Hedda came to stay with us. She made such a difference to our lives. She ran the house for us, which was a tremendous relief as I've never been much of a cook or bottle-washer. I can't change a bed or iron a shirt for the life of me.'

'Ah,' said Ellie. 'Hedda and Raff . . .?'

A nod. 'Hedda and Raff. She was – is – a good girl. She kicked him out when she found him in her bed. She told us she must leave. My wife wept. We didn't know what to do. We'd grown to depend on her, and besides, we were really fond of her. Raff was at a difficult age, about to leave school, impatient to get on with his life. He said he was in love with Hedda and wanted to marry her. Of course, we said he was too young. We asked him to be mature enough to consider what it would do to his mother if Hedda had to leave. He was planning to go into the Army as soon as he left school. We said that if he still wanted to marry Hedda after he'd been away for six months in the Army, then we'd agree to it.'

'And Hedda?'

He shifted in his chair. 'She was in tears most of the time. She couldn't make up her mind what to do. She'd originally planned to come to us for just a year to improve her English, after which she was supposed to return to Germany and go to university. My poor wife was pretty well confined to her bed by that time and didn't want to have to get used to someone else.'

The older couple, anxious and ailing. The young buck, feeling his oats.

The little girl screamed, 'Look at me, Grandpa!' She was on the trampoline, still wearing her roller skates.

Mr Scott got out of his chair in a hurry. 'Darling, you must take off your roller skates before you go on the trampoline.'

A voice floated out through the kitchen window. Presumably, it was the child's mother, Hedda? 'Come here, *Liebchen*. I'll take them off for you.'

The child disappeared indoors. Evan started to grizzle. Ellie scrabbled in her handbag, hoping against hope she could find his dummy, and found the second one, still in its packaging. Relief. Where had the first one gone? Well, never mind that now. She thrust the dummy into his mouth. Peace and quiet descended.

Mr Scott said, 'My wife would never have any truck with those things.'

'I don't approve of them, either, but nothing else seems to satisfy him when he's like this.' She jiggled the buggy, and Evan relaxed, lying back, sucking rhythmically on his dummy, watching the clouds as if they were a peep show laid on specially for his benefit.

Ellie said, 'So when Raff went to the party at the McKenzies, he was feeling frustrated. Why didn't he take Hedda with him?'

'She refused to go. She said my wife needed her. We were relieved because we didn't know how he'd behave towards her if people started to pair off to visit the bedrooms, that sort of thing. He went on his own.'

'On the lookout for another girl?'

'Oh, no. I don't think so. What happened, it was by chance, a terrible mistake.'

'You know what Raff did?'

'He told me when he got back. Half boasting, half sorry. He told me the girl had had too much to drink and was anybody's for the asking.'

'You knew the family well. You knew she was Dan's girl, and that she'd never looked at anyone else. You'd probably met her on one of your social occasions. And, knowing Mrs McKenzie, she'd undoubtedly have bent your ear about how much she disliked Dan's taking up with Vera, just as you in turn confided in her about Raff and Hedda. You must have been terribly shocked when Raff told you . . . boasted to you . . . what he'd done with Vera.'

'Yes. I was. And the worst of it was that Hedda overheard us. We'd both raised our voices, I'm afraid. She came out of her room, demanding to know what had happened. She said she was going to pack and leave next day. Raff was furious with her, said it was all her fault for refusing him. I couldn't think what to say or do. My own son! Acting like that! And then the phone rang.'

Ellie nodded. 'And it was Dan, who didn't know that Vera had been raped or that Raff had been involved. He told you he'd tried and failed to get in touch with his parents. He asked for your help to get him to hospital. You agreed. And took Raff with you.'

'I couldn't leave him alone in the house with Hedda.'

'Your wife . . .?'

'Sleeping pills. She didn't wake. She never knew. We thought it best.'

'So you picked Dan up from his house and took him to the hospital, leaving Raff at the McKenzie's?'

'Yes. Raff hadn't passed his driving test at that time so I drove. Dan was in a terrible state. I thought the hospital should have admitted him, too, but he refused to be examined. He fretted about his cousins and about what his parents would say, and if Vera had got home safely. I knew what had happened to her, of course, but I couldn't tell him that Raff, among others, had . . . I couldn't. I promised him I'd stay at his house till his parents returned. We hoped they'd be back soon, but of course they weren't. Afterwards, I thought of many different ways I should have handled it. I could have gone straight to the golf club and got them out. I could have sent Raff in to do the same thing except, of course, that he couldn't drive and we didn't want to leave the house open. I tried ringing the golf club myself, but they'd switched to an after-hours service.

'So after I'd dropped Dan at the hospital, I went back to the McKenzies'. Raff had found something to drink; there were bottles of the hard stuff lying around, abandoned by the gatecrashers, I suppose. He hadn't even attempted to clear up the mess. I hardly knew where to begin. The thought of Marcella coming home to that . . .! I got some black plastic bags out of the kitchen and a broom and made Raff help me to clear the hall. There was broken glass, plates, and food strewn everywhere. I thought I'd heard somewhere that glass ought to be put in a carton, but I couldn't find one, and all the time I was worrying what to say to Dan, and to Hedda, and how to explain it to my wife . . . how to deal with Raff.

'Finally, Raff said he was bushed and would go and have a kip in the doctor's study. It wasn't too bad in there. Stuff thrown around, but there were some comfortable chairs. He fell asleep, just like that! As if he hadn't a care in the world. I couldn't sleep. The kitchen was OKish, a couple of glasses broken, a bit of mess. I made a cup of coffee to keep myself awake – about the only thing I know how to do in a kitchen. I suppose I must have dozed off. The next thing I knew was someone turning the key in the lock of the front door. I shot out to intercept whoever it was. It was Marcella. I had to tell her that Dan was at the hospital, but not gravely injured, and prepare her for the worst. She had hysterics.'

He paused, eyes shifting. He was going to lie?

He said, 'Raff woke up, asked where the doctor was. Marcella was in a terrible state. I wanted to get her up the stairs to bed, but . . . Raff said he'd go for the doctor, who was the only one who could deal with her when she got like that, but I said no, that he should coax Marcella up the stairs and that I'd go. Break the bad news. I said it would come better from me as one of his oldest friends.'

Liar, liar; your pants are on fire.

'It was an accident,' said Mr Scott. 'He'd been drinking pretty heavily that evening. It was dark. I appeared just as he'd opened the garage doors to put the car away. There was no outside light, but there was a street light opposite. I think he mistook me for a burglar, and before I could speak, he rushed at me. He was off his head from the booze. I was yelling at him, but he wasn't listening. We tussled. I was holding him, trying to quieten him. He stumbled and fell backwards, with me on top of him. Hit his head on the way down. And that was it. He was dead. An accident. Misadventure.'

He shot a glance at Ellie, who sighed and made no response.

He said, 'I couldn't think what to do. Raff was in such a state. I thought he'd probably blurt out everything that had happened that night as soon as he was questioned, and his future would be . . . I couldn't bear to think of it. Then I remembered that there had been gatecrashers earlier that evening. Obviously, they were there for drugs. So I thought that since it had been an accident, and since the police would have plenty of other suspects . . .' His voice trailed away.

Ellie said, 'First: it was you who went upstairs with Marcella, leaving Raff to deal with the doctor. Marcella wouldn't have wanted Raff, who was too young to be inter-ested in her. She would have wanted an older man whom she could charm into cosseting her. Second, the doctor had taken very little alcohol that evening. He was by no means drunk. Third, why should you and the doctor come to blows? Sorry, Mr Scott. You might have thought it a good idea to take the blame for Raff twelve years ago, but there's no point in doing so now.

'Raff was drunk. He blurted out what had happened to the doctor; the gatecrashers, the damage, the youngsters taken to hospital . . . but none of that would have caused them to fight. No, I think Raff went too far. I think he spoke of the rape. It was on his mind. He was one mixed-up kid, wasn't he? Hedda, Vera . . . rape was on his mind, and he let it all out. Dr McKenzie was fond of Vera. He would have been horrified. Perhaps he recoiled from Raff? It was Raff who, conscious of guilt, tried to shout the doctor down . . . and then . . . a chance blow, perhaps? Or the tussle that you've described . . . And it ended badly.'

Mr Scott didn't speak, but looked steadily ahead at . . . something he alone could see.

She said, 'Raff had taken on a lot to drink that night, hadn't he? Marcella was clinging to you, in hysterics. Wouldn't let you leave her side. Raff said he'd get the doctor, who would know how to deal with his wife when she was in a state. I'm sorry, but it was Raff who killed the doctor, not you. I expect it was an accident, as you say. The police will probably agree to pass it off as such.'

'Does it have to come out?'

'You know that it does.'

He was silent for a long time. Ellie thought he might not speak again, but eventually he did. 'I only know what Raff told me, afterwards. He said he'd tried to tell the doctor what had happened but got in a muddle, mixing up Dan being in hospital, and the gang wrecking the place and Vera being raped. You're right; the doctor was sober, but Raff had drunk far too much. He said the doctor couldn't understand what he was saying, said he must ring the police, and Raff thought it was all going to come out about the rape. The doctor tried to push past him, and Raff took him by the shoulders and shook him, and thrust him back . . . He was trying to get him to calm down, to see "sense". The doctor slipped and fell back and hit his head. And that was it. Raff hadn't meant to kill, just to stop him ringing the police till he'd got his story straight. It was an accident.'

'Raff had fair hair?'

'Mm? Yes. Why?'

'Someone saw him. Not to recognize him.'

Silence.

Mr Scott's lips moved. 'Oh no.' And then, 'If there was a witness, why didn't they come forward?'

'I don't think his motives for being out and about that late could bear examination.'

'You mean . . . a burglar?'

'Probably. So, while you were upstairs with Marcella, your son killed your old friend.'

He winced. 'It was an accident. When I came down, Raff was at the drink again. He was mumbling, didn't make any sense. I asked him where the doctor was. He said he was in the garage. I went out there. Yes, he was dead. My old friend was dead. And my son had killed him. I was devastated. I knew I should ring the police. I couldn't do it. Raff shouldn't have to go to prison for an accident. By that time he was so drunk, I was afraid he'd confess to anything if the police got hold of him, so I bought us some time. I got him into our car and took him home, put him to bed. By the morning, when he'd sobered up, I thought he'd be able to give a better account of himself. Then I went back to the McKenzie's and waited till dawn. Only then did I officially discover the body and ring the police. They didn't know Raff had been at the house. The police jumped to the conclusion that the death was gang related, and I didn't tell them otherwise.'

'If you'd both told the truth, Raff could have got away with manslaughter.'

'Not if the facts of the rape came out. I couldn't risk that.'

'So Raff went off into the Army and got himself killed. Did Hedda forgive him?'

'She discovered she was pregnant as soon as he left.'

'So he had forced her, too?'

'I don't know about "forced".'

Obviously, he had. But Mr Scott didn't want to admit it. 'Did they have a chance to marry?'

He nodded. 'Yes, on his embarkation leave. Luckily. We never saw him again. He was killed within his first month on active duty. We helped Hedda to train as a nurse while we looked after the baby until my wife died and the little one was old enough to go to a good kindergarten. Hedda has a good job now at the hospital, and our granddaughter is the light of my life.'

'Happy days for you. A far cry from what happened to Vera.'

'I suppose so.' He didn't give a fig for what happened to Vera.

'Hedda understood what had happened?'

'She has put it behind her.'

'She never thought of marrying again?'

He cleared his throat, uneasy. 'She has a man now who wants to marry her. When that happens I plan to sell this house, give her half and buy a small service-flat for myself.'

'How did Marcella cope? She must have noticed that Raff was there with you when she and the doctor returned from the golf club. Didn't she ever suspect what had happened?'

'Marcella is a charming woman, but she's only ever been interested in herself and protecting her own interests. She believed, as the police did, that the murder had been committed by a member of the gang. She was devastated. I only saw her for a few minutes after that fatal night. She was too distressed to talk, needed full-time attention. Dan was wonderful, put his own career on hold to look after her. Eventually, she got Dan to find her a flat in Knightsbridge, and she moved on, made some new friends. I haven't seen her for years. I don't wish to do so, either.'

Ellie said, 'You understand that I must tell the police what really happened that night.'

'Can't you forget what you've heard? What good will it do to blacken my son's name now?'

'He blackened his own name.'

'And died for it.'

'He'd always wanted to join the Army, remember? He

didn't commit suicide because he'd raped Vera, killed an old family friend and forced your au pair to have sex with him. He did those things of his own accord, and he's left a trail of misery behind him.'

'You are hard.'

'I've had to be. A good many lives were twisted askew because of what Raff did. Dan still mourns. Vera's life was destroyed. *Her* son was brought up without a father, in poverty. Another of the offshoots of your son's action has been to cast an undeserved slur on my husband's reputation. By the way, you weren't surprised when I rang you today. Who told you I was on the warpath?'

'Simon Trubody. He's my sister's son. My nephew. He's been very helpful.'

Ellie sighed. Of course! Simon had probably worked it all out years ago. Simon had seen no evil, heard no evil, and spoken none. Bravo, Simon: you'll go a long way in life.

Mr Scott said, 'I spoke to my solicitor about this yesterday. He thinks it unlikely I'd land up in court for what I did, but that if that did happen, I'd only get a suspended sentence.'

'Dan deserves to know the truth.'

'Oh, I'm sure he worked it out long ago.'

No, he hadn't. Not long ago. Recently, perhaps, he'd begun to suspect . . .? But that was another matter.

Ellie reflected that the seeds of the happenings of that tragic night had been sown long ago. The clinging nature of the doctor's wife, Marcella, and of her niece Daphne, which had hampered and stunted the men in their lives. Dick Prentice's halitosis and acne, his failure to get a girl, leading to his attacks on women. Vera's bright, practical nature and good looks, which had attracted the attention not only of the doctor's son, but also of Dick and Raff, and the others . . . The link between Simon and his sister . . . and his cousin Raff . . .

The elderly dog heaved himself to his feet as the little girl shot out into the garden. 'Grandpa, Grandpa, they're going to let me be the one and only bridesmaid when they get married, and I can choose my own dress!'

A tall, blonde woman came out of the shadows in the

house and stood there, smiling. Behind her came another tall, fair-haired man. Also smiling.

Ellie drew in her breath. Hedda was the same physical type as Vera.

Which meant that . . . had Raff gone after Vera because she reminded him of Hedda? Or the other way round? Vera had said Raff had tried to force her one day at school. Which meant that Raff had taken Hedda as second best . . . or had it been the other way round?

Mr Scott had risen. 'My daughter Hedda . . . this is Mrs Quicke. Hedda, my dear, I have something to tell you . . .'

Sunday evening

Diana bustled in, late, to collect Evan.

She picked him up and dandled him in her arms. 'Has my little chickabiddy had a good day, then? Have you missed your mama?'

Evan crowed with delight. Something dropped on to the floor.

Diana held it up. 'WHAT . . . is . . . this!'

The lost dummy.

Lightning Source UK Ltd.
Milton Keynes UK
UKOC01f0123310115

245401UK00005B/9/P